SPINSTER KANG

We gratefully acknowledge the support of the Canada Council for the Arts and the Ontario Arts Council for our publishing program. We also acknowledge the financial support of the Government of Canada.

Spinster Kang is a work of fiction. All the characters and situations portrayed in this book are fictitious and any resemblance to persons living or dead is purely coincidental.

Cover design: Val Fullard

Library and Archives Canada Cataloguing in Publication

Title: Spinster Kang : a novel / Zoë S. Roy.
Names: Roy, Zoë S., 1953- author.
Series: Inanna poetry & fiction series.
Description: Series statement: Inanna poetry & fiction series
Identifiers: Canadiana (print) 20190094486 | Canadiana (ebook) 20190094508 | ISBN 9781771336055 (softcover) | ISBN 9781771336062 (epub) | ISBN 9781771336079 (Kindle) | ISBN 9781771336086 (pdf)
Classification: LCC PS8635.O94 S65 2019 | DDC C813/.6—dc23

Printed and bound in Canada

Inanna Publications and Education Inc.
210 Founders College, York University
4700 Keele Street, Toronto, Ontario, Canada M3J 1P3
Telephone: (416) 736-5356 Fax: (416) 736-5765
Email: inanna.publications@inanna.ca   Website: www.inanna.ca

SPINSTER KANG

A NOVEL

Zoë S. Roy

inanna poetry & fiction series

INANNA PUBLICATIONS AND EDUCATION INC.
TORONTO, CANADA

ALSO BY ZOË S. ROY

Calls Across the Pacific
The Long March Home
Butterfly Tears

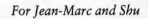

For Jean-Marc and Shu

CHAPTER 1: A SHIRTLESS MAN

O N A SATURDAY NIGHT AFTER WORK, Kang trudged along a snow-covered sidewalk toward Islington subway station. This was her longest workday of the week—three hours teaching Chinese in an after-school program, an hour on the subway, and eight hours behind a Tim Hortons counter. Coffee cups and donuts danced before her eyes in the soft glow of the streetlight, their circular shapes overlapping and swirling with the snowflakes. The biting wind whipped her face and slowed her steps, and her sneakers slid on the snow. It was early March, but it was colder in Toronto than in Beijing.

Several minutes later, she entered the station and boarded an almost empty train. Sinking into one of the soft red seats, she placed her black backpack and pink down jacket on her lap. She stared at her watch: 11:10 p.m. *In twenty minutes, I'll be at home lying in my warm bed.* Thinking about her bed made her feel even drowsier. Her eyes heavy and her head drooping, she dozed off.

Kang had arrived in Toronto six months earlier. Since then, the nickname "Spinster," a label she had reluctantly received and carried in China, had disappeared. In Canada, many women, older than her, were unmarried and might always be; it was nobody's business but their own. Back home, her family, friends, colleagues, and even acquaintances always volunteered to help her get rid of that label by suggesting potential mates for her to consider. She'd found herself being watched and gossiped about constantly, and she'd always wanted to shout, "I don't have a problem! I'm not interested in getting married!" She didn't have any of the skeletons in her closet that people in China normally associated with single women in their thirties: a reputation for being sexually promiscuous or any physical disabilities that might prevent her from being a mother. Her only problem was that she had never been able to trust a man since her sister was raped. So, she simply did not want a man. Any man. Period.

Still fast asleep on the subway, she began to dream. She watched a shadowy human figure stroll along a path in the wilderness. When the figure turned around, she couldn't tell if it was a woman or a man. She noticed the beaming and worry-free eyes, but the vision suddenly began to fade.

"Wake up," said a voice near her ear. "This is the last stop."

Kang opened her eyes. A woman was nudging her shoulder. "Thanks," she mumbled, and quickly stood up. A draft of cold air blew into the warm car from the wide-open door. She read the word "Kennedy"—the east end of the subway line. Sitting back, she yawned, but kept her eyes wide open—she didn't want to miss her stop again. A couple of passengers boarded, and then the train travelled back the way it had come.

Fifteen minutes later, Kang dragged herself toward the five-storey walk-up on Broadview Avenue where she shared a one-bedroom apartment with Fei. Snowflakes drifted onto her face and melted. She licked the snow off her upper lip. To soothe her thirst, she pictured the tall glass of water she would pour herself when she got home.

Mounting the stairs to the fourth floor, she walked to her apartment and heard music and chatter coming from inside. Fei is having a party tonight, she thought. With an audible sigh, she opened the door.

A girl and two young men sat around the table playing cards. Slouching on the couch, Fei giggled with her boyfriend. Her bottle-blonde hair touched her shoulders, and, to Kang's blurry eyes, her glistening red lips looked like a bloody muzzle that might snap at any time.

"They brought me a huge birthday cake." Fei stood and gestured to a large plate on the table. "Want a slice?"

"Happy birthday!" Kang responded, stroking her stomach to indicate she was full. She was too tired to say more, but her annoyance dissolved, and she forgave the noise. *It's her birthday party.* She would've given her a gift if she'd known, she thought as she hung her jacket and backpack in the closet.

The bedroom door was open a crack. She stepped in, and Fei followed her. "Minla is drunk and napping in my bed."

Kang stared at the figure covered with a blanket in Fei's bed beside her own. Fei chuckled. "Can you believe that she got drunk from one cooler?"

At that moment, the blanket moved. Minla sat up, her hair messy and her face red. "I'm okay now," she mumbled, shuffling out to the living room. She rang her fingers through her hair and announced, "I'm going home."

Fei followed her out of the bedroom. "Take some cake with you."

"She might get drunk from that, too," quipped one of the guests. Several people burst out laughing.

They were just twenty-somethings and they seemed to have a great deal of time to waste, thought Kang. Thirty-two-year-old Kang was always in a rush. She always felt like she was chasing something, but she wasn't sure exactly what. When she was a teenager, she often heard older people say they would find time later in life to make up for the things they had missed during those awful years of the Cultural Revolution, such as education, jobs, entertainment, and all the things that are part of a normal life. But that time never seemed to come. Some people had even lost their parents and siblings, and those they would certainly never find again. Kang was five years old when the revolution ended. She had only missed the swings and seesaws.

After years of studies and keen competition, she graduated from Beijing Normal University and was assigned a teaching job at a middle school. These days, in Toronto, she spent a lot of time thinking about the old adage, "time is money," but right now she had neither time nor money. She was very busy working at part-time jobs to pay the rent and then hopefully go back to university and re-earn the credentials she needed to be able to teach in Canada. More than once she had asked herself if she had made the right choice in immigrating.

She closed the bedroom door. After turning the light off, she undressed quickly and climbed into bed. The word "spinster," mixed with stifled laughter from the living room, pricked her ears like a needle. *Will I ever escape the culture of my faraway country?* She sighed, but soon fell into a sound sleep, her slight snoring sounding like ripples on the water.

Kang woke up at eight and breakfasted on a bagel and a glass of milk. Gazing out the window, she saw the snow melting. The lawn in the park shouldn't be icy, she thought, so she grabbed a wooden stick from the closet. It was time for her to practise Tai Chi Stick, a fighting form of Tai Chi that blended rigidity and softness in its movements.

Don Mount Parkette, with its withered grass hidden under a thin layer of glittering snow, was a five-minute walk from her apartment. Occasional joggers panted in the crisp air as they ran around the park. Kang took off her jacket, laid it on the back of a bench, and began to go through the movements she had learned two years earlier while waiting for her immigration application to be processed. Most women practised the short stick form, but she had chosen the more powerful long stick style. She wanted to be in shape so she could defend herself. *If my sister had been able to…*

Kang particularly enjoyed a movement called White Tiger Sweep. The sweep, she imagined, could snap an attacker's leg, but she hadn't had the opportunity to test it yet—she had not encountered any potential threats since coming to Toronto.

When she had completed her routine, she was sweating from the effort. She put the stick back and ended her workout—she had other plans for the day.

Back home, knowing Fei was still in bed, she tiptoed into the bedroom. Before going to shower, she lightly slid the closet door open. As she picked out clothes to wear, a commotion started behind her. She turned around and gasped: a shirtless man was sitting up in Fei's bed. "God!" Kang exclaimed, the clothes in her hand slipping to the floor. Kang wondered if she should get her Tai Chi stick, then recognized Fei's boyfriend, Bing, and sighed in relief.

"Sorry," Fei said, her tousled head appearing from under the blanket. "Bing decided to stay overnight. I didn't want to wake you up to tell you."

"You shouldn't have let him sleep over without telling me," Kang said, stifling her anger. She picked up her clothes and went into the bathroom. Locking the door, she quickly turned on the shower. The warm water soothed her tense body, but her mind was racing. She wondered if she should set some rules with Fei. But it was Fei's apartment and maybe she should just move out, Kang thought. But Kang knew that an apartment on her own would be expensive, and she worried about whether there would be enough left over to save for tuition fees. If she couldn't pay for tuition, she wouldn't be able to get her Ontario teaching certificate. Then the thought of the man sleeping in her bedroom rushed back into her mind. Goose bumps climbed her arms and she suddenly felt nauseous. Shivering, she put on her clothes and went into the living room.

Before she could decide what to do, Bing slipped into the bathroom. She could talk to Fei now, Kang thought as she stepped back into the bedroom where her roommate was zipping her jeans. Kang was blunt. "Bing can't stay overnight."

"I know, but I can't stop him," Fei said. "I don't want to lose him. You know it's not easy to find a guy you really like."

"Does this mean he'll be staying overnight again?" Kang asked, hoping Fei would say no.

"I think so. You should perhaps find another apartment." Fei sat on the edge of her bed. She crossed her legs and looked down at her shoes.

"All right. Give me some time. I'll find a place."

"Okay." Fei sighed with relief, her feet now resting on the floor. Fei felt a little guilty. It was still March and moving was tough in the cold weather. "You can stay till you find a place."

Kang left for the Toronto Reference Library, as she did most Sundays. On the subway, she mulled over her plans. After job-hunting for months, she had realized her B.Ed. in English from China would not land her a teaching position. She had found a job teaching Chinese in an after-school program, but it was only three hours a week. If she wanted to resume her career, she definitely needed to get an Ontario teaching certificate. She had been directing all her efforts toward saving for her studies, but before she could be accepted at a university, there was yet another hurdle: she had to pass the Test of English as a Foreign Language.

The reference library provided facilities for people to learn English, so she had been going there every Sunday to listen to the TOEFL tapes and try the sample tests. If she passed the test, she would be able to start school in September. It had looked promising, but now that this problem with Fei had come up, finding another place to live would have to become her priority.

A memory crossed her mind. When she had arrived in Canada six months earlier, she had lived in a small basement room for a month. It had been a dark and dismal room, but fortunately she didn't have to stay there long. A friend's friend had contacted Fei, who'd agreed to share her one-bedroom apartment with Kang. Not only did this arrangement cost her less, but the place was much nicer.

She got off the subway at Yonge and Bloor and strolled north, enjoying the warmth of the sun. The tree branches looked a little yellowish. There were some anxious buds coming out, but spring still seemed to be shy.

Instead of going to the language section as usual, Kang went to the library's reading area and selected the *Toronto Star* and *Toronto Sun* as well as *Rental Weekly*. Carefully browsing through the papers' rental sections, she focused on the cost and location of apartments. An ideal place would be around York University, the University of Toronto, or George Brown College, where she had sent her applications. Living near school would save her commuting time. She jotted down several names and phone numbers. If this issue had come up a little later, she might have known which university she would be attending, and it would have been easier to decide where to move. But there are no ifs in life, she thought.

After copying down a list of possible rentals, Kang made her way to the language section. She borrowed earphones, tapes, and the TOEFL books, and then entered an empty carrel. She proceeded to bury herself in the sample tests, just like a bird cleaning and combing its feathers before flying out of its nest. In three days, she would take the four-hour test—her last chance to make the May 1st deadline to get into the programs that she had applied for.

With the earphones in, she couldn't hear anything except the tapes. Her worry about finding a place began to fade as she immersed herself in preparing for her future. She focused on speaking and listening, her weaknesses. She had practised speaking English in one of Beijing's "English Corners," where Chinese people often met to practise their English language skills, and she had been sure then that she would have no problem in the English-speaking world. But she was in for a reality check when she arrived in Canada. A few months after arriving, she still could not quite grasp what people were saying, even though she knew most of the words. Practising

English with other people who were also learning the language was one thing, but being immersed in an English-speaking country, and surrounded by those who had spoken English all their lives, was something completely different. Even now, she still had trouble speaking English proficiently and she had to listen very attentively to understand what was being said.

Her stomach growling for food, she left the library. In the lobby, she found a bench to sit on and took an apple and two hard-boiled eggs out of her backpack for lunch. A couple beside her had their arms wrapped around each other's waists, sweet smiles on their faces. Turning her eyes away, Kang stared at the backpack on her lap. She had lost suitors during the past twelve years because of her inability to trust men. She vividly remembered twenty years earlier when her sister, Jian, had come home and sobbed in their mother's arms. Mother had waved Kang away, sent her to her bedroom, and closed the door. Kang had overheard the word "rape," a word that would terrify her for a long time. After that, she had done her best to avoid men. Mother's warning about not going anywhere alone still rang in her head like a constant bell.

She planned to call her sister to find out how things were going with her husband as soon as she finished the TOEFL test. Kang thought of her sister while she bit into her apple. The shadow of her sister's life had become the darkest one in her own life. Jian had suffered so much since that horrific night. Her then fiancé had abandoned her and now her husband was mistreating her. As for Kang, she had become the despised "spinster," never comfortable around men and incapable of forming a relationship with one. Her life was like a still pond, her "spinster" hat floating in the stagnant water. But as undesirable as her single life might be, it was much better than being in a miserable marriage. *If my sister hadn't married...* Kang grimaced.

When she had finished her lunch, Kang went back into the library to continue studying. She had practised a number of writing topics before, and now she focused on this one: "Do you agree or disagree with the following statement? Children should begin learning a foreign language as soon as they start school. Use specific reasons and examples to support your answer."

She composed the following: "I agree that children should begin learning a foreign language as soon as they start school. Children begin to express their basic needs or feelings as soon as they can make sounds. Language is a tool for them to communicate with others. When they reach school age, they study the written form of the language. In other words, language development takes place in their early years."

As language development begins in childhood, Kang stated that it would be beneficial for children to take the same approach to learning a second language. She used her own experience as evidence.

Born in the middle of China's Cultural Revolution, the ten disastrous years of political chaos instigated by Mao, she had started singing revolutionary songs in kindergarten—songs about heroes who had sacrificed their lives for the revolutionary cause. Her sister Jian had sung English songs in secret with her friend Yezi. By chance, Kang had overheard them and, from their facial expressions and body language, she had sensed that the songs were about a boat and a river, animals and plants. Twenty years later, she found out that the songs they had sung were "Row, Row, Row Your Boat" and "All Around the Mulberry Bush."

In Grade 7, Kang studied English by recognizing the written form instead of starting with listening and speaking—the usual method for picking up a language. She guessed that this might explain why, after graduating as an English major and then teaching English for many years, she still had difficulty speaking English fluently.

In her conclusion, Kang wrote that in addition to the language development, there was another advantage to learning a foreign language at a younger age: the child also developed an open mind.

After finishing the writing practice, Kang went home. On the way back, she stopped at the supermarket near Broadview and Dundas Street East for some groceries. Every day, Kang ate sandwiches or donuts between jobs and school or leftovers at home. Real meals were cooked only on weekends. If the kitchen was available, she could make a decent supper, she thought. She wondered if Fei and Bing were still at the apartment, and smiled wryly. The she thought about the list of possible rentals that she had drawn up. She had much to do.

CHAPTER 2: A FREE DONUT

THURSDAY MORNING, after the TOEFL exam, Kang dialled all the phone numbers on her list of possible apartments and arranged viewings. The first place she visited was a house on Jarvis Street. A middle-aged Asian woman was standing in front of the door. "Hi, do you live here?" Kang asked.

"No, but my tenants do," she replied, leading the way through a side door. "Come in. Take a look."

Kang followed her down several steps to a living room. The landlady opened one of the doors off the living room and switched on the light. "Here it is," she said, gesturing towards a bedroom. It doesn't cost very much. You'll have this room to yourself. The kitchen and bathroom are shared."

Kang stepped into the small room, which was crowded with a single bed and a table with a chair. The Chinese phrase "Packed yellow croakers" crossed her mind, and she imagined herself stuck motionlessly between the furniture, like fish crammed into a tin can. She glanced at the yellow walls, then asked, "Where is the window?"

"No window. This is why the room is so inexpensive," the woman grinned. "Like it?"

"I'll think about it," Kang said as she retreated out the door, politely declining the woman's offer to show her another room.

Her next appointment took place at a four-bedroom condominium in a tall, brick building. When she knocked on the door, a man in his early twenties opened it.

A young landlord? "Are you the person I spoke to on the phone?" she asked with surprise.

"Yes, but I'm not the owner. My father is," the young man explained and smiled shyly. "I'll show you the place."

"Is someone already moving in?" Kang asked as her gaze fell on a clutter of cardboard boxes in the living room.

"Those are ours. We just moved in yesterday," he answered, leading the way past two doors to reach the room they intended to rent. "Here it is." He added, "This apartment is brand new."

"Who else lives here?" Kang asked.

"My parents, grandma, me, and my younger sister," he said. At the same time, someone in another room called out. He turned and answered in a language Kang did not understand.

The room was large and Kang was happy to see the big window that looked out onto the street. Kang listened to the family talk and tried to guess the language. *Spanish? Portuguese?* When the young man turned to speak with her again, she asked, "What language does your family speak?"

"We speak Romany," the young man replied, "but my father and I both speak English."

Immediately, Kang knew she would not feel comfortable if she would only be able to communicate with the men in the family. They were interrupted by a knock on the door. It was another person coming to see the sublet. As the young man went to receive the visitor, Kang thanked him and left.

Sunday morning, after breakfast, Kang walked to the closest bus stop where she could buy the *Toronto Star* from the newspaper stand. She also picked up free copies of the *East York* and *North York Mirrors*.

Back in her apartment, she sat down, laid the papers on the table, and pored over the classified section, then marked down a few more phone numbers to call. Thinking about Bing with Fei in the bedroom, she shivered.

At noon, she left for her first choice. It was on a street she had never been to before. The name, Church Street, suggested that the area might be home to several steep-roofed buildings topped with crosses. She conjured up the ad and pictured a single woman seeking another female roommate near a large and imposing church. An image of nuns in black habits flashed through her mind. *Will I become one of them?* The thought amused her. The rent for this particular room was over her budget, but if the space was large enough and if it had a window, she decided she would take it.

She got off at the Wellesley subway station and strode purposefully toward Church Street. The aroma from a Kentucky Fried Chicken floated around the corner of the intersection, and a country music melody, both sweet and sad, emanated from a patio bar. She reached a three-storey apartment building, its front entrance flanked by cheerful flowerbeds filled with pink and white tulips, yellow daffodils, and purple irises. When she knocked on the apartment door, a woman in her mid-thirties with dark hair and fair skin appeared. "Are you here to look at the room for rent?" she asked, sizing Kang up.

"Yes, please," Kang replied, smiling timidly at the woman.

The woman ushered her inside and led the way toward a pair of large French doors. She opened them and then turned back to Kang. "The room is furnished. Hope you like it."

Kang was pleased to see that the room was spacious. A desk with a chair sat under a large window that faced the garden, and a tall bookshelf stood against the wall. "If you take it, I'll put in a single bed." The woman walked over to the closet and slid the door open. "Take a look inside." She pointed to some of the clothes and added, "Of course, I will remove these."

After Kang had seen the kitchen and bathroom, she knew she wanted the place. The rent was was over her budget, but she loved the room and the building. What her mother used to say came to mind: "You get what you pay for." Her almond eyes beamed at the woman. "I'll take it. When can I move in?"

"Have a seat." The woman gestured to the chairs around a

table in the living room. "May I ask you a couple of questions first?"

"Sure," Kang said, making herself comfortable at the table.

"Are you a student or do you work?"

"I have a couple of jobs right now, but I plan to be a student in September."

"How will you pay the rent when you're in school?"

"I have some savings. And I'll find a part-time job, too."

"Another question: do you have a boyfriend?" The woman paused. "Because I don't want any men I don't know visiting my apartment."

"I don't have a boyfriend. I don't even have male friends," Kang answered, feeling relieved that she met that particular requirement.

Kang thought that the expression on the woman's face was a mix of amazement and satisfaction. "Great," she said smiling. "When do you plan to move in?"

"Can I move in right away?"

"You mean today?" the woman asked in surprise. "Why are you in such a hurry?"

Hesitating just a second, Kang said, "My roommate has a boyfriend. He has started to stay overnight. Your ad indicates that the room is available now."

"Right." The woman tapped her fingers on the table. "Okay. Let me get a bed into the room for you. Can you, in the meantime, give me a deposit now?"

Kang nodded and pulled out a chequebook. She wrote out a cheque for the first month's rent and handed it to her new landlady.

"Thank you. Please call me Nancy. And your name is?"

"Kang."

Nancy placed the cheque in her wallet. "I'll need some time to finish preparing the room. Can you come after six? And can I have your phone number in case I need to contact you?"

After jotting down her number and handing it to Nancy,,

Kang hurried away. She needed to get back to the apartment and pack up her things. She walked briskly to the subway, pleased that she'd found a nice place to live.

Once she had moved in, Kang relaxed. There wouldn't be any men sleeping in her room and she wouldn't be getting goose bumps anymore. And she hardly ever saw Nancy either. Most of the time, Kang only saw her at breakfast time. She had learned that Nancy liked Chinese food, so Kang planned to cook her lunch on the upcoming Sunday.

Saturday morning, after teaching her Chinese class in Scarborough, she took the light rail transit—the LRT—to the Kennedy station. By the time she got on the westbound subway train, it was already almost two o'clock in the afternoon. Her Tim Hortons' shift would begin at three. As usual, she took a lunch box out of her backpack and began to eat the sandwich she had made that morning. Suddenly, the only other person in the car, a young woman sitting across from her, stood up and moved to another seat farther away. *Does my sandwich smell?* Inside the sliced bagel were thin slices of ham and cucumber that did not have much aroma. Although she was puzzled, Kang soon forgot about it and enjoyed her lunch.

It was a quiet afternoon at Tim Hortons. Most of the customers bought their coffee or donuts and then left right away. Only a few sat down with their drinks or food. Kang noticed that her line was always shorter than her co-workers. She was faster at serving people, she thought. One of the other servers had started to make fresh soups: chicken noodle, beef barley, split peas and ham, and creamy field mushrooms. Kang took a break from the register and went to the back room to slice tomatoes, onions, cucumbers, and iceberg lettuce to fill the containers for sandwich orders.

When the supper rush finished, Kang's two coworkers went home, leaving her to work the rest of her shift alone. After she cleaned the tables and chairs, she collected the newspapers left behind by customers and stacked them on one of the tables. As she picked up the scattered pages of the *Toronto Star*, a headline caught her attention: "Outbreak of Severe Acute Respiratory Syndrome." She read about Sui-Chu Kwan, a Chinese Canadian woman in her seventies, who had travelled to Hong Kong in February and died of SARS in Toronto. A sidebar stated that the deadly disease was believed to have originated in Guangdong, China, and that the World Health Organization had sent a team of infectious disease experts there.

Now she understood why the woman on the subway train had moved away from her. It also explained why the customer line-ups in front of her had been shorter. It wasn't because she was more efficient, she thought, staring out into the street and watching the occasional headlights flash past the window. She knew that SARS was contagious and could be fatal. She knew too that the disease had emerged in China. That explained why people had been avoiding her, she thought and then sighed. She wished she could simply tell them that she didn't have SARS, and that she hadn't travelled to China recently.

An older woman pushed open the door, walked toward the counter, and stood expectantly in front of her. Kang recognized the customer, a frequent visitor. Glad to see her and remembering her usual order, Kang picked up a medium-sized cup and placed a tea bag inside. After filling it with boiling water, she passed it to her.

The woman sat at the table where Kang had stacked the newspapers. She picked out a few sections and began to read while sipping her tea.

Kang served several other clients, cleaned the counter, added water to the coffee maker, and refilled the hot water under the soup containers to keep the soup warm. Although spring had officially arrived, the snow had not yet completely melted. People were still enjoying steaming hot soup that helped them forget about the lingering cold.

The woman came back to the counter, and Kang refilled

her cup with hot water. She returned to her spot and began to work on some knitting she had brought with her. With no other customers in the coffee shop and all of her chores completed, for the time being at least, Kang turned to her own thoughts once again. Her eyes wandered around the room and then returned to the window and the occasional flashing lights. She wondered what the woman was doing out on such a cold night. *Is she waiting for someone?* Curiosity made her walk toward the woman. A rag in her hand, Kang began to wipe a nearby table. "You're knitting," she said. "Nice colour."

The woman held up the piece in her hands. "It's a scarf," she answered. Her light brown hair shone under the lights, and her hazel eyes gazed proudly at the green-and-white knitting.

"You've been here for a while."

The woman seemed to know what Kang was thinking. "It's cold at home," she said.

"You don't have heat?"

"No, I mean I'm lonely. Sitting here with people around warms me," the woman replied, a half-smile on her face.

A lonely soul like me, Kang thought. Maybe in her home country, she had a family or friends, but in this country, she had to sit in a coffee shop to feel warm and connected with people. Sympathy rose in her. "Would you like a donut? It's free," said Kang. At the end of the day, unsold donuts would be dumped as soon as the new ones became available.

"That's very kind of you. Could I get a chocolate one, please?" the woman said. "I love chocolate."

"Sure." Kang went to get the donut, placed it on a plate, and brought it to her.

After the woman thanked her, she picked up the donut, and chewed it slowly. The glossy chocolate icing reflected the satisfied look on her face.

Kang returned to the counter when other customers started to come in.

At eleven o'clock, Manda arrived to work the graveyard shift after her other part-time job. She was a high school graduate from Brazil. She was happy with the night job because it paid one dollar more per hour.

Kang left for home, noting that the woman was still knitting at her seat.

Outside, the wind was chilly, but she felt some warmth when the image of the lonely woman enjoying the donut crossed her mind. Remembering her plan to prepare a Chinese lunch for Nancy the following day, she quickened her steps toward the Islington subway station.

CHAPTER 3: A KISS

WHEN KANG GOT UP the next morning, Nancy had already left. Instead of practising her Tai Chi Stick, she went to a Chinese grocery store to get the ingredients she needed to make lunch. Back at home, she put the rice on and began to prepare the rest of the food. She soaked black tree fungus, dried yellow lilies, and bean noodles in individual plastic tubs of warm water. Then she shredded pork and diced a chicken breast and a cucumber. Finally, she chopped up ginger, garlic, and green onions for a couple of stir-fry dishes that she hadn't had in a long time. Most of the time, she simply roasted a pork picnic shoulder or several chicken drumsticks. She was used to eating the same thing for several days in a row, but today she wanted to give her new roommate a taste of authentic Chinese cuisine. At the same time, she would eat something that would help assuage her own homesickness.

Kang placed the cooked dishes on the table and returned to the kitchen to finish the bean noodle soup. Perfect timing, she thought when she heard Nancy coming in.

"Wow," Nancy exclaimed, her hand waving at the steam from the kitchen. "Is this a feast?" She ducked into her bedroom and dropped her gym bag onto the floor, then returned to the kitchen, her eyes gleaming.

"This is just an ordinary meal," Kang answered. "Are you ready to eat?" she asked as she began to ladle the soup into a large serving bowl.

"I'm starving. The aroma is making my mouth water," Nancy said. "Let me help." She took smaller bowls from the cupboard and rummaged around the utensil drawer. "Ha! I have two pairs of chopsticks left from the last time I got takeout."

When they sat down at the table, Nancy was amazed at the spread before her. "You call this ordinary? This is a fancy dinner for me."

Kang explained that by Chinese standards, it did not even qualify as a meal for a guest, which traditionally should always consist of three main dishes and a soup. She pointed at one of the two dishes. "Try this one. It's typical Beijing cuisine—pork shreds and eggs with black fungi. I learned how to make this from my dad."

Nancy picked up a fungus with her chopsticks. "This seems different from Cantonese cuisine. What's this dish called in Chinese?"

"*Muxurou*. How about this one?" Kang asked. "I picked this one up from my mother. I warn you. It's spicy."

"Sichuan style. I like that." Nancy seemed to know something about Chinese cooking.

"It's a dish from Yunnan cuisine. It's called chili diced chicken," Kang explained.

"By the way, what does Kang mean?" Nancy asked, as she bit into her chicken.

"Health. In Chinese, it's two characters: *jian kang*. My sister was named Jian and I was named Kang."

"That's very interesting. Are you twins?"

"No. Jian was born in 1966, when the Cultural Revolution started. My mother said many people were criticized or labelled as anti-revolutionaries because of their names, so my parents wanted their children to have politically safe names. *Jian kang* were safe words, and they were also related to my father's occupation as a medical doctor. The only problem was that the phrase by itself did not sound like a real name, so they chose the first character for my sister—*Jian*. When I was born five years later, we were still in the throes of the Cultural Revolution, so they decided to name me *Kang*."

Nancy was curious. "What names could get people into trouble?"

"Well, if someone's name had the character *mei*, it could mean *meiguo*—America. If a name used the character *tai*, it indicated Taiwan. America and Taiwan were considered enemies of the revolution, so names containing such words could easily become targets of revolutionists. Does it sound crazy?" Kang asked. "If I hadn't lived through that time, I would've never believed that people could be afraid of such things, but that was reality during the Cultural Revolution." She shook her head as though to drive the memory out of her mind. "What does your name mean?"

"It's a version of Ann, which in Hebrew means grace. There are many synonyms in English: charm, ease, goodwill, and mercy. You name it."

Then Nancy told Kang that she was the youngest child in her Jewish family. She was considered a black sheep because she chose to study music rather than become a doctor, a dentist, or even a nurse like her siblings. In fact, she had not even had a regular job until recently when she started teaching at an elementary school.

Kang told Nancy that she'd arrived in Toronto the previous year, in October 2002, and that she had been disappointed to learn that she would have to go back to school. But now she was glad to have had the past year to acclimatize herself to life in this new country.

"Why don't you have a boyfriend?" Nancy asked as she finished the chicken on her plate.

Kang had heard this question many times. In the past, she had always replied, "I just haven't met the right person yet." She knew others probably thought: "*You're too picky*" or "*You aren't charming enough*."

"To be honest," she answered, "I'm afraid of men." Then she told Nancy about how Jian had been raped at the age of seventeen, when she herself had just turned twelve. "I had a boyfriend when I was at university, but I left him when he wanted to me to go to bed with him." Kang added, "I have a sort of a psychological problem, I guess."

Nancy stood up, walked over to her, and wrapped her arm around Kang's shoulder. "I understand. Your sister's crisis is still affecting you."

"Thank you," Kang said as she ladled more soup into Nancy's bowl. "I hope you're enjoying the meal."

"Yes! I like everything very much." She tried unsuccessfully to pick up some bean noodles from the soup. Giving up on the chopsticks, Nancy grabbed a fork and at last managed to get some of the noodles into her mouth.

"I had a girlfriend," Nancy said. "We were together for five years, but she left me for a man. I'm happy for her, but my heart is broken. And I'm quite confused."

"Find another one. I am certain that you make friends easily," Kang said. She thought that Nancy must be very fragile to be heartbroken because her friend had found a man. Kang herself was simply glad to have an amiable roommate who did not have a boyfriend. A thought crossed her mind, and she asked, "Are you afraid of SARS?"

"Yeah, a little," Nancy replied. "As long as I wash my hands often, I'm hoping I'll be okay. Are you nervous about it?"

"Not really, but people seem to be afraid of me." She described what had happened to her the day before.

"I've got an idea." Nancy went to her bedroom and returned with a brownish wig. She placed it on Kang's head. "Let's try something to confuse people. I'm good at doing makeup—I can try to change your appearance."

Kang went to gaze at herself in the bathroom mirror. "I look funny."

"It's okay. We can do this next time you go to Tim Hortons,"

Nancy said. "If you go to work looking like a different person, hopefully, people won't be afraid to talk to you."

Early Monday afternoon, Kang sat on the subway with a new look. The shoulder-length brown locks concealed her own short dark hair. Sunglasses covered her eyes though Nancy had applied some light brown eyeshadow. Her cheeks appeared higher with the blush Nancy had dusted them with, and the final piece—dark red lipstick—made her mouth appear wider.

Kang sat quietly with other passengers. Nothing special or interesting happened. Some people read newspapers or books, and others relaxed. No one seemed to be looking at her.

Soon she arrived at the Tim Hortons. When she went to work behind the counter, the server at the cash said, "You can't come...." But then, gazing at Kang more closely, she drew back in surprise. "Sorry. I didn't recognize you. You look so different! But nice."

Smiling back, Kang knew Nancy's efforts had paid off. She took off the sunglasses, hung her jacket in the back room, donned her coffee-brown uniform, and stepped back out to the counter to start another workday.

In the early evening, more customers started to come in. "A black medium and a Boston cream, please," a customer said.

"To go?" Kang asked. After the customer had nodded and paid, she filled a paper cup with coffee, placed the donut in a paper bag, and passed them to the customer.

"*Dos aderezos de miel, por favor*," said a young man who had stepped up to the counter as the other customer had turned and walked away.

"Pardon me?" Kang responded. She assumed he was speaking Spanish, but she did not understand the words.

He switched back to English. "Two honey dips, please."

Kang prepared his order and then, as she passed it to him, she remembered the Spanish words for "thank you" and "good-bye" that Nancy had taught her. "*Gracias, adios,*" she said.

The young man looked puzzled. She thought with amusement that her Spanish pronunciation must have been terrible.

After a couple of days, Kang got tired of the wig and make-up, so she stopped using them. The concern about the SARS outbreak had not, however, abated. Public health guidelines were issued to ensure containment of the disease, including quarantine measures. People only made necessary trips, and a passenger coughing in the subway would scare people out of their wits. The streets appeared less crowded, and fewer customers came to the coffee shop. She felt lucky that she still had her job.

It was Sunday again. After lunch, Kang helped Nancy clean the apartment. Some of her friends were coming over for a potluck dinner. Kang wiped down the kitchen countertop while Nancy tidied the bathroom. She invited Kang to join them. "If you don't feel comfortable, you can stay in your room after the meal."

"What does potluck mean?" Kang asked.

"Everybody contributes one dish to the meal. Each pot contains a different dish. We call it 'luck' because you don't know if it's something you'll enjoy."

"What should I prepare?"

"You don't have to make anything, but I won't object if you want to help me cook my dish." Nancy smiled.

"What will you cook?"

"Jewish chicken soup. I modified the recipe and made it easier."

Curious about her soup, Kang willingly agreed to help.

Nancy dropped chunks of chicken breast into a large pot. Then she poured in three cartons of chicken broth. She washed a bunch of carrots, a celery stalk, a couple of onions, and two parsnips. Once that was done, she started hacking the carrots into pieces with a large knife.

Afraid that Nancy would cut her fingers, Kang took her own knife from the drawer, lined up a stalk of celery on a cutting board, and—*chop, chop, chop*—diced the celery quickly and efficiently.

"You're going too fast," Nancy said, turning to look at her. "You might cut yourself."

"Your way seems more dangerous. I was worried about your fingers," Kang said, grinning.

When everything had been sliced, Nancy scooped it into the boiling soup and added fresh Italian parsley, whole black peppercorn, and salt. "I'll simmer it for an hour. The last part is to drop the matzo balls into the soup. It's easy," Nancy added as she lowered the heat under the pot.

Kang was glad she was learning how to make this Jewish chicken soup, even though it was not completely from scratch. In her mind, homemade chicken soup should not come from cartons of broth.

Soon Nancy's friends—a couple, two other women, and a man—arrived, and she introduced them to Kang. They brought a pasta dish, a fish casserole, a Caesar salad, and a fruit salad. The dishes were placed on the table around a huge glass bowl of cherry punch, and everyone helped themselves. Most of the dishes were new to Kang, but she enjoyed them all.

Listening to their chatter, Kang learned with surprise that Western music and sports had food-related names. Hot Apple Pie was an American country music band; *Fried Green Tomatoes* was the title of a film; and "Too Sweet" was a song by Canadian singer Paul Anka. She was amazed when she found out that Hershey's Kisses were not kisses from Hershey, but flat-bottomed teardrops of chocolate.

They chatted about newly released movies, *The Lord of the Rings* and *How to Lose a Guy in 10 Days*. Kang learned that the Maple Leafs and the Blue Jays were the names of Toronto sports teams. Busy struggling with her two jobs, she did not go to the movies or even watch television. She wished she could stay home in the evening and watch TV.

When the party ended, the guests eventually departed, taking the leftovers with them. Clean-up was simple. Kang and Nancy simply trashed the used paper plates and plastic cutlery. That was easy, thought Kang—back home in China, a host had to do everything from cooking to washing dishes at the end of the meal.

Since coming to live with Nancy, Kang felt her life had become more interesting and that she had more opportunities to explore Canadian society. In this new country, she sometimes felt as if she were a toddler learning to walk. The friendship with Nancy made her happy, and she guessed it was because neither of them wanted boyfriends, but she did not grasp why Nancy felt so upset about her former girlfriend. She knew how hard it had been for Jian when her fiancé had left her after she told him about the rape. But a fiancé is more than a friend—he is a husband-to-be, Kang thought. In this case, Nancy's girlfriend had found a man to be with. Kang was bewildered and thought that Nancy should instead be happy that her friend was settling down.

On a Sunday in early April, Nancy invited Kang out for dinner at a restaurant not far from their home. As soon as they walked in, a well-dressed waiter led them through a dimly-lit entranceway and then downstairs into a pitch-black room. Kang followed the barely visible Nancy, holding her hand in the dark. She thought about the restaurant's peculiar name: O.Noir. It reminded her of the Chinese saying, "You can't see your own fingers even if you place your hand under your very nose." Nancy had explained that, without sight, the other senses were intensified, and that food would taste better. This was why Nancy had brought her here.

Carefully, Kang groped for her chair and sat down. The combination of darkness with soft background music made her feel as though she were sitting in a cinema waiting for a movie to start.

Uncertain and anxious, Kang heard steps coming toward

them. Someone touched the tablecloth, and then a woman's voice explained what was in the dishes that were being placed in front of them. "Here are escargots in cherry tomatoes with garlic butter, marinated shrimp with herbs, and a basket of rolls." Then the steps retreated.

Her hand fumbling with the fork, Kang inhaled the steamy and delicious aroma emanating from the dishes in front of her. "What is an escargot?" she asked.

"It's a French word. It means snail in English," Nancy answered.

"Interesting," Kang said, as her hands found an oval plate that felt warm to the touch and seemed to be heavy-gauge porcelain. Her fork made a little tinkling sound when she touched the plate. She poked at something rubbery, but had trouble picking it up.

"You can use your fingers," Nancy whispered in a voice just next to Kang's ear. She seemed to sense what Kang was doing.

"Right. Nobody can see me," Kang replied with a chuckle. Pinching one creamy, slippery snail with her fingers, she dropped it in her mouth.

"Yum!" Nancy exclaimed, biting into a tasty shrimp. "I remember the first time I went out with my ex. It was a blind date, and we went to a restaurant. I got so nervous and couldn't stop babbling. The dim candlelight helped me relax…. Now, how are you feeling eating in the dark?"

"It's funny. This reminds me of one evening when I was doing my homework with my sister and brother. The electricity suddenly went off. My brother got a flashlight from the drawer and asked my sister to hold it. Then he sketched on a large sheet of paper and cut out three holes. He told us to stay there and close the door, and then he left. We were scared, but also excited, so we sat and waited while I held my sister's hand. A couple of minutes later, there was a knock on the window. We approached it nervously, and then Jian finally plucked up her courage and pulled the curtain aside. We screamed at the sight before us—a skull with two fingers holding the mouth wide open and a tongue sticking out. Light from the flashlight aimed from below the head made the tongue appear red. Then I saw another person behind the skeleton shaking with laughter. It was my brother and his friend playing a trick on us. They probably did it to the other kids in the neighbourhood too."

Kang finished her plate and felt around for the buns.

Nancy pushed the basket near her hand. "Here's the bread."

Surprised, Kang asked, "How did you know what I was looking for?"

"I could sense it," Nancy said. "The escargots aren't enough to fill your stomach."

"Yes," Kang agreed, fingering the small indentations on the plate. "There were only eight snails." She found the butter and spread it on her roll.

"Are you enjoying eating here with me?" Nancy asked as she bit into a bun.

"Very much. This is my first experience eating snails," Kang spoke slowly. "And without light, but with a nice—" But before she finish her sentence, she felt two hands gently holding her face, and then lips pressed softly against hers.

The delicate fragrance told her it was Nancy. Kang was so shocked that she slipped off her seat and onto the floor.

God! She sat on the carpet under the table, completely disoriented by the kiss and her tumble to the floor in the dark.

CHAPTER 4: A TRIPLE BACHELOR

RIDING ON THE NORTHBOUND SUBWAY, Kang thought with shame about how she had freaked out in the restaurant. Knowing little about lesbians, she had never expected she would meet one, let alone be kissed by one. She had first heard the word from Nancy, but had no idea what it meant until she explained.

Kang liked Nancy, but not in that way. It was true that she'd been avoiding men, but that didn't mean she wanted to have a relationship with a woman.

She had expected that her English and educational background would provide her with a better grasp of the Canadian culture than the average immigrant. But now she felt as if she still had a lot to learn.

She knew she could no longer be comfortable living with Nancy, and she thought that Nancy might anyway have a better chance of finding a girlfriend to live with her if she was on her own anyway. Kang had told her she was moving out a couple of days after they had gone to the restaurant. Nancy had not been resentful at the news that Kang was leaving. She had even helped her by suggesting she check the off-campus housing list at York University.

So, once again like a bird, Kang was in search of a nest. She scanned through the lists and marked a few ads. The most promising one was posted by a woman who offered a room in her house in exchange for light domestic duties—no rent.

It's almost too good to be true, Kang thought, but she phoned right away. From the sound of her voice, Kang assumed that the woman offering the room was elderly. Thinking about how her finances would improve if she got the place, she prayed, with her fingers crossed, that the woman named Tania would take her in. Kang recognized it as a Russian name, and she remembered with nostalgia the Chinese versions of some beautiful Russian songs.

Kang got off the subway at Downsview, then took a bus to Steeles and walked north along Dufferin Street. She had checked the map and estimated it would take about fifteen minutes to reach the place.

Many cars sped by, but there were almost no pedestrians. She was struck by how different the pace was from the downtown core; there were houses on big lots and patches of vacant land. The farther north she went, the more meadows and trees she saw.

She shivered in the still cold April breeze. The land seemed half awake; the fresh green of springtime was beginning to appear. Geese waddled on the newly sprouted grass, robins hopped on the roadside, and the sunshine kissed the awakening land. It was so beautiful, she thought, and then she felt a twinge of loneliness. With whom could she share the joy of these new surroundings? She suddenly felt like a speck of dust in an endless and wild universe. She'd been running and running since coming to Toronto, like a chicken with its head cut off. The expression she'd heard from her boss at Tim Hortons flashed through her mind. But now she was like the early bird trying to catch a worm. She smiled at the image of herself as a bird.

She was startled out of her musing by a sudden noise behind her. Before she had time to turn around, a large animal leaped past her leg and turned to face her, dark brown with erect ears. Startled, she lost her balance and fell somewhat ungracefully onto the ground. A whistle pierced the air, and the animal, a young German shepherd, promptly sat down beside her, its tail wagging rapidly. "Sorry about that," said a voice from behind her. "Are you okay?" A middle-aged man extended his hand to help her stand.

"I thought it was a wild animal." Kang felt embarrassed by her overreaction. The dog still sat there panting, its head tilted to one side as if it were trying to comprehend what was being said. Kang stood up and straightened her clothes. "Thanks. I'm fine."

The man and his dog crossed the road, and Kang continued walking until she reached David Lewis Drive. When she turned onto the street, she spotted the house immediately: a bungalow surrounded by several huge beech trees. She knew she was in the right place when she made out the number on the front door: forty-five.

Smoothing her hair, she rang the doorbell. A woman in her sixties opened the door. "Kang?" she asked. "I'm Tania. Come on in."

Tania was tall, with short brown hair and light eyes. She wore a beige sleeveless blouse and matching shorts. She looked younger than her voice had sounded on the phone, Kang thought, as she followed her into a darkened living room. Tania gestured for her to sit down on the couch and then went to the window and opened the drapes. Sunlight poured in and revealed a simple room. Its most notable features were the many large and colourful paintings on the walls.

Tania sat in an armchair across from the couch. "Are you a student?"

Kang hesitated. "I will be in September. What would my duties be? I know how to clean a house. I can cook and do laundry, too."

Instead of answering her questions, Tania asked, "Which program will you be in?"

"A teaching certificate program. I was a schoolteacher in Beijing for many years."

"What place did you say?" Tania asked.

"Beijing."

"Is that Peking?"

"Yes, the same city, but now we use Hanyu Pinyin to spell it."

"I have a postcard of Khrushchev in Peking. I wanted to visit there a long time ago, but...." Tania's voice trailed off. She seemed lost in thought.

"You still can visit it now." Kang encouraged her.

"Okay." Tania returned to reality. "What you need to do is to clean the whole house once a week. Occasionally, I may need your help with my garden." Tania stood. "I'll show you the room; it's a bachelor in the basement."

A bachelor? A single man? What? Kang was astounded, but stopped herself from asking what Tania meant.

"It's in good shape," Tania said, mistaking Kang's confused look for dismay. She led the way downstairs to a large room. Kang made a mental note to check the word "bachelor" in her dictionary later.

There were two windows that faced the backyard, and a large bed, as well as a dresser, a desk, a chair, and two bookshelves. Tania showed her a bathroom in the corner and explained that Kang could share the kitchen upstairs with her.

"It's wonderful." Kang was amazed by the size of the bedroom and pleased by the two windows. "When can I move in?"

"Any time after tomorrow," Tania said. "It's rarely used and will need to be cleaned. I'll let you do that."

"Sure," Kang said, "I'd like to move in next Sunday, but can I bring some of my things in before then?" She clasped her hands, feeling like a lucky bird with a fat worm in its mouth. She had a new job and a free room!

"No problem. Can you tell me more about Peking or Beijing?" Tania asked. Her green-grey eyes were shining and she seemed like a child who wanted to hear a fairy tale.

Kang was reminded of a 1950s song called "Moscow and Beijing," and she wondered if Tania was a Russian communist. She quickly shook her head, trying to focus on what to say. "I love Beijing, especially its historic sites. Heaven Temple and the

Thirteen Tombs of the Ming Dynasty are my top choices. The weather is similar to Toronto's. There are lots of maple trees in the suburbs. The Western Hills are orange red in autumn, just like here."

"That sounds so nice," Tania murmured. She picked up a ring of keys, took one off, and handed it to Kang. "Here's the key to the house."

Kang waved goodbye and left, practically floating on air. The distance to the bus stop seemed shorter now, so she continued to walk toward Steeles, feeling lighthearted and happy.

After she moved in, Kang spent a few hours cleaning her new room. She dusted all the furniture and then vacuumed the burgundy carpet, which felt warm and soft under her feet.

Tania had shown her how to clean the windows by spraying a mixture of water and vinegar on the glass—more environmentally friendly, she had said. Kang admired the fact that Canadians cared about the environment and thought that in this regard Canada was more advanced than China. She smiled contentedly as she dried the glass with paper towels. Now the windows glistened in the sunshine, letting more daylight into the room.

She wiped the shelves of the medicine cabinet in the bathroom with a wet rag while thinking about the other meaning of "bachelor" that she had learned when consulting her dictionary. The word could refer to the apartment like this—a single room, in which a tenant could sleep, shower, and eat. If she had a microwave, she would not even need to go upstairs to use the kitchen. Then there was a bachelor's degree, which she had earned in China.

I'm a female bachelor—more specifically, a spinster. She thought it was funny that the Chinese word *laochunu* was insulting, but in English, the word "spinster" didn't seem to have the same negative connotations. *So, I'm a bachelor with a bachelor's and I live in a bachelor basement!* Amused by this designation that she had granted herself, she wondered why a female university graduate did not earn a spinster rather than a bachelor.

She was also curious about Tania. She wondered if she was married and had children. She had noticed that Tania did not wear a wedding ring, and thought she might be widowed or divorced. When Kang cleaned the main floor of the house, she saw that there were two other bedrooms, both furnished. They had double beds and more pictures on the walls, many of which were prints of classical paintings—she recognized the names of world-renowned artists.

But in the living room, the pictures on the wall were different. As she dusted them, she read the titles on the bottom of the frames: *Autumn Tapestry* and *Autumn in the Northland* by Franklin Carmichael, *The Red Maple* and *Maple and Birches* by A.Y. Jackson, *Autumn Foliage 1916* and *The Pool* by Tom Thomson. They were strange to her with their oddly twisted trees and barren rocks, but she liked them, especially the autumn scenes with their vibrant and reds and oranges. Tania explained that these were famous Canadian landscape painters who belonged to the Group of Seven, which was formed in the 1920s. Kang nodded and wondered why there weren't any photographs anywhere.

After cleaning the bathroom, Kang decided to wash the walls. She held a wet rag and stood on a chair. To make the chore seem less boring, she imagined that she was an artist painting her masterpiece.

To be efficient, she put another chair next to the one she stood on, and then she filled a pail with water and placed it onto the chair. Then she only needed to bend to rinse the rag in the pail nearby rather than come all the way down to the floor. As she wiped the walls, she thought about her sister. Jian had married her husband not because she loved him—she did not even like him—but because she could no longer stand the gossip and loneliness. The gossip seemed trivial, but it had a profound effect on her. Constant whispering, questions, and speculation made her feel inferior. Her neighbours wondered why her fiancé had left her. Did she have a physical problem? Or mental health issues? Did she have a secret so shameful that no man wanted to marry her? Jian wouldn't go shopping or to the movies because she was convinced that everybody knew she had no one to go home to. She lost girlfriends who were busy with their boyfriends, husbands, or children. Some time after Jian's fiancé broke up with her, a friend's relative introduced her to a man named Yaozu. He proposed marriage and he expected Jian to be grateful because he would be doing her a big favour by marrying her.

If Jian had been able to bear the gossip and loneliness, Kang thought, she would never have married him. A Chinese proverb said that if a woman married a rooster, she should follow the rooster; if she married a dog, she should obey the dog. Jian's rooster disliked anything related to words—newspapers, magazines, and books. What he wanted was to have someone cook his meals and clean his home. That was what a wife should do. When Jian fulfilled her other wifely duty by giving birth to a daughter, that rooster considered it her responsibility alone to care for the child, even though she worked full time. Tradition had brought them together—the tradition that said a woman without a husband and children was not a real woman.

Am I a woman? Kang sometimes asked herself. She certainly did not want to be a woman like her sister—feeling shamed as a rape victim, abandoned by her fiancé, and married to a man without love. The tradition had forged bars to imprison Jian. As always, Kang felt heavy-hearted when she thought of her sister.

After changing the water in the pail, she set about mopping the last wall, but she heard steps coming down to the basement. "Kang." Tania stood on the steps, speaking to her. "Come to join me. I've made some chicken soup." Weary from the cleaning,

Kang suddenly noticed her grumbling stomach, so she gladly went upstairs, wondering what kind of soup Tania had made.

On the table were two plates with sandwiches. From a pot simmering on the stove came the aroma of chicken mixed with other unfamiliar scents. "Let me help," Kang said, going over to the stove. She found a ladle, but a look into the pot astonished her. It was a pot of light brown liquid with bits of onion floating in it—no chicken or meat of any kind inside. This kind of clear broth was called "high soup" in Chinese. Why did it have such a strange name? she wondered. Leaning over the pot, Kang could see her face reflected in the soup. Was it because the soup was like a mirror hanging high up on a wall? Kang pondered the name with amusement while she ladled Tania's soup into two bowls and placed them on the table.

"Thanks," Tania said with a smile. "This is my favourite soup. Hope you like it."

Kang spooned some into her mouth. "It's delicious. How did you make it?'

"It's simple. I use a prepared soup package." Tania grinned impishly. "I've been making this sort of soup just for myself for ages."

Just for myself? To Kang, that seemed to affirm that Tania didn't have a husband or children. She wondered if she was afraid of men, too.

"I'm usually too busy to cook," Tania added as she bit into her sandwich.

Kang imagined that there was almost nothing in Tania's refrigerator except for a carton of milk and a jug of orange juice "I can make some Chinese soup for you one day if you like. It has a lot of different things in it."

"That would be nice. And I can give you a ride if you want to go grocery shopping."

"Thanks," said Kang. She had been hoping to get some shopping done that afternoon. Tania was a spinster, too, thought Kang with some satisfaction. They seemed to be a good match.

CHAPTER 5: HACHIKO

AFTER A FEW WEEKS of living with Tania, Kang bought a second-hand bicycle to make the trip between the bus stop and her new home. Tania insisted she install lights on it. "Safety first," she said firmly. Kang complied, even though she thought the streetlights would provide enough protection. As a precautionary measure, she decided to carry a small can of hairspray and use it like Mace to ward off any potential attackers.

She had been checking the mailbox daily. She was crossing her fingers that she would be accepted to York University because it was close to her new home. She also planned to find a job nearby to avoid her long daily commute to Tim Hortons.

By the time Kang woke up every morning, Tania had already gone out with her dog Hachiko. Overweight and with high blood pressure, Tania had retired a month before, though she was only in her early sixties. Free from work, she buried herself in reading and writing in her study all day long.

One Sunday morning when Kang, still groggy and sleepy, turned on the tap to wash her face, she was surprised when no water came out. Wondering what the problem could be, she quickly lifted the lid of the toilet tank to get at least a bit of water to brush her teeth.

Upstairs in the kitchen, she poured some cornflakes and milk into a bowl for breakfast. Tania was usually walking her dog at this time, but Kang heard voices coming from the main floor bathroom—Tania's and a man's. Then she heard a clanking noise as someone banged on a pipe. She finished her breakfast and placed the bowl in the sink. She felt certain they were working on fixing the problem with the water. Since she couldn't do her laundry without water, she thought she might go to read in the library and then do some grocery shopping. It was a nice day to bike, she thought.

Tania came into the living room followed by a young man.

"Kang, meet Brian. He's just fixed the pipes," Tania said. "Sorry about the water problem this morning."

Kang nodded at Tania and then turned toward the repairman. "Hi, how do you do?" Kang greeted him. He was tall and handsome, with slate blue eyes and light brown hair. He was wearing a T-shirt and jeans, and she thought he might be in his mid-thirties.

"*Ni hao!* How do you do?" he replied.

Kang could not believe her ears. "You can speak Chinese! Where did you learn it?"

"Thanks. I picked it up from a friend," Brian answered, putting the tools down on the table. Then he told Tania that he would go to the furnace room to turn the main water valve back on.

"Go ahead," Tania replied. "I'll make some coffee for all of us." She took an espresso pot and a coffee jar from the cupboard, and then she turned on the stove to brew the coffee.

Curious about the pentagon-shaped coffee maker, Kang watched Tania setting three tiny cups and saucers on a tray. She wondered how many of these tiny cups would be equal to a regular cup of coffee. Was Tania trying to save coffee by using these small cups?

Brian returned from the furnace room and turned on the tap over the sink. "It's working now. Can I help you with anything else?" he asked Tania.

"No. Take a seat in the living room. Espresso is ready." Tania poured coffee into the three cups and placed them on the tray with a sugar bowl and some milk. Kang carried the tray to the living room.

Each of them took a cup. Tania added milk to hers; Brian drank his straight. Not fond of the coffee's bitterness, Kang dropped two spoons of sugar into her cup and poured in milk until it was full. She sipped the sweet and milky espresso while Tania and Brian chatted about the Canadian scientists who had determined the genetic code of the SARS virus.

"Have you heard about the international human genome project?" Brian asked.

"No. What is it?" Tania responded.

"It's a huge research effort directed at decoding the entire genetic makeup of the human species. And these scientists are also checking the genomes of nonhuman organisms."

Kang partly understood what they were talking about, but she could not find words to participate. She was surprised that the repairman seemed to also be very intelligent. Finishing her espresso, she excused herself and went back to her room downstairs.

That night, she woke up in the dark and checked the time: three o'clock. She turned and tossed in bed, but could not fall asleep again. She wondered why Brian's face kept popping into her mind.

It rained on and off throughout June. When Kang rode her bicycle, the puddles splashed her pants, giving her more laundry to do. But the sight of the lush green trees and lawn always put the unpleasant muddy stains out of her mind.

One Sunday afternoon, Tania suggested they go and hunt for mushrooms in some nearby woods. "I bet we can find some golden chanterelle and king bolete in Mill Pond Park."

"Ha, I'd like that," Kang said with excitement. "I can recognize some edible mushrooms, but I don't know their English names."

They took Hachiko, Tania's poodle, with them. At Tania's

suggestion, Kang carried two baskets, two knives, and a can of mosquito repellent. Tania also reminded her to bring a sweatshirt. "Is it cold in the woods?" Kang asked.

When Tania said it was for mosquitoes, Kang shook her head. She wondered if they really needed to be that protected. She was doubtful, but brought a sweater with her anyway.

They drove for about fifteen minutes to get to Mill Pond Park. After parking the car in a lot, Tania led the way into the woods while Hachiko leaped around, sniffed at plants, and peed on rocks. Kang found the fresh air mixed with the scent of pine trees invigorating. "Here we are." Tania put her sweatshirt on and sprayed the repellent on her hair, face, and all over her clothes. Kang put on her sweater and sprayed only on her neck, hands, and other exposed parts. She figured that the smell, which made her dizzy, would definitely be strong enough to knock out mosquitoes.

Kang lit up when she peered into the grass under a pine tree and found a yellow, funnel-shaped mushroom. She bent down and cut it.

"Make sure to leave the root in the soil." Tania told her.

"This is a mushroom that we also have in China!" Kang exclaimed, surprised at finding the same species on a different continent.

"Let me see," said Tania, coming to check it out. "Oh, that's a golden chanterelle."

"In Kunming we call it a yellow silk thread mushroom."

"Interesting. Golden and yellow describe the colour." Tania nodded. "In Russia some people call it fox's cap."

"I suppose foxes can be a golden or yellow colour, too," Kang said. "Do you understand Russian?"

"Certainly. After all, I came from the former Soviet Union."

"I know some Russian songs." Kang hummed a melody.

"Wow!" Tania was surprised. "Where did you learn 'Blooming Geider Tree'?"

"From my sister, but I've forgotten the lyrics."

"It's a love song. It was very popular in the fifties...." For a moment Tania seemed to be preoccupied.

"Here's another one!" Kang cried out as she bent down and brushed aside the pine needles with her hand.

"Good. We'll keep looking. There should be lots of them after all the rain we've had," said Tania, making a beeline for a patch of moss.

Suddenly, Kang remembered going mushroom-picking with her sister two decades earlier.

It was the first time eight-year-old Kang had gone with Jian, and her friends, Yezi and Lan, to pick mushrooms. After about a half-hour trek, they reached the woods near the Lotus Pond, where they found many kinds of mushrooms poking up through the pine needles that carpeted the ground. The three older girls bent down to gather them, but Kang was more interested in the butterflies and dragonflies that flitted about.

She picked up a dead twig and scampered after a butterfly until it alighted on a wild rose. Then, tiptoeing toward the bush, she reached out, her hand slightly shaking with the branch. *I can get it. One, two, three.* Holding her breath, she gently pinned the creature down. Then she carefully pinched the wings of the butterfly with her fingers.

She looked at it closely, noticing how the translucent, dark red wings, which were striped and trimmed in black, shone in the sunlight filtering through the tree branches. The butterfly's little round head moved slightly and innocently toward her. *Is it hurt?* Kang wondered, pulling a handkerchief from her pocket and pinching three of its corners together into a cloth cage. Then she released the butterfly and pulled the last corner up to prevent its escape.

At first it fluttered its wings, but then it stopped moving, so she opened two corners of the handkerchief corners and peered inside. The tiny creature lay there, its body curling up and its red wings together, small parts of which now were transparent.

She closed the handkerchief again and then noticed she had tiny red and black dots on her fingertips. She knew they were from the butterfly. *I stole its colours and my handkerchief killed it.* She felt acute remorse at her thoughtlessness as she carefully unfolded the cloth cage on the palm of her hand. Suddenly exposed to the light, the butterfly remained lifeless for a moment, but then it flapped its wings and slowly flew away. Kang released a held breath. It was still alive!

Tania had disappeared into the woods, so Kang continued to gather more mushrooms, some of which were foreign to her. She hoped Tania could identify them for her. Then she spotted more golden chanterelles under some Douglas fir branches that touched the ground. Kneeling down, she lifted one of the offshoots up, stretched her head under it, and was delighted to find so many of her favourite mushrooms. Unfortunately the picking was difficult—a fog of mosquitoes had started to swarm about her head. As she tried to wave them away, she quickly gathered all the mushrooms she had picked and put them into her basket.

On the pine-needle-covered ground, she found a boletus, the species that is known in China as a pine mushroom. Tania had told her that dried boletus from Poland could be found in some stores in the High Park neighbourhood. If she found more of them, she could dry some and see if they tasted better than the fresh ones, she thought as she continued to forage in the damp shade. Another army of buzzing mosquitoes invaded her moment of peace and quiet; she waved her hand around to protect her head against the mosquitoes' dancing. Her face was covered with sweat and dirt, but at least her basket was filled with mushrooms.

"Tania!" she called out, wondering where she could have gotten to. Tania's voice came from a distance, but Kang could not see her. She was trying to find a path to reach her when a sudden rustling noise in the bushes startled her. Was it a wolf?

Or a bear? She recoiled and fumbled for a rock or something to defend herself with. Grabbing a sturdy branch, she retreated to a large oak tree, her legs weak with fear. At that moment, Hachiko jumped into a clearing, his tail wagging. Relieved, Kang bent to pet the dog, the bough slipping from her hand.

Hachiko raced around and around, barking with joy. He went back the way he had come and then stopped to wait for Kang. He was taking her to Tania. Basket in hand, she followed Hachiko, who scrambled through the shrubs and brambles, yelping from time to time to signal his location.

After about ten minutes, they finally reached Tania. "Do you know this mushroom?" Tania asked, pointing to an orange red one with whitish warts on the cap. "I hope you haven't picked one of them."

"Oh, no! I never would. It's fly agaric, which is deadly poisonous."

"How did you know?"

"I learned about it when I first went mushroom picking with my sister and her friends."

"In China?"

"Yes. The first time I saw them, I assumed I'd discovered a treasure. I gathered them all in my handkerchief and ran to show them to Jian. When I opened my handkerchief to display my discovery, she gasped. She told me they were poisonous and asked me to throw them away. I didn't want to, so she got her friends, Yezi and Lan, to back her up.

"Yezi said the mushroom was called fly agaric. Her nanny used it to kill flies. Lan also asked me to get rid of them, but I wouldn't listen to her, either. Their baskets were full of boletus and russula, but I thought my fly agaric was the prettiest."

"How old were you?" Tania asked.

"Eight."

"Such a coincidence. I first went hunting for mushrooms with my cousins at the same age," Tania said. "Where did you pick mushrooms in Peking?"

"Not in Beijing."

"I remember you came from—" Tania paused to mimic Kang's pronunciation—"Beijing."

"I lived in Kunming as a child."

"Where is that?"

"It's the capital city of Yunnan Province in Southwest China. It's where I was born, and where I grew up.

Tania stood up. "Tell me about it."

"The weather there is nice all year round. There are lots of historic spots. On the way home after mushroom picking that day, Jian and her friends took turns carrying me because I was too tired to walk. When we passed the Lotus Pond, Yezi told us the legend of the pond as it had been told to her by her Nanny Yao. About three hundred years ago, during the Ming Dynasty, eight women were renowned for their beauty. One of them was Chen Yuanyuan, who had many talents: dancing and singing, writing in calligraphy, and drawing pictures. She fell in love with General Wu Sangui and became his concubine. During the war, Wu learned that an official of Emperor Li Zhicheng had captured his concubine, so he decided to overthrow the ruler." Kang paused. "Are you following me?"

"Yes. Did Wu love his wife?"

"I'm not sure. I only know that Chen Yuanyuan was his concubine."

"What's her name again?"

"Chen Yuanyuan."

"You've told me about the ruined palace in Beijing. What's its name?"

"Yuanmingyuan." Kang spoke slowly.

"Thanks. I heard 'yuan' in the both names and got confused." Tania patted Hachiko. "There are too many mosquitoes. Let's get out of here, but continue your story."

Kang meandered along with Tania and Hachiko as they made their way out of the forest. "As the governor of Yunnan, Wu eventually became corrupt. Chen felt so disappointed that she became a nun and lived in a temple. When she heard of Wu's death, she drowned herself in the pond. Afterwards, a double lotus grew out of the pond. People said it represented the spirit of Chen's love for Wu."

"It's a bleak story."

"I didn't understand it at the time, but I wondered what would've grown there if she hadn't jumped into the pond. Years later, I still don't understand why Chen Yuanyuan would kill herself for a corrupt man. Do you believe love can be that powerful?"

"I think in old times women depended on men too much. Anyway, love is always beautiful, even though it's sad sometimes," Tania said.

With Hachiko leading the way, they came out of the woods and headed toward the parking lot. No longer bothered by mosquitoes, Kang took off her sweater to enjoy the breeze. She wiped sweat off her face with a tissue and recalled an egg-shaped, white mushroom that she had picked but did not know. She pulled it from the basket and asked Tania if it was edible.

"It's a horse mushroom. It's tasty," Tania said. "I got some, too." Her basket was half full of mushrooms of various kinds.

Kang checked her own basket; it was full, but the mushrooms were mixed with a lot of grass and pine needles. "I don't think we can eat all these mushrooms right away. We have quite a few. What can we do with them?"

"Simple. We can freeze them to use later."

"That's a great idea," said Kang. Thinking about stir-frying mushrooms with shredded pork made her mouth water.

As they talked, Hachiko ran along the path, leading the two women back to Tania's car. Kang praised him lavishly while rubbing his neck and petting his back. Tania started the car. "He was named after the most loyal dog in the world."

She told Kang the tale of the original Hachiko, who had belonged to a college professor in Tokyo. Hachiko would meet his master daily at the Shibuya train station when the professor returned from work. One day the professor died from a heart attack while he was at work. Without knowing of his master's death, Hachiko went to the station at the same time every day and waited for the usual train. He did this every day for ten years until his own death.

Greatly touched by the story, Kang gazed at Hachiko with affection, understanding now why Tania had given him such an odd name. She held him on her lap, stroking his head while he snuggled happily in her arms.

CHAPTER 6: BLACKOUT

ONE DAY TANIA ASKED KANG if she was interested in the upcoming Rolling Stones SARS Benefit Concert. Kang had never paid much attention to rock music, but she had heard about this rock band and was mildly curious.

"They're from England," Tania added, noticing Kang's hesitation. "Do you know Mick Jagger and Keith Richards? I went to one of their concerts a long time ago." She swayed slightly, as if she were listening to their music.

"I don't think I know their music, but okay," Kang said. "I'll come with you. When and where?"

"In the afternoon on Wednesday at Downsview Park—where Pope John Paul II offered a Papal Mass last year."

"How much is the ticket?"

"It's not much. Twenty-one dollars and fifty cents. And I can pay for you if you like."

"No, I can pay," said Kang, thinking that she needed to trade shifts with a co-worker on the Wednesday. She had arrived in Toronto last September, too late to see Pope John Paul II, whose name she had been hearing for many years. But she was excited now that she'd made her decision to go the concert.

Luckily, a co-worker was willing to exchange shifts. On the day of the concert, Kang and Tania headed to Downsview Park after lunch. With all the parking lots full, Tania had to drive around and around until they eventually found a spot to park at a nearby building.

Carrying canvas folding chairs, they stopped to accept bottled water from the volunteers at the entrance and then joined the crowd surging into the park. The concert hadn't started yet, but the huge place was already swarming with people.

Kang and Tania inched their way along until they spotted a space barely large enough for their two chairs. Happily, they squeezed into the space and settled in. Under the bright sun, the canvas chairs were warm to the touch. Although she was dressed in shorts and a T-shirt, Kang sweated. Everyone was hot. There were no trees to provide some shade from the sun. Around her, thousands of sleeveless arms were pumping up and down in excitement. To Kang, they looked like little sails in a throbbing sea of human beings.

People were cheerful, chatting and laughing. A group near the fence looked upward and suddenly screamed. At the same moment, Kang felt cool drops on her face. She looked up and discovered that the water was coming from a hose wielded by one of the volunteers. The crowds cheered their appreciation for this brief relief from the scorching sun.

The woman next to her told Tania about being in the same location the year before, when Pope John Paul II had started his speech by mentioning the rain showers that had already soaked the crowd twice. "I remember," Tania reminisced. "The Pope said everybody there had been baptized by nature."

"I got wet from the rain, but I didn't get sick. So maybe it was holy water." The woman laughed.

Listening to their conversation and imagining the shower she had missed the year before, Kang thought about a Chinese expression: *hu feng huan yu*. It was a call for wind and rain. She smiled at the thought that Pope John Paul II was so connected to a higher power that he might have actually been able to make the rain fall to cool down the people in the crowd.

At that moment, the stage announcer's voice boomed through the loudspeakers, and then a couple of different bands appeared on a large screen and began to perform. The human sea started to pulse to the beat of the music. All around her, people laughed, cried, or joined in the singing. Kang felt as if she was floating up and down on the rock-and-roll waves.

Suddenly, she saw a woman, naked above the waist, jumping up out of the crowd. Then another one, not far from her, took off her blouse and stood. Her uncovered breasts shimmied when she raised her hands. Kang gaped at them, speechless. The woman's pale, plump, and sweaty breasts glistening in the sun shocked her. She turned to Tania to see her reaction, but Tania just smiled and said, "A rock concert couldn't happen without bare breasts."

Kang thought the women were really bold. She wondered what freedom really meant. Would she ever feel free enough to bare her breasts in public? She thought not.

As dusk fell, the stage was lit with striking and colourful strobe lights. A middle-aged man in a bright red shirt emerged on the screen and shouted, "This is the biggest party in Toronto's history, right?"

"Right! Mick! Right!" the audience cheered, arms pumping up and down. Their roar echoed as the man continued, "You're here. We're here."

Some of the audience chanted along with him, "Toronto is back, and it's booming!"

Clasping her hands, Tania murmured, "He's getting older...."

"Who is he?" Kang asked.

"You really don't know?" said Tania. "That's Mick Jagger, the lead singer of the Stones." Her eyes were fixed on the large screen, and her body swayed to the rhythm of the music.

Kang stared at the singer; his face was full of wrinkles, and his big smile seemed to arouse hysteria among his fans. Gradually, she immersed herself in the music and the enthusiastic shouts. At the end of the concert, she stretched her arms, waving with the others in the cheerful sea.

Days later, the music of the concert still echoed in her head like thunder. The downpour of the rock and roll had stopped, but the echo still hovered.

Accepted into the program she had applied for, Kang chose York University without hesitation. She started job hunting near the university, but had no luck, so she decided to continue working at Tim Hortons until just before her classes started in September.

One afternoon, she passed a cup of coffee and two chocolate chip cookies to a customer and punched the amount into the cash register, as usual, but no number appeared on the screen. She blinked, wondering what had happened. The cash register had stopped working.

The customer answered her unspoken question. "The power is out," he said.

He was right. Kang noticed then that the whole shop was dim, and the background music had stopped. Some people in the line walked away, but others remained, hoping their orders could be filled even without power.

The man placed the money on the counter and took his coffee and cookies. "Don't worry about the machine. I always buy the same things. "It's two-forty-five, right? Here's two-fifty. Keep the change."

"Thanks." Kang wrote down the amount of the money on a slip of paper so she could punch it in later.

"Sorry everybody," said the assistant manager, who had come over to the counter. "No electricity. Cash only, please. Sorry for the inconvenience." She opened Kang's cash register with a key. "Try your math skills." She grinned as she went to unlock the other machine.

The next person in line asked for four large cups of coffee and four donuts. As Kang filled the cups, she made the calculations in her head and then used a pen and paper to add the tax.

"That's nine dollars and sixty-six cents including the taxes," she told the customer.

"Wow," the woman said, "you're quick." She passed the money to Kang.

"Thanks. Next please." Kang's face was sticky with sweat and her shoulder-length hair was stuck to the back of her neck. It was hot now that the air conditioner had stopped working.

Twenty minutes later, the manager arrived. He told everyone that he had heard on the radio that the blackout would last a long time, so he had decided to close the shop. He told the servers to give away the food in the fridges and on the shelves. "This is a good time to give our customers some treats," he said, and the customers clapped their hands.

Kang and the others passed out coffee, tea, donuts, and cookies until nothing was left. "No more work today," the manager told them. "See you tomorrow." He handed each of them a bag of donuts and cookies that he had prepared for them while they were serving the customers.

That was nice of him, Kang thought with appreciation as she put her bag in her backpack. She left the coffee shop with Susan, co-worker, who asked, "Where do you live? Do you need a ride?"

"In Vaughan," Kang answered. "I'll take the subway."

"But there's no subway service now."

"How do you know?" Kang asked. She had noticed an empty streetcar on the track not far from the shop, but she had not linked the electricity problem with the subway.

"It's a blackout. The TTC trains can't work without electricity," Susan replied with a smile. "I can give you a ride to the Dufferin station, but then I'll have to go south to pick up my daughter."

"That's very kind of you. Thanks." Kang followed Susan to her car in the parking lot. She was very nice, thought Kang, even though they'd hardly ever spoken. "I appreciate your help. Without you, I wouldn't have even realized the subway was shut down," Kang said.

In the car, Kang saw ordinary people directing traffic at the intersections along Bloor Street West. Crowds of people filled the sidewalks. It looked like the streets in Beijing—full of pedestrians, thought Kang.

"It's like a festival, isn't it?" Susan said, checking her watch.

"Yes. I've never seen so many people out on the street before," Kang replied, noticing Susan's worried face. "You can drop me here. I'll walk to Dufferin or any subway station where I can get a bus."

"Are you sure? The buses must be crowded. Do you have any friends who live around here?"

"Yes. I might stay with one of them if I can't get home," Kang said, thinking about contacting Nancy or Fei.

Soon the traffic was bumper to bumper. Susan slowly moved her car into the right lane, turned at a corner, and stopped. "The station should be in the next block. Sorry to drop you here."

"Thanks a lot," Kang said as she got out. She watched Susan's car turning right on the next road. Then she joined a pack of pedestrians across the street and headed east. Everyone was friendly, smiling, talking to one another. Old or young, men or women, they all seemed to be cheerful rather than worried. The city without electricity seemed more electric.

She planned to contact Tania and tell her it would takes ages for her to get home. Kang started looking for a phone booth. If the subway didn't start running again soon, she thought she could phone Nancy to find out if she could stay with her.

Spotting a phone booth, she went in and got her address book out of her backpack. She dropped a quarter into the slot and dialled Nancy's number, but all she got was the answering machine. She hung up and put another quarter into the slot to telephone Tania, but now there was no dial tone. She heard the coin drop into the box. Staring at the screen, she saw nothing. The phone line had died on her.

With a sigh, she left the booth and strode along the packed street. When she arrived at Dufferin station, she asked a TTC worker if the service would resume soon. Chances were slim, she was told, so she continued walking north on Dufferin Street. She wondered whether she should try to flag taxi, but she hadn't noticed any on the roads. She also wondered if she would have to find a hotel room, but that would mean that using up all her grocery money for the next two weeks. She checked her watch. It was 5:41 p.m. She decided to keep walking. She would probably get home before eleven o'clock. That wasn't so bad, she thought. Normally, she would've just finished work by that time.

At a corner, some people stood with a few cases of bottled water piled beside them. They offered free water to passersby. Kang thanked them and took one. The water soothed her tongue and mouth. She licked her dry lips and realized she had been overwhelmed with excitement and stress. Before she finished her bottle of water, a car pulled over to the curb beside her. Then she heard someone call out, "Kang!"

Surprised, she turned her head and saw a minivan with the words Toronto Hydro. A man in the passenger's seat stuck his head out the window and waved his hand. "Hop in." The side door behind his seat opened.

Do I know him? Kang was puzzled. The passenger pointed to the driver, and she spotted a smiling face.

"Brian!" She remembered the repairman she had met at Tania's house.

"Join us," Brian said.

As Kang climbed into the van, a woman squeezed over to make room for her. A few more people were sitting inside.

As they drove, Kang tried to figure out who these people could be. It seemed from their conversation that they had not known each other before. She assumed they were not workers with Toronto Hydro and that they were probably getting a ride just like she was. But Brian must work for the company, she thought, otherwise he wouldn't be driving the van.

Gazing out the window, she noticed that volunteers were still directing traffic at the intersections. In some gridlocked places, instead of leaning on their horns as they might have done on a normal day, drivers signalled for cars to go around them or patiently waited their turn. The blackout seemed to have shortened the distance between people. Kang marvelled at the thought that this was the second ride she'd been offered that day. And it had been a pleasant surprise to see Brian again.

Soon the van stopped in front of a high-rise office building. "This is as far as I can bring you, everybody. Good luck with the rest of your journey back home," said Brian.

Kang slid open the side door and got out of the vehicle along with the other passengers. Brian got out, and everyone thanked him for the ride.

"You're more than welcome," Brian responded and then smiled at Kang. "I still have a couple more jobs to finish, but then I can drive you home," he said to her. "If you'll wait for me, that is."

"That's okay," she replied. "It's not too far now. I'll be able to get home much earlier than I thought."

"Good luck. Bye!" Brian said, lifting his toolbox from the van.

Kang heard her stomach growl and realized she was hungry. She suddenly remembered the bag of donuts, so she took off her backpack and pulled the package out. "Before you go, would you like some donuts?" she asked Brian.

"Sure, I'd love one."

She opened the paper bag and he reached in. "Ha! Chocolate—my favourite!"

"Take more." Kang insisted.

"One's enough. Thanks!" Brian said and then hurried into the building.

Kang left and joined the crowd surging forward on the sidewalk. She took a donut from the bag and bit into it, savouring its soft texture and sweetness.

"Would you like one?" she asked, holding the bag out to a girl with a ponytail walking next to her.

"Thanks," the girl said with surprise as she eagerly took one.

By the time Kang reached Steeles Avenue West, it was dark and there were fewer people around. Near the bus stop, she retrieved her bicycle, which she had locked to a chain-link fence. As she cycled along, feeling more lighthearted than she had all day, she noticed that the stars in the sky seemed much brighter than usual. The moon shone like a huge light bulb, guiding her through the darkness. Softly, she began to sing an old Chinese song: *"The moon is bright. My true love—"* She paused and grinned. Did she have a true love? she asked herself as Brian's face popped into her mind.

CHAPTER 7: A NEW JOB WITH TANIA

KANG REACHED HER STREET and Tania's house finally came into view. Silhouetted in the moonlight, with ivy leaves on the walls rustling in the evening breeze, the bungalow suddenly reminded her of the gloomy and foreboding setting in *Wuthering Heights*. It was in that house that Catherine married Edgar, but fell in love with Heathcliff. Kang walked up the steps and put her key into the lock. She wondered if Tania had ever had a lover. Maybe he had left her, like Heathcliff had left Catherine. The questions crossed her mind like a flash in the darkness. Why was she comparing Tania to Catherine? She shook her head to get rid of this odd notion, then shivered slightly and felt a sudden pang of loneliness.

She unlocked the front door and pushed it open, calling out, "Hello? Tania? I'm home."

"Thank goodness!" Tania cried out from her bedroom. "How are you?" She emerged in the glow of the oil lamp in her hand. Hachiko followed his mistress, barking in greeting and wagging his tail.

"I'm good," said Kang, reaching out to take the lamp. They fumbled carefully through the shadows cast by the dim light and sat down at the table in the living room. The sense of loneliness disappeared. Kang was happy to be with Tania.

But sitting in the dark brought a childhood memory to mind. Years before, she had been awakened in the middle of the night by a thunderclap. "Mom!" a young Kang had cried out in fear.

"Don't be scared. I'm here with you," her sister Jian had said, sitting up in bed, gently patting Kang's head. Their parents had been away, as they often were those days, and had left Jian to look after her. Kang had not understood why their parents, like some of the other teachers and staff at their school, had had to receive thought reform at another school, the May Seventh Cadre School. Many such thought reform schools had been established across the country. That night she had asked her sister what their parents were doing at that school, and why they'd had to go.

"They are learning to work with the soil and fertilize it. They sow seeds and harvest crops," Jian had explained.

"But they aren't farmers."

"Chairman Mao wants to re-educate them."

"Do we have to go there when we grow up?"

"Maybe...."

"I didn't even notice the blackout until five thirty when I tried to turn on the stove to make some soup." Tania's voice broke into Kang's musing. "Luckily my radio is battery-operated, so I heard the news." Tania held Hachiko on her lap; his hair appeared fluffier in the candlelight. "How did you manage to get back without the TTC?"

Kang told Tania about her day's adventures.

"So you didn't have supper," said Tania, turning the knob on the lamp. The flame lengthened, and the living room became brighter. "We have some canned food in the kitchen. Take whatever you like from the cabinet by the fridge."

Kang did not feel hungry, but she was thirsty. She filled a glass with cold water and sat back down with Tania who now started to reminisce about a power failure she had been through in her teen years, several decades earlier.

Born to a medical school professor's family, Tania had grown up in the suburbs of Moscow. Every time a power failure happened, there would be no running water, so the local residents would go to the Moskva River with their buckets.

One freezing January morning, the water pipe was dry once again. With no water to use for cooking, the family made do with canned food. When Tania and her sister, Nadya, came home after school, their parents had not yet come back. Coal was burning inside the iron stove, keeping the sitting room warm, but the electricity had not yet come back and the taps were still dry.. Tania decided to go to get water from the river; she had seen people drilling holes in the ice to reach the water, and she was curious about the process.

"Mama told Papa she would get it if there's still no water by the afternoon," Nadya had said, sitting down on a padded wooden chair. She wanted to read Mikhail Lermontov's *A Hero of Our Time*.

"I'll go myself if you don't want to," said Tania, going to the kitchen to get a tin bucket and a wooden stick. Nevertheless, preferring Nadya's company, she offered a bribe. "If you come with me, I'll lend you Pushkin's *Eugene Onegin* and give you some beads." She bent over to put on her rubber boots. From the corner of her eye, she saw her sister standing up. She knew Nadya would go along with her.

Tania hung the tin bucket on the middle of the stick, holding one end and passing the other end to Nadya. Then she led the way to the riverbank and picked her way down towards a hole in the ice, following a trail of footprints. Many people had been going to the frozen river to get water, Tania noted. On the way there, her hand pinched the bread crumbs she had put into her coat pocket, and she wondered whether she would be fortunate enough to get a fish through the hole—she had heard that some boys had caught a few.

The ice glistened in the afternoon sunshine, and skaters glided in the distance. Reaching the jagged edge of the armchair-sized hole, Tania squatted and peered into it. Nadya stood by, watching the skaters and waiting for Tania to fill the pail.

Tania dropped crumbs into the water, and immediately a few small fish opened their mouths to swallow them. An idea occurred to her. She held the handle of the bucket with her hand and slowly pushed it into the water, deep enough that the fish could swim over into it. Her other hand got more crusts from her pocket and dropped them little by little into the water that had filled the bucket. Two fish swam into it. One, two, three! Tania yanked the pail out of the water.

But suddenly, her feet slid, and the weight of the bucket pulled her down into the hole. "Hel—!" Before she could finish the word, she plunged into the icy river. Her hands flapping, she struggled to keep her head above the water. "Nadya!"

Nadya had already picked up the stick they had used for the bucket and was now stretching it out for her sister to grab onto. "Mama!" she cried out, her teeth chattering. "Help! Help!" Her screams carried over the frozen river.

Tania grabbed the stick and tried desperately to heave herself onto the ice. The icy water soaking through her clothes felt like a dull knife cutting her. Though her body had become completely numb, her mind was still clear enough to be aware that pulling too hard on the stick might drag Nadya into the water, too. Her lips trembled, and her voice, calling for help, became as light as thin threads.

Time froze. Then she felt her arms being lifted. That was the last thing she remembered. Only later did she learn that a skater had come to her rescue.

"I almost lost my life," said Tania, a wry smile crossing her face in the dim light. "But I learned a lesson. Listening to Mama is always the right thing to do."

Kang pondered Tania's story and compared it with her own experience over the past few hours. She was so lucky to have run into Brian. Thinking about him, she could not help but ask, "Is Brian single? He's such a nice person."

"He's charming." Even though Tania could not see Kang

clearly, she could guess the reason for her curiosity. "You seem to like him. I'll tell you a secret, but don't feel too disappointed."

"What is it?" Intrigued, Kang leaned her head toward Tania.

"He's gay."

"How do you know?"

"I've figured it out. Since he broke up with his girlfriend five years ago, he hasn't had another one. I asked him about it several times, and he said he just lost interest in girls. Once he visited me with a young man, his housemate. They seem to get along very well. 'Don't ask and don't tell'—that's my philosophy. Even though he's my nephew."

"He's your nephew!" Kang exclaimed.

"Yes. Didn't I tell you that when he came here last time?"

"No." Kang shook her head. "I have met a few gay people here in Canada," she said. The news left her with mixed feelings. She was relieved to think that she need not be afraid of him, but she didn't fully understand why she also felt a smattering of regret.

Kang didn't think she had ever met any gay people back home. She told Tania that many Chinese people did not even know what the word "homosexual" meant.

"I think there are many gay men and women everywhere," Tania said. "It's just that in some countries it's not accepted, and so people are forced to hide who they are, which is terrible."

"Yes, that is terrible," answered Kang.

"As for Brian, I wish he were married and had a child, so I could be a great aunt," she said. Then she let out a long sigh. She smiled at Kang, and added, "Well, he could also marry a man and adopt a child!"

Kang had not known that this was even possible, and she suddenly felt very happy to be living in a country where people had the freedom to live their lives as they chose to.

When classes at the university started, Kang quit her two jobs. Since she saved three hours on the commute, she now had the time to clean the house on Saturday mornings. But after paying her tuition, she had very little left in her savings account, so she had to find another job soon. She checked newspaper ads and help wanted signs on campus and near home, but had no luck.

She assumed that since Tania had been a professor at York, she might have some suggestions to help her find a job.

When she joined Tania in the living room, she said, "I've applied for a job at the cafeteria, the bookstore, the gym, and the computer labs, but I haven't got any responses."

"It takes time," said Tania. "Have you checked with the International Student Office? I know you're not a visa student, but they might be able to help you."

"I'll try it. And if you hear of anyone at the university who is hiring, please let me know."

"Hmm," Tania replied, something crossing her mind. "Do you think you could proofread?"

"I think so," she answered, thinking it would be marvellous if she could get paid for doing a job like reading. "Where can I find this kind of work?"

Tania hesitated for a second. "You can do it for me. I'm working on the final revisions of my memoir. I can't pay you much more than the minimum wage. But then I don't think you have any experience with this kind of work."

"No, I don't. But I think I can do it, and I'll try my best." Kang was intrigued about the prospect of reading Tania's manuscript and learning more about her, especially about her early years in the former Soviet Union. Like many Chinese people, she had some familiarity with the Russian culture. Her father had even studied there, though he never talked about it. In fact, she would have been willing to proofread for free if she had not needed the money to survive. "When can I start?"

"How about in late December? I plan to finish writing by the end of this year and have it proofread in the following months. If you need some money, I can pay you in advance."

"That would be great! Thanks so much!" Breathing a sigh of relief, Kang decided to get some books from the library about proofreading the following day. She wondered whether there would ever come a day when she did not need to worry about a job, when, just like Tania had, she could help others by offering them work. Her mind now at ease, she had a decent sleep for the first time since her classes began.

Saturday, after cleaning the house, she visited Scott Library at the university. Searching through the catalogue, she borrowed two books: *Handbook for Proofreading* and *The Canadian Style: A Guide to Writing and Editing*.

After supper, Tania went out with Hachiko. With two pillows piled against the headboard, Kang lay down on her bed and opened one of the books about proofreading. After reading through several pages, her mind started to wander. She thought about Sigmund Freud's theories of psychosexual development, which she had studied in one of her psychology courses. She wondered if she had developed a strong sexual interest in the opposite sex during the final stage, what Freud called the genital stage? She recalled that she had once hiked with a young male friend on the Western Hills in the suburbs of Beijing. When they'd reached the last stone step leading to a pavilion, Kang had cheerfully recited a line by the Tang Dynasty poet, Wang Zhihuan: "To have a bird's eye view, one should reach the top of the tower."

The young man had turned and hugged her tightly. Kang had felt her face flush and her heart start pounding. When he had kissed her, his tongue thrusting into her mouth, she'd felt as if a claw had seized her heart. She'd pushed him away, and her twisted face had startled him. He'd stumbled and fallen. "What's the matter with you?" he'd shouted, his face flushing red.

Kang remembered reading that according to Freud, if development is arrested in what he called the phallic stage, a girl becomes a woman who continually strives to dominate men, either as an unusually seductive woman with high self-esteem or as an unusually submissive woman with low self-esteem. Kang did not consider herself either seductive or submissive. Whenever a man started to get close to her, she put up a wall. And she knew with certainty that it had nothing to do with high self-esteem or low self-esteem. Her development had been halted when she was twelve; when Jian was raped.

She went to the bathroom and splashed some cold water on her hot face. What did she need a man for? Was she crazy? Did any of this matter? In this country, she could be whoever she wanted to be without worrying about other people's opinions. She dried her face on the towel. She checked her watch. It was seven o'clock. She returned to her bed and picked up the book she had started reading.

Suddenly the phone rang, startling her. It was most likely for Tania, she thought.But it kept ringing and then Kang remembered Tania was out walking the dog. The phone stopped. After a few seconds, it rang again.

Who is this stubborn person? Why not leave a message? She jumped out of bed and reached for the phone on the wall.

CHAPTER 8: MEETING, NOT DATING

KANG PICKED UP THE PHONE and was surprised to hear a familiar male voice. "Is this Kang?"

"Speaking." Her heart seemed to skip a beat. Why was Brian calling her?

"Could we meet for a coffee?"

Hesitantly, she asked, "When?" She felt her face get hot.

"How about now? At Tim Hortons on the corner of Dufferin and Steeles? I can pick you up," he said. She detected a slight tremor in his voice.

She pictured his smiling face. This was not a date, she told herself. *He's gay. Why not meet him?* She could practise her English. "Okay," she said. "When will you be here?"

"In twenty minutes. Is that okay?"

"Yes, I'll see you soon." Kang went into the bathroom to get ready. While she combed her hair, her hand trembled. She had just agreed to meet a man for the first time in many years. But he's gay, she repeated to herself.

Half an hour later, Kang sat with Brian at a corner booth at Tim Hortons. The coffee shop looked exactly the same as the one she had worked at—the colours of the tables, chairs, floor, and the counter were all familiar, and she felt relaxed. Noticing his jumbo coffee cup, she asked, "Doesn't coffee keep you awake?"

"Definitely. I drink two or three cups every day, and I feel like I'm alive." He grinned. "Tell me—what part of China are you from?"

"I came from Beijing, but I was born and raised in Kunming."

"Have you ever seen *Five Golden Flowers*?"

"Oh yes. I like it," said Kang, astonished that he was familiar with that particular movie, a love story based on Yunnan folklore. "It's a story from my home province."

"Oh, tell me more about it."

"It's about the Bai people, one of the minorities in Yunnan," she explained. "When did you watch that film?"

"That's a long story." He sighed. "My ex studied Chinese and used to watch Chinese movies. *Five Golden Flowers* was her favourite. I watched it with her a couple of times." He looked at Kang and smiled. "Besides the Bai people, there must be other ethnic groups in Yunnan."

"You're right. There are many, but most of the population is Han Chinese." She hesitated for a few seconds. "As a matter of fact, my mother is Hmong, but I don't usually tell people that."

"Why not?" He stopped sipping the coffee, his eyes wide open.

"Minority people are sometimes looked down upon by others," she said, wondering why she was talking about something she usually tried to forget.

"Do you mean racism?"

"Well, ordinary people can be prejudiced against other ethnic groups in China, but there are government policies to try and counteract discrimination."

"How?"

"In my case, I had an extra ten points added to my total scores on the entrance exams for universities because of my mother's ethnic background. The higher points helped me get accepted to Beijing Normal University."

"Sort of like some Canadian government policies that aim to help minority groups here, I guess." Brian smiled, and added, "Would you like to hear my story?"

Kang nodded and listened with interest as Brian told her

that he had been a senior student majoring in engineering at Colombia University, where his ex-girlfriend Ingrid majored in history. Later Ingrid had switched into the East Asian Studies program and fallen in love with her Chinese professor, which led to their breakup.

Kang could sense how heartbroken Brian had been when his girlfriend left. Looking into his slate blue eyes, she felt sorry that he'd had to go through that, but she couldn't help but wonder how the experience had made him a gay man.

Before she had a chance to try to respond to his story, however, his cell phone rang. He turned to her and with a slight grimace said, "So sorry. I've got to go. My housemate lost his key and he's locked out. But I'll drive you home first."

Kang enjoyed the psychology course she was taking. For one assignment, the students had to form discussion groups before writing individual papers on a particular topic. Kang's group discussed how childhood experiences affected them as adults, and she was amazed at how open her fellow students were about their own experiences.

"I remember when I was five years old, my parents used to go to the movies on Saturday night," said Luke, always an active participant. "They hired a teenage babysitter to take care of me. Her name was, let me see, Mickey. At seven o'clock, she turned on the TV and found *Land of the Lost* for me to watch. Then she told me she was going out for a few minutes. 'Don't leave me! Take me with you!' I begged her.

"'Shh!' Mickey put her finger on her lips. 'If you're good, I'll tell you an awesome story.' So I agreed to watch TV, but I asked her to come back in five minutes. I followed the Marshalls on the screen into the mysterious world they discovered at the bottom of a scary waterfall. I was suddenly afraid that my parents might have been taken to some strange world like that, and I started to scream. Mickey came back into the room and sat beside me, looking very annoyed. I didn't care much for the expression on her face, but I held on to her arm tightly as I watched. Anyway, I think this childhood experience had a strong impact on my psychology." Luke paused. Kang was all ears.

"That's why I don't like science fiction," he continued. "And whenever I feel nervous I smoke."

"Hey, what's any of that got to do with smoking?" asked one of the participants.

"Oh," Luke added, "I forgot to mention that my babysitter was fired because my neighbour told my mom that Mickey always smoked cigarettes outside our house whenever she babysat. I smoked when I was a teenager, maybe because of her influence. I think that counts as a kind of psychological damage from childhood."

Kang was surprised that he thought behaviour he had not actually witnessed would have affected him. It seemed more plausible that the fact that he was frightened while watching a science fiction television series made him dislike science fiction.

When she was five years, Kang's family did not have a television. She played with hand-me-down wooden blocks from her brother and sister. And, her siblings were her babysitters. On Saturdays, her parents had to attend political studies classes, mandated by the Mao government, instead of going to the movies. Had these things in her childhood affected her psychological make-up? She wasn't sure.

Then Mary told a story about her teenage years. She had asked her father if she could join her friend who took a class in Yiddish, the language her parents sometimes used at home. Her father had refused her request. "Speak only English!" he had shouted.

"It was confusing. Canada is a multicultural society, but my dad didn't want me to learn his mother tongue," said Mary. "I only understood what he meant when I got older."

"What did your dad mean then?" one student asked.

"His parents had brought him and his little sister to Canada to escape the Nazis during World War II. He knew what it meant to be a disliked minority, so he hoped that I'd be regarded as a Canadian and he wanted English to be the only language I knew."

"How about French? Canada is a bilingual country," said Kang.

"My dad didn't think about that much. To him, a person who spoke English fluently was a Canadian, and not an immigrant. And that idea was based on his childhood experiences of growing up in Germany where he was considered an immigrant and an unwanted minority."

"So it was actually your dad's childhood experience, rather than yours, that had an impact on your adulthood," another student pointed out. "And how about you, Kang?"

"I'm still thinking about it." She thought it would be too personal and embarrassing to discuss her sister's rape and its strong impact on her own psychology, so she tried to think of something less serious to share.

At last, after everyone in the group had spoken, Kang shared a memory. "When I was three or four years old, radio announcers in China were always denouncing the bourgeoisie and American imperialism. I had no idea what those words meant, but I figured that everything beautiful must be denounced, because it seemed to belong to the bourgeoisie and the imperialists. My sister's friend had received a dress as a gift from her grandma in America, and one day my sister tried it on. My sister didn't want me to touch it because my hands were dirty from burying sunflower seeds in a pot. I got upset and screamed at her, 'Down with American imperialism!' I really frightened her with those words. I had not realized how powerful they were. Now, I can see that I was obviously influenced very strongly by the media and my education."

"Ha," said Mary, clasping her hands. "But did it impact your adult life?"

"Of course. I didn't feel comfortable wearing nice skirts and dresses, even when I went to college. This was partly because of the social and political pressure, but it was also because of my family background—my father was labelled a rightist in the 1950s. I always did everything I could to avoid attracting attention and getting criticized."

"What is a rightist? What did your dad do?" Luke asked.

"Why would someone criticize you? And how?" Mary asked.

To answer these questions, Kang had to explain the Anti-Rightists Campaign and the Cultural Revolution, during which educated people were persecuted. She told them that "rightists" were mostly professionals and intellectuals who questioned Mao's policies. Mao used the Anti-Rightists Campaign to purge his political rivals and bring Chinese people under his control after the communists' takeover in 1949. The campaign lasted roughly from 1957 to 1959, and many people were accused—including her father—and subsequently punished with formal criticism, forced hard labour, and sometimes even execution.

At the end of her story, silence fell. Everybody was obviously moved by what she had said, and some felt even a little embarrassed that their troubles in their childhood seemed so trivial in comparison.

Kang knew she had been lucky. If she'd been born earlier, she would've been even more impacted by the Cultural Revolution. She sighed with relief. At least she hadn't been totally psychologically damaged by her chaotic childhood.

The group discussion had given Kang some good ideas for her paper. Besides using her own experience, she wanted to make Brian her guinea pig by interviewing him, so the two met once again at Tim Hortons, this time on a Saturday evening. At the same small corner table, she sipped tea, and he, coffee. Kang glanced at the bare maple tree outside the window, on which only a few tough golden yellow leaves were shivering in the early winter's wind. She turned her attention to Brian. "Do you have any unhappy childhood memories?" she asked. With a pen in her hand, she arranged notepaper and charts on the table.

"Whoa, why don't you start with a happy one?" he protested. "By the way, I hope you won't mention my name in your paper."

"I'll use a pseudonym," she said. "Okay then, what was your happiest moment?"

His eyes twinkled. "On my sixth birthday, when I blew out the candles on my cake. I wished that I'd marry my mom when I grew up."

"What?" She gasped. Was this a real case of an Oedipus complex? "Are ... are you serious?" She chuckled. "Can you speak slowly? I need to take notes."

"Sure," said Brian, scratching his head. "A child can have all kinds of wild ideas. On my next birthday, my wish was to kill my dad in order to marry my mom." He burst out laughing before she reacted.

"You're kidding, right?" She narrowed her eyes. "Do you know what an Oedipus complex is."

He nodded. "Sure I do. I'm just teasing you. Actually I love my dad. One of my other joyful moments was going on a fishing trip with him. I was so thrilled whenever I got a bite. I loved holding the fish in my hand and throwing them back into the water."

"So you had many happy times. Can you tell me about any unhappy ones?"

"Let me think." Brian looked serious. "Here's one. When I was five, my mom got pregnant. Then one day when my mom came home with my dad, I noticed that her belly was not as round and full as it had been. 'Where's the baby?' I asked. 'It ... it's gone.' My mom's voice was tremulous, and she started to weep. Dad helped Mom sit down in an armchair and he tried to soothe her as she wept.

"I didn't dare ask what had happened, but I knew that the baby was gone. She was, in my grandma's words, 'with God.'

That was my most traumatic moment," he said, his eyes his eyes fixed on the cup in his hand.

"That's really a tragedy for a child who is expecting his parents to come home with a sibling." Kang nodded.

"It was a girl. So, I would have had a sister. The worst thing was that for several years I kept dreaming that my baby sister grew up in heaven, first crawling and then walking, but unable to come down to visit us. I couldn't make out her face, and I didn't know her name. In my dream she would cry out that she wanted to see our mom and dad. Then I would wake up in tears." Brian placed his elbows on the table and placed his head in his hands.

Kang sighed, her eyes misting over. "I'm sorry. That must have been very hard." She pictured little angels with white wings flapping among the clouds like something out of a commercial for soft bathroom tissue.

"Hey," said Brian, "are you still interviewing me?"

"Oh yes! So, how did that moment affect you?"

"Quite a lot, I think. When I was younger, I avoided dangerous situations. I wouldn't try any of the more risky things that boys generally get up to, like jumping off the roof, or riding a bicycle down the stairs."

"So you feared death," Kang nodded as she made notes. "I understand."

"Let me put it this way: I understood how precious life was."

"I have one more question. Do you think that unhappy moment affected your learning ability in school? And speak slowly please." She flipped to a fresh sheet of paper.

"Yes and no." Brian sank back into his memories for a while. "Sometimes the dream would make me so heartsick that I couldn't focus on what I was doing in class. When the teacher asked me questions, I would sit mute, with no idea what she'd been talking about. On the other hand, curiosity about life and death and wanting to get to the bottom of it got me interested in science. I studied a lot of biology, and then that

led me to math and physics. In the end I became an engineer."
He chuckled. "So maybe I wouldn't have gone into this career
without the loss of my unborn sister. But who knows? Anyway,
if you hadn't asked, I would probably never have wondered
about any of those memories, good or bad. And I wouldn't
have thought about relating them to my learning abilities.
Fascinating. Maybe I should ask you some questions, too."

"Wait a second." Kang arranged her notes. "I just want to
verify what you've said. You mean the sorrowful memory had
a positive impact on you, right?"

Brian smiled. "Well, yes. I think so—at least in my case."

"Can you tell me why?"

He drained his coffee. "I'd say I had a very happy childhood
surrounded by loving parents and grandparents. I'd forgotten
that particularly sad moment until you forced me to think about
it." He noticed her confused look and added, "I'm kidding. You
didn't force me. I wanted to answer your questions. I should
add that the unhappy experience also had the effect of making
me very interested in and fond of children. I love them."

Kang listened carefully. He loves children, she thought, but
won't be able to have his own unless he adopts one. "Maybe
you should consider being a teacher," she said.

"Maybe," said Brian.

"By the way, you mentioned your grandmother. Did you
live with your grandparents, too? I thought family structure
in Canada tended toward the nuclear type."

"Do you mean an immediate family? He paused. "I lived
with my parents and saw my grandparents often, but we didn't
live together."

"Now I see. Thanks for all your helpful answers."

"You're going to do great on this project. Would you mind
if I ask you similar questions next time we meet?"

Next time? Kang was pleased he wanted to see her again.
She enjoyed chatting with him. "That's a good idea. Yes, let's
do this again."

CHAPTER 9: PRACTICUM

KANG SPENT AN ENTIRE DAY in the Scott Library on the weekend, going through several journals and books on cognitive development, children's ways of learning, and the impact of childhood experiences on adult behaviour. All the research was for her paper entitled "The Impact of Unhappy Experiences on Children's Learning Abilities."

Impressed by how Brian had been able to make something positive out of his adverse childhood experience, she tried to identify whether she had made a similar transformation. Her conclusion was yes. In Grade One, some of her classmates would not let her join them when they jumped rope, because her father was a disgraced rightist. At the time, Kang did not know what things someone labelled a "rightist" might have done, but she knew the word "rightist" meant a bad person.

At home, she asked her sister Jian, "Is Dad a rightist?"

"Who told you?"

"Some of my classmates. They didn't want to play with me. What did Dad do?"

"Mom said Dad made a big mistake in 1958, but he's still a good man. But don't tell people Mom said that." Jian patted Kang's shoulder.

"I won't, but I don't understand."

"Rightists belong to the Five Blacks group."

Kang knew the Five Blacks; landlords, rich farmers, counter-revolutionaries, bad influencers, and rightists were considered the "enemies" of the Revolution who should be denounced in public, but she didn't understand how their dear father could be involved with those evil people. Puzzled, she stared at Jian.

"Chairman Mao said, 'Political attitudes and behaviours are important.' So if we don't have opinions that are different from others, our attitudes are okay," Jian continued. "If people say it's good, don't say it's bad. Don't argue with anyone. Understood?" But Kang hadn't understood. It wasn't until many years later that she learned that the term "rightists" simply referred to all those did not believe in Mao's "revolution."

After that, whenever Kang was excluded from playing, she never protested. Instead, she used the time to read or do extra math exercises. As a result, she received the highest marks in her class at the end of the year.

Thinking about that episode in her childhood, she recognized that that unhappy moment had lead to a positive outcome. An idiom she had heard not long ago flashed through her mind: *every coin has two sides!*

A week later Kang started her practicum at DuPont Public School. She was assigned to teach math to Grades 3 and 5 and physical education to two fifth-grade classes. But on the first day, she was to observe all the classes. As soon as she followed the math teacher, Mr. Arrigo, into a classroom, some of the students called out greetings. "We have a Chinese teacher!" exclaimed one student, grinning at her. Children have sharp eyes, Kang thought. They weren't like adults who had to ask what other language she spoke to discover her ethnic background. She noted that the number of students in this Canadian class was much smaller than the ones she'd had in China. Fondly, she recalled the school where she had taught. During recess, there had been so many voices floating around her that she had felt as though she were drowning in their twittering sounds.

"Good morning! Everyone," said Mr. Arrigo. "This is our new teacher, Ms. Wang. She'll teach our class tomorrow."

"Good morning, Mr. Arrigo and Ms. Wang," the students chimed in unison.

"Nice to meet all of you," Kang responded, feeling less nervous. They seemed like lovely kids.

During recess, she went to another classroom.

"Hello Kang." A familiar face appeared in front of her in the hallway. She was delighted to see it was her classmate, Luke.

"Are you here for practicum, as well?" she asked

"Yeah. I'm teaching English and Music. How about you?"

"Math and Physical Education."

"We can exchange notes later. Good luck." Luke smiled widely.

"See you around," Kang said and continued to walk to the next classroom. Luke looked happy and she was certain his students would like him. She was a bit anxious about teaching physical education as she did not have experience in that area. She thought of a phrase she had learned from a Jamaican classmate: *monkey see, monkey do.* The expression amused her, bringing to mind the ways in which monkeys often imitate the actions of people. *I guess I'm a monkey now.* She chuckled, thinking that she would have to copy the actions of the school's regular physical education teacher.

The following day, Kang stood nervously in front of the students in her math class. Taking deep breaths, she felt her heartbeat slow down to normal. Soon, she was ready to start the lesson.

"Girls and boys, let's review what we've learned before." She held up a diagram of a pie chart card divided into three equal parts, one of which was shaded in green. "What is this?"

"A pie!" some students answered.

"What do you call the shaded parts of the pie?" she asked.

"One over three!" a student said.

"Three over one!" Another one got a different idea.

"One over three is correct," she affirmed.

Then she explained that the total parts were three, the denominator, and the part was one, the numerator. She wrote down *1/3*. She then asked the students to read flash cards as she held them up one by one. Most of the class got correct answers. Only two children had difficulty.

She asked the students to do the fraction exercises in the textbook, and then walked around the room to see who needed help. When she came to one of the boys who looked like he was struggling, she crouched down next to his desk and gently asked, "Neil, can I help you?"

There were numerous sketches all over Neil's opened text book. Kang pointed at a pie chart. "Can you tell me how many parts are here all together?"

Neil moved his finger over the picture of the slices one by one. "Five."

"Very good," said Kang. "How many parts are shaded?"

After his finger crawled over the diagram, he answered quietly, "Two."

"So what's the fraction?"

"Five. No. Two over five."

Kang praised Neil and asked him to try another chart.

"I hate fractions!" another boy yelled. Some of the children giggled.

She should've gone to Mike first, Kang thought with a pang. She remembered that Mr. Arrigo had mentioned a child with a learning disability. She walked over to Mike's desk next.

"Min doesn't know fractions." Mike pointed to the girl sitting behind him and then gazed at Kang. "I like your hair pins."

Surprised, Kang almost touched her hair, even though she knew she was not wearing any hairpins. Later, Mike offered more compliments. "I like your skirt," he said, although she was wearing slacks. She wondered if Mike had heard people say similar things to praise others, and was imitating them, without knowing if his remarks were appropriate or not. She noticed that Mike's eyes shone with innocence. When he spoke, he smiled broadly, and his hands fluttered around his body, touching his pencil, his book, or his clothes.

"I'm sure you will be able to learn fractions well," she said to the boy as she helped him with a problem. Within a few minutes, Mike could name some of the fractions with confidence. He needed attention and help, Kang thought while she continued to move around the room to check on the rest of the class.

In the gym, the students were organized into two groups. Mrs. Goldberg, the class's regular gym teacher, took one group to play basketball and let Kang work with the others on floor exercises. Kang led her group to the fitness room where two crash pads were lined up together. "Girls, I'll show you what to do, and then you can try it." Taking a deep breath, she stepped toward the head of the mattress, placing her hands firmly on the pad, and executed a first forward roll without difficulty. On the second one, however, she went too far and ended up rolling off the mat, onto the floor.

The children laughed. "She did it on purpose," said one girl.

Kang stood up. "I made a mistake. The only way to learn is to do it again." She grinned sheepishly, stepped back onto the pad, and rolled forward again. This time she was successful. "Come on." Kang beckoned to the first student in line. "Don't be afraid of making a mistake."

The girls tried. Some rolled forward, but others went sideways. One girl simply stood there watching the others. She was covered from head to toe with a lengthy scarf that blanketed her head and neck, and she had long sleeves that even concealed the backs of her hands. Her stockinged feet peeped out from a floor-length dress, and her hands held the ends of her headscarf. Kang was worried that the scarf and dress might impede her movements, or worse, that she would get tangled up and hurt. "Can you take off your scarf, Afia?" asked Kang.

The girl shook her head. "I can't take off my hijab."

"Would you like to try?" Kang asked, reaching her arm out to Afia. She recalled that Mrs. Goldberg had mentioned this young girl's reluctance to participate in the exercises.

"She's never done this," said one of the girls.

Afia withdrew and stood against the wall. "I just want to watch."

Kang let her go and supervised the other girls who were now practising rolling backwards. Some wobbled off the mattress, and others were unable to roll over at all. They just lay there kicking their legs in the air. Girlish giggles filled the room. Even Afia joined in the laugher.

One afternoon, while Kang was marking assignments in the office, Luke stopped by. "Can you please help me out, Kang?"

"What is it?" she asked. She was curious as to why he would need her assistance.

"I have a boy from China who doesn't want to write the composition I've asked for like everyone else. He always says 'yes' to me, but I'm not sure if he really understands what I'm saying. If you have time, can you come to my class and talk to him?"

"Sure. I'm free until next session. Which room?"

Luke was relieved. "Room 305. I'll see you there, and thanks."

Kang put away her work and headed to Luke's class. As soon as she entered the sixth-grade classroom, Luke led her to the boy. "Guang, this is Ms. Wang. You can speak to her."

Guang's eyes beamed. "Can you speak Chinese?"

Kang nodded. "Follow me, we can talk in private."

Luke continued speaking to the rest of the class. "Girls and boys, today we're going to read some of your writing out loud...."

Kang gestured to Guang to sit next to her on a bench in the hallway. "Do you understand English?" she asked him in Chinese.

"Some," Guang spoke Chinese delightfully. "Do you enjoy speaking English?" he asked in turn, his hand fishing for something inside his pocket.

"I certainly do. What about you?"

"Not much." Guang said, finally pulling a calculator out of his pocket.

"Why?"

"Well, if I learn English, I'll forget how to speak Chinese."

Kang watched Guang playing with the calculator. "You can remember both," she said, trying to understand why Guang would be afraid of forgetting Chinese. "How long have you been in Canada?" she asked.

"Six months."

"Do you like it here?"

Nodding, Guang scratched his head. "School is easier."

"Why do you think if you learn English you will forget Chinese?" Kang patted his shoulder, hoping to encourage him to open up.

"My dad said if I learned English well, I wouldn't be able to speak Chinese anymore. When I go back to see my grandparents in China, how will they understand me if I can't speak Chinese?"

"What?" Kang understood the boy's problem now. "You live in Canada, right? If you don't learn English now, it will be hard for you to study it in the future. When you become an adult, you'll have to work, so you won't have lots of time. Does your dad want you to go to college?"

"Yes, he says education is important. He wants me to study mathematics. I like the calculator." Guang's fingers moved quickly on the number keys. "I do mental calculations and then I use the calculator to test my results. This time I think it's one thousand two hundred and eighty-seven." He pressed the keys and showed the display to Kang. "Am I right? Five plus six times ten, then add seven, and multiply by eleven."

"Wow! You're really good at math," said Kang, amazed by the boy's agility with numbers. "But let's talk about learning English. If you can't write English well, how can you go to college here? Maybe you would prefer to go to college and study in China?"

"No, no. My dad says I won't be able to take college courses there after high school here."

"Well, then, you must improve your English—speaking, reading, and writing—if you want to go to college here."

"What should I do?" Guang's eyes left his calculator; he turned to Kang, listening.

"Work on any assignments given by your teacher. Read as many books as possible. Do you want me to call your dad? I can talk to him."

"No." He shook his head. "He'll think I'm making trouble in school."

"If you want to keep up your Chinese, you can go to an after-school program. I'll find one that's near you and I can give your dad the information."

The boy nodded and replied in earnest "Okay, I'll try to learn English well."

"Good," Kang said in English and smiled. "What did your teacher ask you to write yesterday?"

"Hmm, he say..." Guang followed her into English. "What I learned in English class."

"It's about what you have learned in English class."

"Oh yes! How do you knew it?"

"How do I know?" Kang corrected his English. "It's 'know,' not 'knew.'"

"My teacher taught us past tense. I remember 'knew.'"

"Very good. Did you know him? 'Did' indicates past. You don't need to change know to knew." She was glad Guang was trying. "Tell me what you have studied."

"I have studied some words and sentences. Sometimes I study grammar. Sometimes read stories. Ms. Wang are— Ms. Wang is talking to me. She speak Chinese good and speaks English more better."

"Go on."

"One day. A classmate spoke to me and said, 'I know you. I don't know Mandarin, but I've eaten mandarins.'" Guang paused and asked in Chinese. "Ms. Wang, what does mandarin mean?"

Kang still spoke English. "Mandarin means *pu tong hua*—standard Chinese. But 'mandarin' in English also means a kind of orange."

"Wow. I understand what he meant now," Guang spoke in English.

"What else do you learn in class?"

"I write some English sentences."

"Okay. Write what you've told me in English and give it to your teacher." Kang pulled a pen and a slip from her pocket. "Here's my phone number. Tell your parents that English is very important for you to learn. If they have any questions, they can call me. If you have questions, you can come to my office, Room 200, on the second floor. Do you understand me?"

Guang put the slip and the calculator carefully in his pocket. Kang asked him to repeat what she had said and sent him back into his classroom.

On the way back to the office, she thought about Guang. She had understood his experience very well. He had listened to the confusing ideas from his father, and so he had stopped himself from learning English. Hopefully he would eventually be able to speak English as well as he played his calculator game, she thought.

On the bus home, the babble of different languages made her think about Guang again. She wondered if children's learning abilities and motivations changed in a second language environment. She had always thought that children picked up new languages quickly and easily, but it did not seem so easy for this child, especially since his father wasn't encouraging him to learn.

Suddenly she overheard a blonde woman, in the seat across from hers, speaking Chinese. She glanced over and realized the young woman was Asian—her hair was dyed blonde—and she was speaking Chinese to her friend. She grinned. She gazed out the window and watched big snowflakes land on the glass and slide down slowly. In two weeks, it would be Christmas. She was looking forward to a rest.

CHAPTER 10: THE SIXTH STAGE

KANG SAT WITH BRIAN at their usual table in Tim Hortons. When she thought about her own childhood, and then what had happened to her sister, she felt like she was on an emotional roller coaster—elated one moment, scared the next. Her childhood had been happy, until Jian had been violated. She had become much more reserved after that, but she had warmed to Brian and found she could open herself up to him.

"Did you have some happy times as a child?" Brian asked, a lopsided smile on his face.

"Of course," Kang replied and grinned. "One day, when I was feeling ill, I woke up to find some candied fruit on a stool near my bed. My mother had come back from work to prepare lunch and had brought the candied fruit home for me. I was so happy. I picked up a piece and popped it into my mouth. I can still taste it—sweet and sour."

"How old were you then? Who was with you before you woke up?"

"About seven. And I was alone in the house, sleeping."

"It's illegal in Canada to leave a kid younger than twelve alone at home," Brian commented.

"I guess my parents committed a Canadian crime without knowing it," said Kang, her mouth curving into a grin. She flipped her shoulder-length hair back with her hand. "Isn't a seven-year-old old enough to sleep alone at home?"

"No, not in Canada. If I'd been left alone at home when

I was under twelve, and if the authorities had found out, it would've been a cheerless time for me and my folks. Did your parents bring you to your family doctor when you were sick?"

"My family doctor?" Kang chuckled. "Nobody had a family doctor. When you got sick, you saw any doctor on duty in the local hospital. Anyhow, my father was our family doctor."

"Wait a second. Your dad is a doctor?"

"He was, but he's retired now. He worked at the on-campus clinic at Spring City University. The staff and their children usually went there when they were ill. If the case was serious, the doctors would send them to other hospitals. I had a fever that morning. My sister noticed it first because we slept in the same bed. She told our mother that my face was bright red. My mother touched my forehead and asked my father to check on me. Father took my temperature, and then listened to my lungs with a stethoscope. He gave me a couple of pills to take and put me back into bed. It made me really unhappy to stay home and miss school. My head throbbed, but when I thought about the assignments I'd miss, I felt even more miserable. That bitter moment was around the same time as the joyful moment of enjoying the candy my mother had brought home as a treat. Maybe I should say they were mixed moments," Kang laughed.

"Do you mind if I comment on your English?"

"Go ahead."

"'Mixed moments' sounds like a math term to me. A moment in math means a quantitative measure. Mixed moments are moments of multiple variables. Okay, you may say it was a moment of mixed emotions."

"Thanks."

"In my opinion, everything is relative. A great moment for one person might be a dismal moment for another." Brian said, clasping his hands in front of him.

"That's very philosophical. To me, an unhappy time seems to be always related to a happy time. For example, after a rainfall, there's always sunlight. If someone doesn't experience of unhappiness, then how do they know what happiness is?"

"Do you think that sad memory had an impact on your adult life?" asked Brian. "I'd like to play the part of the Freudian now."

"As an adult, when I recall that unhappy moment, I can't complain. I know I was generally a happy child."

"The way I see it, in different cultures, kids in the same situation might have very different reactions to that situation."

"What do you mean?" Sensitive to any comments referring to cultural difference, Kang asked, "Can you give me an example?"

"As a kid, if I wasn't allowed to go out, I'd feel miserable. But in another culture, a kid might feel bad if he or she wasn't allowed to go home when they wanted to. How about you as a kid?"

"I didn't experience anything like that, but when my brother misbehaved he was sent outside. I think he probably felt unhappy, because our neighbours and his friends would know he was being punished for something bad he'd done."

"Understood. I'm back to the same question. Did that sad moment you spoke of earlier have an impact on you?"

"It's funny. That experience of being ill left me with a sort of sweet memory compared to other more terrible recollections." Kang paused as she thought back that time, and then to her sister's horrible experience. "When I was ill that time, it resulted in something that made me happy: the candy."

"So your childhood experience had a positive impact on you, regardless of whether it was cheerful or sad. Would Freud agree with that?"

"My problem isn't with Freud, but with Erik Erikson's theory of stages. I believe other experiences affected my psyche."

"What experience? The Cultural Revolution?"

"No. I meant experiences with men." Kang hesitated. "Well, actually it was something that happened to my sister, but her experience also affected me."

His eyes dimmed, and he leaned in a little closer. "What happened?"

Hesitantly, she told him about her sister's rape, and how, as a result, she had become frightened of men.

"Did your sister or parents report it to the police?"

"My father wanted to, but my mother stopped him. They didn't want anyone to know. Rape brings shame to a woman and her family. I overheard my parents discussing this. They didn't want people to gossip about Jian."

"It seems to me that they didn't care very much about bringing the rapist to justice."

"They cared more about protecting my sister's reputation."

"Her reputation? She did nothing wrong."

"That's easy for you to say," Kang responded. Suddenly she felt nauseous. "After that, my sister fell apart, and I fell through the cracks. That is my most horrible memory," she said, her eyes blurring with tears.

"I'm sorry for bringing this up." Brian picked up her cup and placed it into her hand. "Have some tea."

"I'm okay. Getting it off my chest is making me feel better." She sipped the tea and then continued. "My psychology course has also helped. It's given me a better understanding of how that event affected me. In China, I took a psychology course and learned about Freud, too, but we were told the theories of Western psychologists must be read with a critical eye, and only parts of what they theorized should be used. But I didn't have the opportunity to read the original works—only some translated sections."

"So you aren't afraid of men now, right?" Brian tilted his head.

"Well ... I haven't finished my story. More traumas in my sister's life affected me as well." She took a long breath. "The rape happened when Jian was in Grade 11, but she still managed to graduate from high school and attend university. She fell in love with one of her classmates, Pan. After graduation, they found good jobs, got engaged, and planned to get married as soon as Pan was assigned an apartment in the following year. We all liked him, and we were thrilled for them. But then, suddenly, Pan stopped coming around, and Jian looked depressed. When my mother asked her why, she said Pan had broken up with her because she'd told him about the rape."

"Why would he break up with her?"

"According to Chinese tradition, a good man should marry a virgin. Only virgins are considered honourable women. Pan couldn't accept Jian since she wasn't a virgin anymore."

"This is very strange to me." Brian sighed.

"The breakup hit Jian like a thunderbolt. And it stunned me. My distrust of men started then. I graduated from high school at eighteen. According to Erik Erikson, this age represents the sixth stage of psychosocial development, when a person begins a life of intimacy or isolation. If a person develops a romantic relationship with another person during this stage, they will find intimacy. If they fail, they will live in loneliness and isolation. I think I stumbled in that stage, hopelessly."

"How was Jian?"

"Worse. She totally changed. She hardly spoke and she stopped singing." Kang paused, a faraway look in her eyes. "I learned so many songs from her—some of them in English. She had picked them up from her close friend, Yezi, whose mother taught them English in secret. They would sing songs together when they finished their homework, and I would sit at the table playing with toy blocks. Those were sweet moments for me." Coming back into the present, she looked at Brian as if she had just noticed him. "Sorry. What was I saying?"

"You were telling me about Jian."

"Yes. She was twenty-four when Pan broke up with her. Many of her friends had boyfriends; some of them were already married. You might think that she was still young and could have easily met someone else, but she'd been psychologically destroyed and she didn't trust men anymore. That year I left to study at the university in Beijing. When I returned home a year later, she was like a ghost. She moved about silently and stayed in her room with the door closed most of the time. She hardly spoke to me, even though we only saw each other once a year. Her only friends seemed to be the piles of books she had stacked on the shelves in her room.

"My mother worried about her and tried to find a match for her. In China, it's a red flag if a woman is still single by the age of thirty. It means she's too old to find a boyfriend. Jian lived in the same place where she had been born and raised, surrounded by people who knew her. Some of them were my parents' colleagues who had watched her grow up. All the people who had gone to school with her, from kindergarten to high school, even from university, gossiped about her and began to call her "*laochunu*"—spinster. Classmates of her classmates, friends of her friends, and colleagues of her colleagues—they all seemed to have formed a large spider's web, and poor Jian was like a fly. To be invisible was a way to protect herself from being watched and gossiped about. I think that's why she became so ghost-like." Kang paused. "Maybe I'm talking too much. Tell me more about yourself."

"Why me?" Brian sighed, obviously interested in Jian's story. "You're a good storyteller. I feel like I'm right there with you and Jian. Life in China isn't what I'd imagined. It sounds like women there are still shackled by a tradition that doesn't value them if they're unmarried. Did the Communist Party change this tradition or these ideas?"

"Maybe only at a superficial level. I think traditions change slowly."

"So your sister is one of those shackled women."

Kang envisioned a human figure bound by clanking chains. "If you were in her situation, what would you do?"

"Hmm...." Brian tapped his finger on the table. "It's hard to put myself in the place of a woman in another culture. One can only hope, I suppose, that the shackles would sooner or later rust and crumble. Well, you asked for my story. Here it goes. You can try your Freud or Erikson on me."

"Good," said Kang, breathing a sigh of relief. She didn't want to think about Jian anymore.

"I don't know if you've watched the movie *M. Butterfly*."

"It sounds familiar. Isn't it about a love affair between a Japanese girl and an American navy man?" she said, confusing it with Puccini's opera, *Madama Butterfly*.

Brian shook his head. "No, it's a love story between a Chinese Beijing opera singer and a French diplomat."

"Mei Lanfang?" she asked. "The famous Beijing opera singer?"

"No. It isn't about Mei Lanfang."

"So is the French diplomat a woman?"

"Nope. Why do you assume the Beijing opera singer is a man?"

"Most of the famous Beijing opera singers are men. Male singers who play female characters are known as *Dan*. So what's the movie about?"

"Here's the story. Gallimard, a French diplomat in Beijing, falls in love with Song, a beautiful Beijing opera performer, who gives birth to his son. Years later, Song joins him in Paris...."

"I've never heard of this movie. When did it come out?"

"In 1993. I saw it on opening night." He looked into Kang's intense eyes. "It's just a movie. Don't take it too seriously. Anyway, both of them were arrested as spies. Only then did Gallimard learn that his lover was a man."

"But you said they had a son!" Kang's eyes widened. "How could a man carry a baby? And how could Gallimard not know Song was a man? After all, they had a relationship for so many years."

"Because Song appeared and behaved like a woman. He actually worked as a spy for the Chinese government. He got the baby from somewhere to help with the deception. Anyway, in prison, Gallimard agreed to perform in a show put on for and by the prisoners. At the end of his performance, he actually commits *seppuku*—a form of Japanese ritual suicide. It's an incredible scene."

"It's hard to believe such a thing could happen in real life, but it's fascinating."

"It's really amazing." Brian lost himself in thought.

For him, it was great love story between two men, Kang thought. She could not help but ask, "Do you believe it?"

"Yes, it's based on a true story. I watched the movie with Ingrid. I told her she was my butterfly. She was in East Asian Studies and knew the butterfly legend very well. But not long after the movie, my butterfly flew away from me. I think I understand why Gallimard wanted to kill himself."

"Did you ever dream about that movie?" asked Kang, hoping to try out some of Carl Jung's theories.

"Good question. Yes, I did. But I don't know if I can still remember the dream." His fingers tapped impatiently on the almost empty coffee mug.

Kang searched her mind, trying to recall some of what she'd read by Jung. A person's superego worked hard to protect the conscious mind from being disturbed. She concluded that Brian needed to forget the gloomy story of M. Butterfly.

Kang looked at Brian carefully. His face was bathed in sunlight from the window, and his eyes squinted in the glare. "You're trying to take yourself away from the depressing movie ending. Am I right?"

"Do you mean I'm trying to forget my dream?" Brian grinned. "I dreamed that I became a butterfly, fluttering around with another one. Nice, right?"

Kang nodded, curious about what his dream might mean. She resolved to learn more about the psychology of dreams. "You really know a lot about the Chinese culture," she said.

"That's a result of my relationship with Ingrid. Do I fit into any of Freud's or Erikson's stages?" He chuckled.

"Not yet," Kang said jokingly.

Like most Canadians, he had an easy life, she thought. And

she could have an easy life here, too. There were no social pressure—she could live any way she chose. He was gay and he was happy and free to live his life any way he wanted. His smile stirred warm feelings in her. "Are you content with your life?" She blurted out the question without pausing to think.

"Yes, as far as I can tell. Chatting with you is a kind of fun way to learn about Freud even though I don't really believe his theories."

"Why not?"

"He said girls go after their fathers, and boys, their mothers. But I'm a chip off the old block. I even became an engineer, just like my mom. And I certainly never had any weird ideas about taking my mom from my dad. What did Freud call that?"

"The Oedipus complex."

"Yeah. That's the one. Killing my dad in order to marry my mom."

"But my experience matches the theory," Kang recalled. "Once I saw a photo of my father alone sitting on a rock in a park, and I felt like crying. I was about five years old. That day I browsed through lots of my parents' photos. In some photos my mother was alone, too, but I only felt sad for my father. And that feeling lasted for a long while. I think that was some sort of an Oedipus complex. It was my earliest feeling of affection or sympathy for my parent of the opposite gender."

"Wow! You are a real disciple of Freud."

"I enjoy chatting with you about these things. It's good therapy."

"Glad I could help." He noticed her glance at her watch, so he said, "I'll take you home."

They walked out of Tim Hortons and climbed into his car. Brian dropped her off at Tania's and waved good night.

She went into the house, remembering in particular something he had said earlier that evening: "I always live in the present, never in the past." Kang thought that she herself sometimes lived far too much in the past.

CHAPTER 11: JIAN'S MARRIAGE

WHEN THEY MET AGAIN, Kang decided to tell Brian the rest of her sister's story. She hoped that sharing the story would finally free her from the shadow of Jian's tragic life.

"Jian was single till the age of thirty-three, until she could no longer resist my mother's matchmaking attempts. She finally agreed to marry a man whom many others had considered a good match for her: a thirty-five-year-old technician. He was quiet and got along well with others, but he didn't have a university degree and was quite a bit shorter than average. But Jian, a thirty-three-year-old spinster, didn't have much going for her either. Higher education was not considered to be that important in a woman—youth and virginity were what counted. Being over thirty and not a virgin, Jian was undesirable in many men's eyes. There were plenty of young single women for them to choose from.

"I was relieved when, after all she'd been through, Jian finally got married. She had been under pressure from her family and friends, not to mention society, for so many years. I had a better situation—I was living in a larger city where fewer people knew me. I did the right thing by getting out of the small social lab and going to university in another city."

"What social lab?"

"I mean 'society.' I learned the word 'lab' as a child. I used to go to my dad's lab—I would examine everything in the tubes and jars, and ask tons of questions out of curiosity. I think people in society watch others just like I observed the items in the lab."

"Go on," Brian encouraged.

"My acquaintances were a couple of colleagues and former university classmates. We were equals. There were no colleagues and friends or acquaintances of my parents, who had watched me grow up, whom I was supposed to call uncle or aunt, or whose advice I had to listen to with respect. Furthermore, I had no younger siblings for whom I was expected to set a good example.

"Years later when I came home for a visit, many people dropped by to see me—friends, former classmates, my parents' colleagues, and their friends. They always asked if I'd found a boyfriend or not. They praised my sister's husband and her daughter. I knew I was about to become the fly in the spider's web—by this point I was thirty years old and still single! At the beginning, I cracked a smile and responded to the visitors' questions cooperatively. But the interrogation went on and on, and at the end, when I was supposed to add more tea to the visitors' cups, I felt like throwing it on their faces. I did it many times in my head. I knew I was being seen as an object; I was being examined by all these curious observers and in many ways, judged.

"But I understood their curious minds, and I could forgive them, especially since I didn't live there and only visited my family once a year. The social lab I was associated with was larger—I was new and almost invisible among the greater number of human beings in Beijing. Many lab volunteers in the larger city already had their items to examine and didn't have extra time or energy to observe me."

"Wow! That's a vivid metaphor—social lab!" Brian ginned. "Now welcome to our human meat grinder!"

"Human meat grinder? I've heard this phrase from somewhere. Who said that? What does it mean?"

"Maybe an American sociologist. The idea is that we human

beings are products of this human grinder—society."

"From a social lab to a human meat grinder, it's like from a cage to a machine. Ha, what product will I become? I feel like I've escaped that lab; I'm free as a bird here. Many women are like Tania—career women. They can decide what they want to be, whether they want to get married or be a so-called spinster."

"My aunt is a special case. It doesn't mean many women would do the same," Brian said cautiously.

"Don't most men in Canada treat women equally?"

"Yes, men are supposed to treat women equally. But we still have some old-fashioned men, and women still suffer from unequal treatment and unequal pay."

"Hmmm.... I haven't noticed a lot of that," Kang said. "Anyway, that's why I decided to come to Canada. I wanted to choose my lifestyle for myself, without being examined or shaped by others." Kang tucked her hair behind her ear. "It's funny—when I'm talking to you, it feels like we understand one another easily. It's almost like we're the same gender."

"That scares me." Brian chuckled. "Tell me whether your sister is happy in her marriage."

A wry smile appeared on Kang's face. "Here's a Chinese saying—there is no lucky star over my sister. After getting married, Jian and her husband seemed to do well, at least in the eyes of outsiders. But they started having problems after their daughter was born. Her husband was raised to believe that his most important duty, as a man, was to keep his family's name by having at least one son. His name is Yaozu, which means 'glorifying the ancestor.' You must know about China's one-child policy. Having a daughter meant that he would never have a son to carry his family name to the next generation, so he believed that Jian ruined his chance to honour his ancestors. Jian is content being a mother, but Yaozu doesn't help take care of their daughter. Sometimes he even says to Jian, 'You are of no use, because you can't bear a son.' My mother told me that Jian fought back, and I can imagine how sharp her words were. Unable to win verbally, Yaozu chose violence to exert his power. That became an even bigger problem."

"Is there any place Jian can get help?"

"Not really. She would sometimes bring her daughter to my parents' place, but Yaozu wouldn't want to lose face. He'd apologize and bring Jian and their daughter back home. However, his attitude remains the same. He always says to Jian, 'You have a better education and a better job, but it's me who rules the roost. You must obey me.' He also repeats his favourite Chinese proverb: 'after marrying a dog, you follow the dog. After marrying a rooster, you follow the rooster.' I think I'm lucky because I don't have to follow a dog or a rooster." Kang grinned, then she let out a sigh of relief from the bottom of her heart.

"It's interesting that Chinese marital relationships are represented by animal imagery. Does this mean that the wife should bark like the dog husband and crow like the rooster husband?"

"Yes, something like that." Kang burst out laughing, imagining a woman hand in hand with a dog or a rooster, dancing the tango. "Traditionally, husbands are supposed to dominate their wives, and wives are supposed to obey their husbands."

"Do most Chinese families function that way?"

"It depends on the education level of the couple. In my family, for example, my mother usually has the last word."

"Your sister and her husband are both educated, but it seems like her husband has the upper hand."

"Erikson's theory might explain Yaozu's behaviour. Children pick up things from their parents and environments—he was raised in a rural area where his family, neighbours, and peer groups all were influenced mostly by Confucian traditions that see men as superior and women as inferior."

"Is that what Confucius taught?"

"Yes. To him, women were the same as villains."

"So Confucius was a sexist."

"Some Chinese traditions are rooted in Confucianism. I chose

English as my major because I prefer the English culture, which treats women equally."

"Do you mean the British culture?"

"I mean the Western culture. Now I realize that people who have a background in science are generally precise in their definitions." Kang chuckled. "Anyway, Yaozu grew up in a more traditional environment, so his education didn't help him to understand the concept of equality between men and women."

"Hmm, I have a story for you." Brian paused.

"Go ahead please." Kang urged him.

"Last summer, Eric's sister brought her child to visit Toronto after her divorce. She seemed to be happy. She made the wrong choice when she got married, but she had the opportunity to correct that mistake and she took it."

"I agree that a divorce might be the way for my sister to end her unhappiness, but it's hard for her to escape the tradition in which women are supposed to sacrifice themselves for their marriages." Kang sighed. "I'm lucky I left."

"Was that your reason for immigrating here?" Brian asked, sipping his coffee.

"Right. I hated being labelled a 'spinster,' but I didn't want to change my spinster status. So I'm here."

"To be honest with you, I've hardly ever hear the word 'spinster.' It reminds me of an elderly woman in an old fairy tale." Brian grinned. "You're not that old."

"Any unmarried thirty-year-old woman in China is labelled a spinster."

"Do you mean you've gotten rid of that label here?" he asked with caution.

"Nobody would call Tania 'spinster'—right? I'm in the same boat. In Western culture, women have more freedom to choose their lifestyles. Don't you agree?"

"But I would think women in China also have more choices now than before."

"Not really. Although, nowadays in China if women are still

unmarried at the age of twenty-seven, they're called 'leftover women,' which I think sounds better than 'spinster.'"

"What does 'leftover women' mean?"

"It means they're undesirable. Most of these women are well educated and have careers."

"They're undesirable because of their education?"

"Mainly because of their age." Kang took the last sip of tea. "By the way, does Eric's sister have a career?"

"She's a nurse."

"Financially, my sister could be independent, but tradition and peer pressure make the situation harder. I'll have to think about how I can help her," Kang said, her mind beginning to wander.

Kang returned home, and, picking up a pile of letters from the mailbox, immediately noticed her mother's handwriting on an envelope. As soon as she opened the door, she dropped Tania's mail onto the living room table and went downstairs to her bedroom. Tearing the envelope open, she pulled the pages out and devoured them, she was so starved for information from home.

Dear Kang,

We have not heard from you for a while. How are your studies? Hopefully your hard work will lead you to a good teaching job.

Your brother has been promoted; he's now the director of the Department of Engineering and Applied Science. He is busier, but his wife is a great help at home. Jian's dark cloud finally has a silver lining: Yaozu met a younger woman, and has finally agreed to a divorce. He's hoping to have a son and an obedient wife.

Since September, I have been enjoying my retirement so much, unlike your father who took so long to adjust to his retirement five years ago. Sometimes he would even pick up his briefcase after breakfast as if he had to go to work. When he realized he didn't have to go anywhere, he would look like he got lost.

I am thinking about you learning to eat salads and drink cold water. You might get sick if you eat raw vegetables. Why do Canadians have this childish habit? Is it because they are too busy to cook? Raw vegetables and cold water in winter's sub-zero temperature may upset your stomach. You are alone in a foreign country, and I cannot help you. You need to take care of yourself.

We do not have email addresses. Your father did not trust the Internet, so he did not think about buying a computer until recently. I will try to open an email account when we have a computer.

Love, your mother

Kang wrote back immediately.

Dear Mother and Father,

I started my practicum at a school three weeks ago and will finish in a week. Then I'll have the second part of the practicum next semester. The university schedule here is different from the one in China. Classes finish by the end of April. It means I'll graduate if I pass five more courses and do well in the practicum. Prospective graduates start to hunt for jobs in December. I'm going to apply for jobs after I get my practicum evaluation next month.

I'm glad to hear about Jian's good news. I think that leaving Yaozu is a good choice for her, even though it's hard for a divorced woman to bear the gossip and prejudice that might arise. Women have more choices in Canada. They don't even have to get married if they don't find Mr. Right, or if they prefer to live by themselves. My landlady is a retired professor. She has never married, but she lives a satisfied and happy life.

Eating salads does save me time. It also provides me with more vitamins. Now I'm as lazy as you can imagine. I only cook two or three times a week, not three times a day! I drink juice or tap water instead of boiled water. The running water here is safe for drinking. I'm healthy, and I haven't even caught a cold. Don't worry about me.

I hope you will start to use email soon. It will save you time and postage. And it's fast! My email address is kang.wang@ yorku.ca

Oh, I almost forget to tell you that I sent a letter to Yezi at the address that Jian gave me, but it was returned. The stamp stated that the receiver moved. I think even if her grandmother is still alive, Yezi can't still be living with her. It's been more than two decades since Jian got that address. I can hardly believe that our family has been living in the same apartment for twenty years! Here, I have already moved a few times.

Anyway, next Saturday will be Christmas, which is as important as Chinese New Year. Some people begin to decorate their homes in November. They string tiny lights on doors, windows, and trees. Some have life-sized ornaments on their lawns, such as Santa in a sleigh pulled by a reindeer or a shepherd with a lamb. At night when the lights are on, everything looks like a fairy tale. I enjoy walking down the street to admire the lights and the decorations.

I'll have Christmas dinner with my landlady and her friends. I'll learn how to cook a turkey. Do you remember seeing turkeys in the zoo? They have a red comb and dewlap around the neck. Roasted turkeys are served on Christmas and other holidays in North America.

I have a lot to tell you, but I've got to stop now. It's late now, and tomorrow I need to prepare my lessons for next week.

Please send my best wishes to Jian.

Love, your daughter Kang

After writing the letter, Kang fell into a deep sleep. She dreamed that Jian was walking toward Santa in his sleigh. Kang ran after her. "Wait for me. I'm going with you." She tried to open her eyes, but she could not. Kicking her feet, she leaped forward and she spotted Linling sitting on Santa's lap. Her pigtails, tied together with a red ribbon, shook against Santa Claus's long white beard. She clapped her hands, and her giggles rang like jingle bells. *Oh, my dear and cheerful niece,* Kang wanted to call out to her, but her lips moved without making a sound. At that moment Jian's smiling face appeared beside her daughter's. Then they both waved at Kang.

CHAPTER 12: PLUM PUDDING

FRIDAY WAS THE LAST SCHOOL DAY before the Christmas break. In the second period, Kang entered the fifth-grade math classroom. She scanned the room and noticed that only three students were absent. "Do you remember what we're supposed to do today?" she asked as she walked along the aisles, distributing worksheets to each student.

"We're going to review decimal problems. Right, Ms. Wang?" several students asked at the same time.

Not hearing Cira's voice, one of the top math students and usually an active participant, Kang glanced towards her seat. She was there, but she was holding her head with both her hands and her eyes were staring blankly at the blackboard.

"Are you okay, Cira?" asked Kang

The girl's eyes blinked rapidly and then she lowered her head.

"She's leaving school," a girl answered for her. "Her family's moving back to Mexico."

"Is that true, Cira?" Kang went to her.

Tears welling in her eyes, Cira nodded. "My dad can't find a job. We're leaving."

"Can you go to school there?"

"Yes, but I love my school here." Cira wiped her eyes.

Kang patted Cira's shoulder and placed a handout on her desk. "Let's talk later, okay?"

She turned to the rest of the class. "Let's work on problem-solving now. Then we'll compare our answers."

Some students had questions about the math problems on the worksheets. Kang walked up and down the aisles to help them. She found a common mistake that some of them were making, so she addressed the class. "Please pay attention. When we add or subtract decimal numbers, we should line up the decimal point and the numbers in columns."

She went to the board to illustrate this and explained the calculations to the students. Then we need to add the numbers in each column," she added. "Understand?"

"Ha, I was right," one of the students said with palpable satisfaction.

As usual, Cira finished her assignment first. Kang checked her results and was pleased to see that all of her answers were correct. She got an idea. "Since this is your last day, would you like to come to the front to tell the class how you solved the problem? I'm sure everybody would like to hear how you did it."

"Can I just say it at my desk? I don't feel like going up there."

"Okay," said Kang. Remembering the red-and-white pep-permint candy canes she had brought with her, she took some out of her handbag and gave two to Cira and one to each of the others.

"Is everybody done? Cira has solved every problem cor-rectly. I'm sure some of you have also done everything right, but today is Cira's last day, and I'd like her to tell us how she solved them."

Encouraged by the other children, Cira explained how she had done each operation while Kang wrote what she said on the board.

When Cira had finished, everybody applauded. Some stu-dents placed pencils or sharpeners or pens on Cira's desk for her to keep.

"This is mine," one girl said. "I'll miss you."

"Don't forget me." Another one gave a picture of herself to Cira.

Other students made a farewell card, and everyone signed it. Their colourful names were spread across the card like birds fluttering their wings across the sky, singing goodbye.

Touched by the children's friendly gestures, Kang gave her calculator to Cira. "I hope you don't mind that this is a used calculator. And I hope that you'll continue to love math and do well in your new school."

"I'll remember all of you. And I hope I'll come back to Toronto when I grow up."

As the bell rang, the children gathered around her and asked her to autograph their notebooks. At last, they began to walk out of the classroom, waving goodbye to Kang.

"Merry Christmas!" "Happy Holidays!" Many students cheered.

Luke had asked for Kang's help in his English class, so she rushed over, delighted to be asked to come in again. When she got there, Luke placed a pile of handouts on his front table.

"You're Scrooge," said one of the students, pointing to her friend.

The girl laughed. "I'm the Ghost of Christmas Past."

"Hi, Kang," Luke said, his eyes beaming.

"What should I do?" she asked.

"Please help my new students. They don't seem to understand the story. We've read a simplified version of *A Christmas Carol*, and today we just want to review it by asking and answering questions."

"I have something for the class." Kang pulled the package of candy canes from her handbag. "Can I put them in there?" she asked, pointing to a jar on his desk that was filled with bell-shaped chocolates wrapped in red or green foil paper.

"Sure. Thanks. We can give them to the kids when the lesson is finished."

"Okay." Kang felt someone tug at her sleeve and turned her head.

It was Guang. "Ms. Wang," he said with a grin, "my English is better now."

"I'm glad to hear that." She turned to Luke. "Is he trying harder?"

"Yes. He writes much better, too." Luke pointed at several names on his class list. "These second-language kids need more help."

He started the lesson by asking students to describe the events in *A Christmas Carol*. Kang helped some of them with the vocabulary and explained the story, which she had prepared the day before. She thought some might have watched the movie, which would help them understand the story better.

"Can you use five adjectives to describe Scrooge?" Luke asked the class.

"Scrooge's friend died. He was squeezing, wrenching, grasping, scraping, and clutching," one girl answered.

"Is that a good answer?" asked Luke.

Some said "yes," and some said "no."

"Why not?"

Another student answered, "Mina should say 'Scrooge' not 'he.' I thought 'he' was Scrooge's friend."

"Suzie has a sharp ear. Anything else?"

"I would say Scrooge was a cheapskate businessman. 'Scrooge's friend died' was true, but the sentence doesn't say anything about who Scrooge was."

Kang nodded. This student had critical thinking skills.

The lively discussion continued until they heard a knock on the door, and the secretary popped her head inside the classroom. "Excuse me. Luke, you've got an emergency call."

Luke's face turned pale. He handed the few sheets in his hand to Kang. "These are the questions. Can you continue the discussion?" He left in a hurry.

Kang stared at the questions on the sheet, but could not concentrate. Even the children were silent. Finally, she went to the desk and picked up the jar of candy. "These treats are from Mr.—" Too late, she realized she couldn't remember Luke's surname. "From your teacher and me," she said hastily as she passed out two bells and one candy cane to each of the students.

A few minutes later, Luke opened the door and beckoned Kang to come out into the hallway. "My girlfriend is in the hospital. Do you think you can manage the class?"

"Of course, I can. You go."

"If you have any problems, talk to Mrs. Taylor, my supervisor. She knows you're here."

As she nodded, he rushed into the room to get his briefcase. "Sorry, class. I have to leave for an emergency. I wish everyone a happy holiday!" he said and then hastened out the door.

Kang asked the next question: "Who visited Scrooge on Christmas Eve, and what did Scrooge say to them?"

The class continued, but the students were not very enthusiastic. Before Kang was able to get to the last question, a girl raised her hand. "Why don't we sing a Christmas song?"

"Yeah!" several children responded in unison. "We can finish the assignment at home," they added.

Kang glanced at her watch. There were six minutes left. Why not? It was the last school day before the Christmas break. "Okay. What do you want to sing?" she asked.

"'We Wish You a Merry Christmas,'" the girl said as she stood up.

"Yeah!" The students were enthusiastic and some clapped their hands. The girl started to conduct the class using her candy cane as a baton. Kang joined the singing and forgot about Luke for the moment.

As she rode the bus home, the cheerful words of the song still echoed in her ears. But suddenly a flicker of worry flashed through her mind and she hoped that Luke's girlfriend was okay.

Kang woke up at seven as usual. It was Christmas morning. She reminded herself that she didn't need to go anywhere and snuggled back under the blanket, leisurely going over her to-do list for the two-week holiday. She had promised to help Tania with the Christmas dinner and had offered to make Chinese dumplings for everyone. She thought it was funny that people in Canada called them ravioli. Suddenly, she remembered that she needed to thaw a package of *jaozi* wrappers and the ground beef she had bought a week earlier. She jumped out of bed quickly.

In the kitchen, her eyes widened at the counter piled high with mushrooms, onions, celery, garlic, parsley, potatoes, carrots, green beans, turnips, and a bag of croutons. A food processor, several jars of spices, a knife on a cutting board, and a vegetable peeler on a paper towel were also spread out on the kitchen table.

"Good morning. Are you running a restaurant?" Kang chuckled.

"This is my battle. Haven't done it for ages," said Tania as she got a tub of margarine from the refrigerator. "Have your breakfast first. Then help me."

Even though many of the ingredients were different, stuffing the turkey, peeling potatoes, and chopping vegetables all reminded Kang of the time she had helped her mother prepare a big meal for Chinese New Year's Eve.

"It would've taken me forever to do this without you," Tania said appreciatively.

"Is this what you usually make for Christmas dinner?" Kang checked the clock on the wall and decided she would make the Chinese dumplings after lunch.

"Years ago, I used to have Christmas dinner with Brian's parents," Tania recalled wistfully. "Have I told you that Brian's mother was my younger sister, Nadya?"

"I figured it out after you mentioned he's your nephew. Why have you stopped joining them for Christmas?"

"They died in a plane crash. That's why Brian moved to Toronto from New York."

"I'm so sorry," Kang said, placing her hand for a brief moment on Tania's arm.

"Since then I've always gone to friends' homes or to a restaurant with Brian. But now I'm retired and have time I felt like having some people over. My friend and her husband and Brian and his housemate will be here."

"I'm glad I'm learning how to cook a Canadian Christmas dinner."

"Someday you can cook it for your own family." Tania grinned. "Don't live alone like me."

"Why not?"

"I envied my sister her husband and child, but I wanted to pursue my own dreams." Tania sighed. "Don't get me wrong, I've never regretted my choice. Under the circumstances, getting a Ph.D. was my preference. But this is a different era, and you have more opportunities...."

"I'm not sure if I'll have my own family. You know my issue."

"If you get to know people, you may change your mind about men." Tania grinned. "I've lived in my own world for too long, but you have many years ahead of you to explore life. Anyway, I need a nap before I can help you with your Chinese stuff."

"Don't worry. I can do it myself. Just tell me what else I should do for the dinner."

"We can put the potatoes and vegetables on at four. The timer will beep when the turkey is ready. It should take about five hours," replied Tania as she entered her bedroom. "By the way, there's some chili in the fridge. You can have it for lunch if you want. I'll just have some soup a bit later."

"Thanks," said Kang as she headed downstairs. She had just remembered she needed to return Fei's phone call.

As delicious aromas filled the house, the two women set the table. No sooner had they finished than the doorbell rang. The first guests arrived.

Tania introduced Kang to Lynn, her former colleague, and

her husband David, and then she pointed to a large plate of biscuits. "Enjoy Russian caviar." She took the ice-cream cake that Lynn had brought with her into the kitchen and placed it in the freezer. David put a bottle of red wine on the table.

Lynn picked up a biscuit and bit into it. "Wow! This tastes really great."

Having read about caviar in a Russian novel, Kang had often wondered what it tasted like, so she eagerly picked up a biscuit. She tasted the strange delicacy, and, fighting the urge to spit it out again, swallowed it with difficulty.

"Amazing," said David, as he, too, tucked into the biscuits with enthusiasm.

Kang thought she would have preferred a cracker with cream cheese. The taste of caviar was not what she had expected.

The doorbell rang again, and Tania escorted the next guest into the dining room. "This is Eric, Brian's friend."

"Nice to meet you all." Eric laid a bag on the table and shook hands with everyone. "When we were about to leave, Brian got an emergency call from work, so I'm afraid he can't make it. I brought his pecan pie though, and my plum pudding." He removed the two items from the bag.

Kang eyed the bell-shaped pudding. "Did you make it?"

"I wish. I wanted to get one made in England, but I had to settle for one made in Toronto," Eric said. "In my family, a plum pudding was always part of Christmas dinner."

"It looks great," Kang said, feeling lucky. She had read about plum pudding in *A Christmas Carol* in her classroom just the other day. And now the pudding had come her way.

By the time they were ready to eat, the guests were already chatting like old friends. Kang listened most of the time. To her surprise, she learned that Lynn and David were newlyweds, even though they appeared to be in their fifties. Eric was in his forties and completing M.A. in Library Science. He had earned a B.S. in England and a B.A. in Australia. "I am a professional student," he said and laughed.

As everyone enjoyed the food and drink, Tania described her earliest memory of Christmas. "In 1944, I was five years old. Russian Christmas is celebrated on January seventh, according to the Julian calendar. However, all Christmas celebrations, orthodox or not, had been banned since the October Revolution in 1917. But that year, my mother said we should celebrate our first Christmas back in our Moscow home, following our evacuation during the war. There was a food shortage at that time, so our festive meal consisted of kidney beans, white bread, and a small five-layer honey cake. I hadn't tasted any kind of cake for ages. I still remember how that sweet smell made my mouth water!

"Suddenly the electricity went out. My mother held my little sister on her lap while my father searched for a candle and matches. In the dark, I managed to find the honey cake and slid beneath the dining table with it. When my father lit the candle, my parents found me sitting on the floor holding the only remaining layer of the cake."

Kang thought the evening had been perfect. The food was excellent and the people had been warm and friendly. She wondered, however, why she hadn't tasted any plum in the plum pudding; she didn't know that plum pudding was made with raisins instead of plums.

CHAPTER 13: TANIA IN MOSCOW

DURING THE CHRISTMAS BREAK, Kang started to proofread Tania's manuscript. The story took her back more than half a century earlier to the Stalinist era in the former Soviet Union, which seemed very similar to Maoist China.

***

April 3, 1953 was a Friday. After school, Nadya and I helped our mother prepare a dinner for several of my parents' Jewish friends, including the widow of Yakov Gilyarievich Etinger, a physician and a professor at the Second Moscow Medical Institute. I had not seen these people for years. Because of officially sanctioned anti-Semitism, any gatherings might catch the KGB's attention, and any participants might be charged with anti-Soviet activity. Like many Jewish doctors, my father had avoided any gatherings with other Jews, especially after the Doctors' Plot affair, during which Stalin had accused Dr. Etinger and others of committing malpractice so as to kill off the Soviet leadership. As a result, Etinger was arrested in November 1950. Subjected to heavy interrogation and torture, he died in prison in March 1951. Whenever I touched the doll he had given me for one of my birthdays, the image of his round face and smiling grey eyes would appear before me.

I felt excited by all the preparations, but I was also nervous about the possible danger involved. "Are you sure they'll come?" I asked my mother.

"I guess so. After all, Stalin is dead."

Once the guests had arrived and sat around the table, my father opened one of the two bottles of Palwin, kosher wine that my mother had bought from the black market. Pouring the wine into each goblet, my father announced, "I have important news." Then he held his goblet up. We clinked our wine glasses together and made the traditional toast, "*L'chaim!*"

Taking a sip of the sugary wine, I listened to my father's news eagerly. "This is the first Passover after Stalin's death," he said solemnly. He paused, and then suddenly broke out in a broad smile. His eyes beamed, and his normally furrowed brow became smooth. "Here is my good news. The Doctors' Plot is finished! All those imprisoned because of it will soon be released!"

There was a moment of silence. Everybody was shocked, but soon they all cried with joy, "*Baruch Hashem!* Thank God!" Our wine glasses clinked cheerfully again. I was fourteen at the time, but it was the first time I had heard my father sounding so carefree.

"How did you know this, Professor Shapirovski?" asked Mrs. Etinger, her eyes filled with hope. She had lost her husband, a fact that even the good news could not change. It would, however, alter the fate of their adopted son, Yakovlevich, who had survived the Holocaust but was still in prison.

"I have reliable sources," my father said with hesitation. "But keep this to yourselves. Let's wait and see."

"If only my son could return home soon," Mrs. Etinger said, dabbing her eyes with a handkerchief.

Other guests sighed with relief. "No more constant worry about losing my job or going to prison."

I suddenly realized where my father had gotten his information. He had always seemed rather timid to me, but something had happened only a few days before to make me wonder about him. I had awoken in the middle of the night and gotten up to go to the washroom. I had left the lights off so as not to disturb anyone, and in the darkness, I had noticed a dim light coming from under the door of my father's study. I had thought my father was working late again. But then I had heard someone speaking in English. As I listened, I had recognized that the voice was coming from our radio. He was listening to the Voice of America or the BBC! I was very frightened because I knew that people could be jailed for this. Those countries, we were repeatedly told, were our enemies.

On tiptoe, I went to the washroom and quickly returned to the bedroom I shared with Nadya because I didn't want Father to know that I had seen what he was doing. I did not know much English, but I had understood several of the words I had overheard: "Soviet Union" and "Jews."

Now I gazed at my father with mixed feelings. He was brave to listen to news from outside the country. I thought he was probably engaged in anti-government activity. I recalled reading an article in *Pravda* a few months earlier. The title was "Vicious Spies and Killers Under the Mask of Academic Physicians." The article claimed that a group of doctors had been recruited by American intelligence. I shuddered and had told myself to never tell this to anyone. I felt lucky that my father had not been put behind bars like other Jewish doctors.

That night, the good news relaxed me. So, my father would never be arrested, and the show trial that Joseph Stalin had ordered would no longer happen. Years later I learned that the real reason that Dr. Etinger was arrested was because of his dissatisfaction with Stalin. He was a member of the Jewish Antifascist Committee, and most of the members were executed under Stalin's regime.

I looked at my father's brown eyes that were full of vigour, and I felt proud of his courage. I was glad that he could relay this crucial information to his friends. Mrs. Etinger continued to be very emotional all the evening. Tears trickled down her wrinkled face. "If only my Yakovlevich would come home soon," she kept repeating.

A few days later, on April 6, an article entitled "Socialist Law Is Inviolable" was published in *Pravda*, proving that what my father had heard on the Voice of America broadcast had indeed come from a reliable source. It confirmed that all the imprisoned doctors had been falsely accused. I could imagine how thrilled Mrs. Etinger was, even though her son was not released until the following year.

***

After correcting a few typos she had found, Kang stopped reading for a moment to rest her eyes. The memoir interested her greatly. She considered what she had read, intrigued by how similar the conditions in the former Soviet Union were to those in China during the Cultural Revolution. She had learned about that period from reading or listening to others' stories rather than from her own experience. She thought about what it was like in China in the 1950s, and she wondered why her parents never spoke of those years. She was eager to read more, but she had many other assignments that needed to be completed, so she had to stop for the time being. She was relieved that Tania's family had avoided trouble so far.

Several days later, Kang took up the manuscript again.

***

In 1957, I was a high school senior, and Nadya was two grades below me. My family had moved from the Moscow suburbs into a two-bedroom house on Lebedeva Street in the Sparrow Hills area, which was called Lenin Hills at the time. I adored our new home even though it was smaller than our old house. It had a small garden filled with several mock-orange bushes that, when they bloomed in June, sent a pleasant scent wafting in through the windows.

My father could walk to his office at the Faculty of Medicine in Lomonosov Moscow State University, which was now called Moscow State University. My mother began to work as a clerk in a campus library after being transferred from a teacher's job at an elementary school. She felt content with her new job which, like my father's, was also close to our new house. My goal, meanwhile, was to study at the same university just a few steps away.

I first heard the name Viktor Liu from my father, who supervised the first-year graduate program in the Intense Clinical Training department. He was a Chinese graduate from Peking Medical University. Over dinner, my father praised his intelligence and diligence.

"I hope Tanechka and Nadenka are able to achieve his level," Father said, smiling at me and my sister.

"Why do you compare me with him?" I protested. "I'm not interested in science, so why should I do what he does?" I knew my father was trying to steer me toward a medical degree, but my heart belonged to the arts: literature, painting, and music.

"I can be as good as him," said Nadya, who was planning on becoming a nurse.

Father shook his head and did not resume the topic, but Mother said, "These are smart girls; they will choose the right things for their future." Every time my parents discussed our future, I could sense the worry in my father's voice.

I didn't understand why he was concerned. Stalin was long gone. And the year before, Soviet Premier Nikita Khruschev had acknowledged that the accusation against Jewish doctors lacked solid evidence. The Doctors' Plot was dropped a couple of years ago. What made my father worry so much? At the age of seventeen, I did not realize that the dictator's death did not mean the system had changed.

Even though I had grown up under a degree of oppression because of my Jewish background, I had dreams and ambition at that age. I didn't understand why my father still acted submissive. I presumed that it was in his nature to be frightened. In fact, it became his way of protecting us.

I listened to music by Pyotr Ilyich Tchaikovsky, Sasha Argov, and Reinhold Glière. My preferred poet was Alexander Pushkin. I burst into tears when I read *Eugene Onegin* and imagined a man like Onegin fighting a duel over me. I did not enjoy Anna Akhmatova much—I didn't think her novels were romantic enough. I was fond of *Fathers and Sons* by Ivan Turgenev and dreamed of writing a novel entitled *Fathers and Daughters* someday.

One Saturday morning in February, when my parents went grocery shopping at the market, I lay on my bed reading *Red Love*, a novel by Alexandra Kollontai, a well-known Soviet author. I had gotten it from my class monitor, Ana, who thought every girl should read it and learn how a good Soviet woman should behave. "You'll find out about sexual morals," Ana had said in a serious tone.

I was less interested in the revolutionary story than in the sexual morals. The protagonist, a Bolshevik named Vassilissa, read and relished Tolstoy—that got me interested.

Vassilissa received a letter, the long and hungrily expected letter from her man, her comrade, her lover. They had been separated for months. This was heady stuff for a young woman like me. I wondered where her lover was. Then the doorbell intruded on my imagination, but I assumed that Nadya would get it.

"The Revolution is no game; it demands sacrifices from everybody. Vassilissa, too, has to make a sacrifice to the Revolution," I read. I was curious about whether or not Vassilissa would sacrifice her love. The doorbell's insistent ringing interrupted my thoughts. I wondered who it could be. We never had visitors on the weekends, and especially in the mornings. I inserted a bookmark into the novel and got up to answer the door.

Walking past the sitting room, I realized that Nadya had left. So I opened the door a crack, and peered out cautiously. I saw the back of a man with a medium build. He was descending the stairs of our front stoop. Hearing the door open, he turned around and addressed me: "I am here to talk to Professor Shapirovski."

"He's not at home. I'm his daughter," I said, opening the door a little wider. The chilly wind made me shiver. "Is there a message I can give to him?"

"My name is Viktor." He took off his hat—known as a fur *ushanka*—and bowed his head. I noticed his side part shining white in the sunlight. "Miss Shapirovski, please tell your father I am sorry. I did not submit the laboratory report to him last night because I did not finish it until early this morning." The Chinese man pointed at the door. "I left my report in the mailbox."

His bloodshot eyes, wan face, and sleepy voice, combined with his odd politeness, amused me. Father always said that an intelligent student needs to be buried with work. Now I understood why my father praised him.

"Thank you. I'll tell my father." Watching him walk away, I noticed he was wearing a pair of thick black cloth shoes instead of warm boots—known in Russian as *valenki*. This man, Viktor, didn't seem to be afraid of the cold. He was not wearing *valenki*, although he had an *ushanka*. I had the funny thought that maybe his head felt cold, but his feet did not.

I retrieved a manila envelope from the mailbox and took it to my father's study. The large desk was piled high with papers. Adding the envelope to a stack, I noticed a few pages marked with red ink. It was a paper written by Viktor Liu. I turned to the last page—my father had written a note praising Viktor's work. I could see that my father really liked him.

* * *

When Kang read this part, she began to think about her own relationship with her father. Tania was lucky, she thought. She had escaped the communist regime, so she was able to write freely about her life.

Kang wished her father would write a memoir, if only to help both her and her sister to get to know him better. But Kang doubted he would ever do such a thing. He'd never even said a single word about his past. Kang understood that he didn't want his experiences to have a negative impact on his children. But still, she would have liked to know what had happened to him. She hoped that the day would come that she could ask him why he had been labelled and persecuted as a rightist.

Yawning, Kang stood up and got ready for bed. Liu, she thought, was an interesting character and she was looking forward to learning more about him. As she drifted off to sleep, Tania's story was still spinning in her mind. Tania had described her father as a typical Russian Jew with curly dark hair and brown eyes, but Tania's hair was light brown, and her eyes were greyish green. She seemed more like her Slavic mother physically. Her bolder personality was also similar to her mother's, Kang thought. It seemed to her that Tania didn't fit Freudian theory who'd said that daughters generally inherit traits from their fathers.

Falling asleep, Kang dreamed of a star shining on a centre tower of the "Stalinist Gothic" building. It was flanked by two clock towers, like the main building of Lomonosov Moscow State University that Tania had described in her manuscript. Then she saw a figure trudging along a snow-covered road on the university campus, wearing a grey coat and carrying a pile of books under his arm. From the way the figure walked, she realized it was a young man. She wondered if it was Viktor Liu, but she couldn't see his face. She continued to watch him. Suddenly, he fell, and his books scattered in the snow. A strong gust of wind blew one of them open. She was close enough to catch a glimpse of a picture of a microscope and test tubes, and some Russian text, before the falling snow gradually blanketed the page. The man got up, stamping his black cloth shoes to shake off the snow. He was Viktor. But where was Tania? Kang tried to call her, but couldn't make a sound.

Kang struggled to open her eyes. At last, she woke up in

the dark. The drapes were not quite drawn, and dim light was filtering in from the corner of the window. She got out of bed and opened the drapes to look outside. It was snowing, and the translucent snowflakes decorated the window. She hurried back to her warm bed, and soon she was dreaming of snow-covered Moscow once again.

CHAPTER 14: A SUMMER PARTY

ONE OF THE MAJOR ITEMS on Kang's holiday to-do list was to prepare a report on her practice teaching experience. She knew that when school resumed, she would have to give a presentation about it that would make up a significant part of her grade. She knew it was better to get to it right away while the experience was still fresh in her mind. After sketching out a quick outline, she spent two days reviewing the new skills she had learned in her courses: critical thinking, teaching internationally, and teaching interculturally—a new way of teaching that integrated disciplinary knowledge with intercultural developments. It was all very exciting for Kang and she had made many notes during her practicum that helped her understand and evaluate the relationship between practice and theory.

When she got down to the task of writing the report, she noticed her mind occasionally straying back to Tania's autobiography. She kept telling herself that she had to finish her paper before she could continue working on Tania's story.

Once her first draft was finally completed, she opened Tania's manuscript again, and the story brought her back to the summer of 1957.

***

I graduated from high school in July and was accepted into the Department of Foreign Languages at Lomonosov Moscow State

University to study English Language and Literature. Cheerful and relaxed, I relished the summer holiday. Sometimes I went to visit friends, but most of the time I worked on English grammar and vocabulary. I also read any English novels that my mother could find for me. She had asked the advice of a professor of English at the Department of Foreign Languages and obtained a list of recommended literary works. Then she had managed to find some of them in the library's small collection of classic English novels. The first one I attempted was *Jane Eyre* by Charlotte Brontë. It attracted me immediately, even though I needed to consult my English dictionary for many of the words.

It was certainly much more fascinating than *Red Love* by Alexandra Kollontai, which I had found very confusing. I just didn't understand the relationship between Vassilissa, a Bolshevik, and Vladimir, a former anarchist who had spent years in America. Why, at the end of the novel, did Vassilissa leave Vladimir, even though she was happy that she was pregnant with his baby? Was it because she felt that, while love could be lost, the Communist Party would always be there for her? I thought about what Vassilissa had told her friend Grusha: "*I haven't stopped loving Vladimir. He's still in my heart. But my love has changed.*" It was true that the conflicts between the two lovers were caused by their different values, but it was hard for me to grasp why Vassilissa did not listen to her heart. I felt sorry for her. So, all in all, I did not care much for the story, even though I lived in the same society. Only years later, when I read Kollontai's *Selected Writings*, did I come to understand why the love between Vassilissa and Vladimir had ended that way. Kollontai's point of view was that love should not be seen as a private matter between the two people, but rather as a social emotion.

Reading *Jane Eyre* was a completely different experience. I did not need to think about who was right and who was wrong. I was immediately drawn in to the experience of the poor little orphan mistreated by her aunt and three cousins. My heart went out to Jane when I read about the cruel woman locking her up in the red room where her uncle had died. I burst into tears when I read about the death of Helen, Jane's friend, in the bleak boarding school to which her aunt had banished her. I felt elated for Jane when she finally graduated from the school and became a governess at Thornfield.

That was as far as I had gotten in the book when, one Sunday, my father invited his students to come over for a small farewell party. One of them had been assigned a job as a doctor in a Saint Petersburg hospital upon his graduation from the Master's program. In the early morning, Mother prepared dough and filling for *pirozhki*—oval shaped buns stuffed with a mixture of shredded onions, mushrooms, cabbage, and cheese. Nadya and I filled and shaped the buns, and Mother deep fried them. Then, when there was only enough filling left for two, an idea occurred to me. I got a bottle of vinegar from the kitchen cabinet.

"What's that for?" asked Nadya.

I covered her mouth with my hand and whispered. "Just finish wrapping." When she saw me pouring the vinegar into the filling and adding more salt, she understood what I was doing and made a face, but did not say anything.

"Let's see who will be *lucky* enough to eat them," I said, imagining the twisted mouth of whoever got the sour *pirozhok*.

A small wooden table to hold the food had been set up in a corner of the sitting room. There were two plates of *hvorost*— deep fried pastries sprinkled with powdered sugar on them—a tray of *pirozhki*, a pot of strongly brewed tea, and a *samovar* of boiling water for diluting the concentrated tea according to one's own preference.

The six visitors arrived. Two of them were Ph.D. students, three were in the Master's program, and the last one was the guest of honour. The Chinese student, Viktor, was among the guests. Like the others, he wore a *rubashka*—a cream coloured short-sleeved shirt—and dark green shorts made of khaki, as

well as black cloth shoes that seemed thinner than the ones
he wore in winter.

They greeted us and sat on the sofas, wicker chairs, and
a bench that had been brought in from the garden. Nadya
served the *pirozhki* from the tray. I filled cups halfway with
the strong tea, brought them to everyone, and invited them to
add water to the tea from the *samovar* on the table. I didn't
like this type of work, but my mother loved to train Nadya
and me. She wanted us to learn proper etiquette and good
manners in order to become excellent hostesses. When visitors
praised us for our polite greetings and tea service, my mother
would grin from ear to ear, proud of her daughters and sure
that her domestic training would make us good wives in the
future. I wondered if I would be a good wife. The thought
amused me.

I placed the last cup on a saucer and brought it to Viktor,
who sat at the right end of the bench. As I held the saucer
with the tea cup out to him, he stood up and said, "Thank
you very much."

"Not at all," I responded. "Please enjoy the tea." His formal
manners reminded me of an old-fashioned knight bowing to
a noble woman.

As I walked toward my mother, who was sitting in an armchair, I noticed my father bite into a *pirozhok*. His mouth
twisted, and he choked. Mother gazed at him, a worried look
on her face. "Are you okay?"

"Toothache..." he gasped and went to the washroom.

I felt sorry because I knew that Father did not have a toothache. I knew that there were two *pirozhki* on the tray with a
a horrible taste, and he had gotten one of them! I shouldn't
have pulled such a cruel trick. I told myself over and over that
I'd never do anything like that again.

Glancing at all the guests who seemed to be savouring their
refreshments, I took one of the buns and bit into it carefully,
worried that it was the other doctored one. I was ready for

the sour and salty taste, but the one I picked tasted great, even better than any *pirozhki* from restaurants.

Father, returning from the washroom, looked puzzled when he saw everybody happily savouring their *pirozhoki*. Then he swallowed some tea and joined in the chatting.

As they discussed laboratory test results, I got tired of listening to the chemical formulas and medical jargon. I had something more enjoyable to do—reading *Jane Eyre* in my bedroom. I was eager to discover whether Rochester would find out about Jane's love for him and how he would respond to her. But before I retreated to my bedroom, I wanted to see who the other victim of the sour and salty *pirozhki* would be.

I observed everyone closely. Vasily went on about his dissertation-in-progress, an unfinished *pirozhok* in his hand.

Others seemed to have taken at least one bite of theirs. Only Viktor had not touched his. I wondered if maybe he did not like *pirozhki*. But I thought to myself that he should still try it. After all, the old adage, "when in Rome do as the Romans do," is just as appropriate at a Russian tea party as it was in fourth-century Italy. Then I saw him taking a bite of it—a big bite. I closed my eyes and imagined his surprised face. When my eyes opened, I noticed his mouth was tightly closed and his eyes were squinted as though to avoid bright sunlight. His throat moved slightly as he tried to swallow the *pirozhok*. Such a gentleman! He didn't even make a sound during his struggle. I wondered if he thought this was how Russian pastries were supposed to taste.

Viktor finally managed to eat the entire *pirozhok* and washed it down with some more tea. As I watched his facial muscles moving to cooperate with his mouth and not show any signs of dismay, I vowed not to play such a trick ever again.

Suddenly someone said, "We should sing to celebrate Lev's graduation."

"Yes!" responded Daria, the only female student, clapping her hands in delight. "Andrei, get your *bayan* out."

Andrei, who was sitting next to Viktor, stood up and lifted a case from behind the bench. I decided to watch his performance before retreating to my bedroom.

Viktor held the accordion almost tenderly and began to play "Farewell of Slavianka." Soon the others, including my parents, began to sing:

With our faith to defend Russian land
In our hearts we compose many a song
To glorify our native ground
We always love you no matter what
You are our holy Russian land.

Nadya and I joined in the applause when the song ended. I thought the music was very powerful, even though I didn't like the lyrics much. They were too revolutionary and political, I thought.

Then Andrei passed the *bayan* to Viktor. I wondered if he could also play the instrument. I could not wait to find out.

Not only could he play the instrument, but he also sang a strange Chinese song. The melody sounded solemn too. It seemed everyone liked it, and they clapped. I concluded that scientists didn't have much artistic taste.

Then, to my surprise, Viktor began to play a familiar melody, and Daria, standing near him, started to sing:

Viburnum blossoms in bloom
Are growing near the stream
In love with a fellow I am
God knows if I should keep mum....

The song, "Viburnum in Bloom," came from a movie, *The Kuban of Cossacks*. The lyrics were written by Mikhail V. Isakovsky. It was my favourite song!

I wondered where this young Chinese man had learned this

particular song. As I listened to Daria's sweet voice, I pictured the slender girl in the movie, standing by a stream. But I imagined that it was me, not Daria, who was singing with Viktor. When the singing ended, the room erupted into applause and I returned to reality.

"Sing another one!" someone cheered.

Viktor handed the *bayan* to Andrei. "It's your turn now."

Andrei played a cheerful melody, and someone sang "The Ural Rowan Tree."

I picked up the tray of remaining *pirozhki* and walked around the room, offering them to our guests. I went to Viktor first. He stared at the pastries with hesitation before picking another one up. He waited. I figured that he did not want me to notice his trouble with the awful *pirozhok*, so I moved on to another person. Out the corner of my eye, I watched as he cautiously bit into it. He looked surprised but satisfied. I turned to him and asked "Do you like this *pirozhok*?"

"Very much." He smiled. "Thank you, Miss Shapirovski."

I was glad he'd had the chance to try authentic *pirozhki*. Then, with pleasure, I carried the tray to the others. When I offered one to my father, he shook his head. "No," he said, taking a pastry from the plate Nadya served. "I'll have a *hvorost*."

I wanted to tell him that the rest of the *pirozhki* were normal, but I didn't say anything. I knew I would never make such mischief again.

I enjoyed the music and singing at the party, and I began to think that these medical students were quite interesting. Viktor playing the *bayan* was especially charming. I felt a little jealous of Daria. Although I kept thinking about Jane and her plight, I didn't return to my room until all the guests had left.

* * *

The ring of the telephone brought Kang back to reality. She checked her watch. It was almost ten at night. She thought the call must be for Tania and did not bother to pick up the phone. Then she heard footsteps on the stairs, followed by Tania's voice. "Kang, a phone call for you."

"Thanks!" She jumped out of her chair and picked up the receiver on the wall. "Hello."

"It's Fei. I want to remind you about our party tomorrow."

"Thanks, but I told you last Friday I wouldn't be able to come. I've got an assignment to do."

"Come on. Tomorrow is New Year's Eve. Everybody needs to have fun! Even our Chinese God of Wealth will take a break. No matter how busy you are, you need a rest from making money. And you need to eat, so come and eat with us. Bing and some other friends will be here. We're going to make *jaozi*. You don't need to do anything. We'll prepare everything. You shouldn't forget your Chinese friends." Fei did not give Kang a chance to answer. "And we have a surprise for you."

"What?"

"I won't tell you. You have to come find out." Fei said. "I promise you'll enjoy the party. Plus, I'll make some black sesame dumplings."

Kang smiled at that. "They're my favourite, as you know. Okay, I'll come."

"Great. Try to get here around five thirty?"

"Okay." Kang placed the receiver back on the wall. The call made her realize how much she missed speaking Chinese and eating Chinese food. She suddenly felt very affectionate towards Fei, who had even sent her a birthday card when she was too busy to remember her own birthday. Kang thought Fei was right. She shouldn't cut herself off from her Chinese friends. In this new country, these friends were like relatives.

Yawning and stretching, she decided to call it a day and got into bed. She was curious about what the surprise might be. Nothing would really surprise her unless her parents showed up at the gathering, but she knew that was impossible.

CHAPTER 15: A WINTER PARTY

KANG SPENT THE FOLLOWING MORNING revising her report. When she completed it, she flipped through the clothes in her closet, wondering what to wear to the party. She knew that many of the people there would be younger than her and she didn't want to look old.

Most of her clothes were white, grey, dark blue, or black. The one exception was a red silk blouse her mother had given her. She put it on and stared at herself in the mirror. She thought she looked awkward in red and she had never really liked the blouse, but her mother had insisted that she bring it with her to Canada. "Red is the colour for us Red Hmong people, and wearing red in the New Year can protect you from illness and evils," she had said. Kang recalled seeing a photo of her mother wearing a red pleated skirt with cross-stitch embroidery on its hem, a black wide-sleeved blouse, and a huge red headdress. As a child, she would gaze at the photo and imagine that her mother was a princess of the Red Hmong people who had run away from home to marry her father. Except for that photo, her mother had never shown her anything related to her ethnic background. She had never spoken about that part of her life.

Kang had learned from her sister that their mother had been born to well-educated Hmong parents who worked and lived in Kunming. According to Jian, everything her mother knew about the Red Hmong people had come from a few visits to their grandparents' hometown in Funing County. Kang recalled that their grandparents dressed just like the Han Chinese people, the major ethnic group in China.

She had taken for granted that her parents did not need to tell their children about their past, but now she regretted knowing so little about their lives. It seemed obviuis to her now that both her parents had secrets buried in the past that would be hidden forever if she didn't attempt to dig them up.

She put on the red blouse with a pair of grey pants, and, staring at herself in the mirror, she suddenly felt inspired. Opening the drawer, she pulled out a black knitted vest and put it over the red blouse. The blouse and the vest were a perfect match. Her eyes beamed. It was a perfect holiday outfit, she thought.

Tania offered to drive Kang to Downsview station. "Look at you, so beautifully dressed. You'll sweep young men off their feet at the party."

Kang blushed, but she was feeling proud of her appearance and she enjoyed the flattery. She asked Tania, "Could you drive me to Yorkdale station instead of Downsview? I can do a little bit of shopping beforehand."

"Sure. I'm ready for my party, too. Let's get going."

By the time Kang arrived at the five-storey building on Broadview Avenue, the streetlights were already on. She climbed to the fourth floor and was immediately drawn towards the aromas of Chinese food that drifted from Fei's apartment. She assumed that she could probably find the apartment with her eyes closed, simply by following the smell. As she went forward, she began to hear familiar music. She recognized the melody from the movie *Five Golden Flowers*, and she was suddenly reminded of the old days back home. She took a deep breath, and suddenly thought of Brian. She wondered if he would like this music and she imagined him enjoying New Year's Eve with Eric and his other friends.

Before she knocked a second time, Fei opened the door. "Good to see you!" She pulled Kang in. "Everybody is here now."

Kang handed her a bottle in a paper bag. "Champagne for the celebration!"

"You poor student—you shouldn't have bought anything," Fei said and then introduced her to everyone. She recognized Minla, who had gotten drunk on one cooler on Fei's birthday.

When Kang recognized Mrs. Chen and her husband, she wondered if this was the surprise that Fei had mentioned. She had met Mrs. Chen at the airport. They had been waiting to board the same airplane, and Mrs. Chen, who was bringing her son with her to join her husband in Toronto, had felt nervous about changing planes in Vancouver. She didn't understand English, so Kang had volunteered to help her make her connection.

"How are you? How is your son?" Kang shook hands with her.

"Good to see you again," said Mrs. Chen, smiling. "Our son is in high school now. He didn't want to come with us—he went with his friends to the New Year's celebration at Nathan Phillips Square."

"That's nice. I'm sure he'll have fun," said Kang. "Thank you both so much for helping me find Fei's apartment when I first arrived in Canada. I will never forget the kindness you showed me as a new arrival to this country."

"Oh my dear, please, that was never a problem." Mrs. Chen hesitated, then added, "You look lovely tonight. I like your red blouse, but..."

"But what?"

"Maybe you should take off the black vest—I think it would be nice to let everyone see your beautiful blouse."

Kang looked around. No one else was wearing a black shirt or blouse. Two of the women were in red skirts.

"Thanks for reminding me." Kang suddenly remembered that in China black was an ominous colour associated with death, and she realized why everybody else had sounded a little uneasy when they greeted her. Not wanting to spoil the cheerful atmosphere, she took off the vest and hid it in her coat.

The guests were invited to sit down around the table. In the kitchen, Fei ladled *jaozi*, Chinese dumplings, into the bowls, and Bing and a man named Shang served the bowls to the guests. Kang offered to help, but Fei declined. "Don't move. It's too crowded. You might turn the table over!" Her giggling amused everyone.

Mr. Chen, by virtue of his age and his job as a professor, was the most respected. He proposed a toast. "We are a lucky bunch," he said as he stood up. "Fate has brought us together to celebrate the New Year of 2004 right here in Fei's home in Toronto. We should be thankful. Thirty years ago, at the age of fifteen, I was dispatched to receive re-education in the countryside. During those difficult years I never dreamed that someday I would be living in Canada, a country of opportunities. Cheers! Drink till the bottom of your cup is up in the air!"

"Bottoms up!" everyone shouted.

Shang, who was sitting next to Kang, passed each of the dishes on to her. When the dessert—a fruit cake and black sesame dumplings—was served, he handed her the bowl of dumplings without asking her if she would like some. He seemed to be in his late thirties. When Fei had introduced him, she had mentioned that he was an IT programmer.

She thanked him for the dumplings but couldn't think of anything else to say.

Shang broke the ice. "Fei said you're working towards a teaching certificate. Do you think you'll find a job?"

"I have no idea. But I think my teaching experience in China may help."

"Fortunately, I got my job after a year of training in IT," Shang said, his mouth full of the sweet dumplings.

"You like dumplings?" asked Kang, noticing that he was the only man eating them.

"I studied for my B.S. in Shanghai, so I got to like Shanghai-style cuisine."

Fei then offered them slices of the cake. "You know, you

two have something in common." Both of them gazed at her, listening. "Kang from the south studied in Beijing. Shang from the north studied in Shanghai," she said. "And now you're meeting in Toronto, which means a meeting place in the Mohawk language."

Suddenly Kang realized that Shang, not the Chens, was the surprise. She felt a little embarrassed, even though she appreciated that Fei was trying to help.

"I'll let you chat," Fei said, winking slyly at Kang before she hurried away.

"Is your job very demanding?" asked Kang.

"Not really, but I do have to keep up with all the new software versions that are always coming out."

They ate their dumplings in silence, again at a loss about what else to say to each other. Eventually the silence was broken when one of the guests asked, "Do you want tea or coffee?"

"Coffee, please," Shang answered. "How about you, Kang?"

"Neither," she responded. "But a glass of juice would be good."

"Would anyone like to listen to Kris Phillips?" Minla asked.

"Of course," said one of the guests.

"Me, too," another chimed in.

"Both of us do," Mrs. Chen answered. "Let's sing 'Clouds of My Hometown' with him. That song was his first hit."

Several people, including Kang, joined the Chens as they began to sing: "*A cloud from my hometown at the edge of the sky keeps calling me/ The cries for returning home join the breezes past me...*"

As Kang sang, she felt a memory stirring. In 1987, the Chinese-American singer, Kris Phillips, appeared on the national television program for the Chinese New Year celebration and became the most popular star across China overnight. A lot of time had passed since then, but it seemed that Kris's song was still fresh in the minds of people of various ages, even here in Canada, she thought. At ten thirty at night, Kang told

Fei, "I'd better leave now. It will take me about an hour and a half to get home."

Fei winked her eyes. "Oh, you're not enjoying my party?"

"I am. But you know how far away my place is."

"What do you think about Shang?" Fei asked.

"He's nice," Kang answered, "but—"

"Shang!" Fei called out. "Would you mind driving Kang home tonight?"

"I'd be pleased to do so," Shang said, walking toward them.

"Why don't you stay until the countdown?" Mrs. Chen suggested. "The we can give you a ride, if Shang cannot."

Kang looked at them, nodding. "Okay. In that case, I can stay."

Bing passed some tea and coffee to the guests. "Let's have some stories before midnight. Who will go first?"

"You go—it's your idea." Someone laughed.

"I'll go first," Minla said. "It's my earliest memory of New Year's, when I was four. We call New Year's Day "Yuandan." Yuandan, as you know, is a homophone, so as a child, to me the word meant a round egg. Everybody was so busy getting ready, preparing lots of candy, fruit, food, and new clothes. I could tell this round egg that they were all talking about must be very important. On New Year's Day, I checked everywhere inside and outside our apartment, but I couldn't find a round egg anywhere. At the dinner table, there were many dishes— upside-down pork, steamed fish, chili chicken, and so on. When a bowl of egg drop soup was placed in front of me, I knelt on my chair instead of sitting and craned my head over the table to see if the round egg was hidden somewhere.

"My mom asked me to be careful and not to fall. My dad asked what I was looking for. I told him that I wanted the round egg and kept repeating *yuandan, yuandan*. My mom asked me if I wanted to celebrate New Year's Day—the *Yuandan* Festival in Chinese. I said 'No celebrate! I want a round egg.' I put my hands together to form a circle. 'Like this.' My parents laughed. My mother kissed me and told me she'd cook an egg for the next meal. My father burst out laughing."

"Funny," said Bing. "It's my turn now. Five years ago, I was a freshman at the University of Toronto. Once I saw people fishing in Tommy Thompson Park—I didn't even know the name of the park then, but I knew I wanted to fish too. As soon as exams were over, I biked there on a Saturday with a homemade fishing rod. I managed to catch five carp, each about a half pound, from a pond near a bridge. I had enough fish for several meals after that."

"Where is Tommy Thompson Park?" Minla asked.

"At the waterfront. It's also called the Leslie Street Spit. I'd never caught fish so easily before. So I invested fifteen dollars in a fishing rod and went there again on the following Sunday.

"I checked around a few ponds and spotted lots of carp and bass in one spot. So I parked my bicycle near a grove of bushes and started fishing. In no time at all, I caught a big fish, put it in a large string bag, which I had attached by a cable to a metal bar on the shore, and submerged it in the water.

"I was focusing on the next bite when I heard a female voice behind me say, 'How are you doing?'

"'Very well.' I turned my head and saw a woman in a green uniform with a large brown-and-green badge on her cap. I wondered if she was a soldier or an actress. I asked her if she was fishing, but she responded by asking me if I had a licence.

"I didn't understand why I would need to drive a car to get here. I pointed to the bushes and told her, 'No. I came on that bicycle.' She then told me that she was a wildlife conservation officer, and she wanted to know if I had a fishing licence. I stared at her badge and read the words *Ontario Natural Resources*. Slowly I grasped what she meant and said, 'I'm sorry. I wasn't aware that I needed a licence to fish.'

"She asked, 'How long have you been here?'

"'About an hour,' I said and wondered how much she would fine me.

"'No,' she said, 'I mean how long you have been in Canada?'

When she realized I was a newcomer, she chuckled and then gave me a pamphlet from the bag hanging from her shoulder. 'Read it and learn how to apply for a fishing licence. Fishing without a licence is illegal. I won't charge you this time since you didn't know.'

"I was very nervous when I found out how easy it was to do something illegal without knowing it in this new country. I thanked her, pulled my fishing line out of the water, and set the fish free from the string bag."

Kang laughed along with other listeners.

Then Shang told a tale that took place during the Cultural Revolution. "Twenty-eight years ago, my elder sister, after she'd finished high school, was sent to the countryside to a place called the Dabie Mountains."

"I remember a movie called *The Dabie Mountains in Snowstorms*," said Mrs. Chen.

"Me, too," Kang added.

"The Dabie Mountain area functioned as a communist base for Mao's revolution, but people there still lived very hard lives. My sister, Ying, insisted on going there because she wanted to follow in Mao's footsteps. She learned how to grow wheat and corn, and how to plough fields with a hoe. And she learned to eat corn meal porridge with pickles. In her second year, she fell off a cliff during a mudslide. A young local peasant bravely climbed down the mountain to search for her. He saved her life, and eventually she married him. When most of the re-educated youth were able to return to the city, she wasn't allowed to bring her husband and son back to Zhengzhou City, where she was from. Without a residential permit, they couldn't receive rationed food and other necessities, and her husband couldn't legally work there. So they had to stay in the Dabie Mountain area. She's still there, but she sent her son to our parents so the boy could get a better education. He graduated from college last year, but my sister sacrificed her youth for Mao's revolution." Shang sighed. "Mr. and Mrs. Chen know how hard life was for those re-educated youth."

"Oh, yes. Sometimes I try to tell my son about our experience, but it's hard for the younger generation to understand," Mrs. Chen said, sighing. "Young people here—do you know anything about the re-education camps that were established in rural areas during the revolution?"

"Well," said Minla, "it's interesting to hear about it, but really, to us it all seems so far away, so foreign. We live in a different time and even a different country."

"Let me turn on the TV. It's almost midnight," Fei reminded her guests. "We can open the champagne Kang brought."

As the guests downed their champagne, and their cheers mingled with those of the crowds on TV, Kang felt the thrill of those last moments before the New Year.

She did not decline Shang's offer of a ride home that night.

CHAPTER 16: "MOSCOW NIGHTS"

K ANG WENT BACK TO PROOFREADING Tania's manuscript the following day. She was curious about what happened after the party at Tania's parents' house.

* * *

The party was over, but I always wondered about Viktor. The way he had reacted to the *pirozhok* made me feel guilty, and his playing the *bayan* to "Viburnum in Bloom" amazed me. I felt curious about his black cloth shoes—both the padded ones he had worn in the snow when he came to hand in his report and the thin ones he had had on at the party. Did Viktor prefer cloth shoes to leather ones?

The following day, Nadya started her two-week military training with the Komsomol, the All-Union Leninist Young Communist League. As an enthusiastic participant in each of its activities, she left in the early morning and came back in the late afternoon. I was a League member and would remain so until the age of twenty-eight, but I only participated when it was required. Since I had graduated from high school, I was free from any of the Komsomol's activities.

I decided to take on some self-directed work: every day I would read English aloud for half an hour, do English grammar exercises for two hours, study Russian history and math for an hour each, and read any books for as many hours as I wanted. I also decided to write diary entries a few times a week.

Since Nadya was out most of the time, I only went to swim in the Moskva River if a friend asked me to. One afternoon after some grammar excises, I was bored, so I decided to take a walk to the campus. It was very subdued—most of the students were away for the summer holidays. I approached one of the buildings in the school of medicine; the Department of Surgery was on the second floor and my father's office was in the Department of Anatomy on the third floor.

I loitered around the building, not sure if I should go inside. It seemed I had no reason to do so. What would I tell my father if I ran into him? What would I say to Viktor if I saw him? After a while I decided to leave.

Sitting back in my chair, I immersed myself in *Jane Eyre*. Mr. Rochester finally announced his love and proposed to Jane, and I could feel Jane's bliss. Her love and effort were finally rewarded. The misery in her childhood had not turned her into an unhappy person, but a charming person with determination, morals, and, now, true love. I compared her life to my own. I felt very lucky. I had loving parents and a lovely sister, and in September I would go to university. At my age, Jane had taught for two years at Lowood Institute, a boarding school for girls, where she had studied before becoming a governess at Thornfield Hall. I imagined her teaching at the girls' school, but I didn't think I could manage to do so. It occurred to me that I had been somehow spoiled by my mother, who did a lot for me and Nadya, including cooking for us and taking care of our clothes.

The following day, I told my mother I would cook supper. "What supper?" Mother asked.

"Any supper."

"You should spend your time studying," said Mother, "but you can help if you wish. Why the sudden interest in helping around the house?" She gazed at me, puzzled.

"I think I'm old enough to take care of my—my family." I felt a little bit awkward saying so.

"Ha, a grown-up girl. That is very good."

In the afternoon, I went out for a walk. After wandering about for half an hour, I sat on a bench in a garden and pulled out a folded page of newspaper to read. My eyes were fixed on the paper, but my mind was somewhere else. I wondered where Viktor was at that moment, and what he was doing. Then I wondered why I wanted to see him.

All of a sudden, I heard a woman calling from a nearby path. "Viktor! Wait a moment."

Then I heard Viktor's voice. "Please tell me." He had a slightly strange accent, but his deep voice woke me from my day dream.

"Don't forget that we'll be at Auditorium A at a quarter to seven." The woman's high-pitched voice sounded familiar, and I realized it was Daria speaking.

"Yes, thank you," Viktor said as he strode past the hedgerow of the garden.

I seized my chance. I stood up to say something to him, but I lost the courage when I noticed Daria walking toward him. I sat back down and watched them over the hedge. Daria turned left at the corner while Viktor walked toward the library. When I stood and watched him from the back, it thought I heard Daria singing, "*I fell in love with him/ It's hard to put into words.*" My heart tightened, and I could not move.

Finally, I returned home. Mother had not yet come back from work, but I remembered what I had promised her. So I checked the basket in the kitchen corner and found a few potatoes and onions, as well as a covered bowl in the cupboard. I lifted the lid and saw that the bowl was partially filled with cooked beef kidney left over from lunch. I decided to make *rassolnik*, my father's favourite soup.

First, I sliced onions and pickled cucumber, and then I mixed them with the leftovers in a large bowl, filled a pot with water and pearl barley, lighted the gas stove, and placed the pot on it. Then I picked up several meal coupons from a drawer, lifted the handle of a two-tier enamel lunch pail, and went to the canteen. I bought several slices of *borodinsky* bread and two dozen *pierogies*. After putting the food into the pail separately, I saw the clock on the wall read five forty-five, so I rushed out of the canteen carrying my purchases.

I heard Anna's voice behind me. "Wait, Tania," she called. She was carrying a small enamel basin filled with *pierogies*. "Are you going to watch *Carnival Night* tonight? It's playing at the auditorium. I'll go with you."

"No," I answered quickly. "I've watched it before." I didn't want to change my plans in order to go see it again.

"Me, too. But I want to watch it again—it's so funny! Let's go together. Alina will come too."

"Next time," I said, thinking about my pot on the stove and quickening my pace.

"Movies are more interesting than novels." Anna's voice drifted behind me.

I turned toward our house. "Enjoy the movie. Goodbye," I said, opening the door. Nadya was home, but Mother had not returned.

The pot on the stove was steaming. I lifted the lid and saw that there was no more water in the soup, so I added some more and stirred the boiled pearl barley. I signed with relief. Even though some of the soup had spilled and dried around the pot, at least I didn't burn it! Five minutes later, the water started to boil, and I poured in all the ingredients.

When everybody had sat down at the table for dinner, Nadya spooned the *rassolnik* into her mouth. "Strange! Why is it sugary?"

I tasted the *rassolnik*, which was sweet and sour, and I realized I had added sugar instead of salt.

"Not bad. It tastes like Chinese soup," my father said, smiling. Maybe it reminded him of the year he had spent in Shanghai as a child.

"Tania has created a new recipe," my mother said and smiled.

I was delighted. Somehow my mistake had worked out for

the best. I had made Chinese sweet and sour soup without even knowing the recipe!

After supper, I told my mother I had decided to go to the movie that Anna had mentioned and I left home quickly. I didn't want Nadya tagging along with me.

I walked hurriedly past a few buildings, trying to avoid anybody I knew, and approached the road leading to the back of Auditorium A where the movie was playing. When I got to the entrance, I didn't see either Daria or Viktor. Feeling more relaxed, I stepped into a garden surrounded by hedges, where some people seemed to be waiting for the door to open. I strolled back and forth, keeping an eye on the few paths toward the auditorium, as people in twos and threes approached the entrance. When I saw my mother and Nadya arriving, I sat down on the lawn and hoped they wouldn't see me. I hadn't expected them to show up.

Several minutes later, still peeping through the hedge, I saw Viktor appear at the end of the path on the right side. It was my chance to speak to him. After my mother and Nadya were out of sight, I left the garden and made my way over to Viktor.

"Hello!" I wasn't sure what to say, and I felt awkward. Viktor stopped and gazed at me with surprise. "Miss, do you need help?"

"I'm Tania. Don't you remember me?"

"I know you, of course," he said, smiling.

"Can you come with me?" An idea had suddenly popped into my head. "I.... My father asked me to bring you to his office."

"What's happened?" His voice betrayed his worry. "I'll go right now."

I was tense. "Let's go."

"You don't need to go. I know where his office is," he said, hurrying away.

I quickened my steps to follow him. "I hope you don't mind if I go with you."

He said nothing, just continued to hurry towards the building.

I noticed that he was wearing leather sandals, not cloth shoes. Was he wearing those nice shoes for Daria? A sour feeling rose in me, and I kicked some small stones out of my path as I went.

Neither of us spoke. The air seemed to be frozen. We reached the building and climbed the stairs to the third floor. My heart was beating quickly. I stumbled, unable to see in the dim light, and fell down, moaning in pain.

Viktor turned and stepped down to the stair. "Have you hurt your foot?"

"Yes."

"Which one?" He squatted. "Can I touch it?"

"Sure." I pointed to my left one.

He lifted it slightly. "Does it hurt?"

"No."

He held my ankle with one hand, cupped my foot with the other, and pressed on it gently. "Does it hurt now?"

"Yes."

"Can you move it?" He flicked my ankle. "Maybe I should carry you to the clinic, but…"

"But what?"

"I should go to your father's office first."

"He's at home." I had to tell the truth.

"What? How do you know?" He raised his eyebrows.

"Sorry. I lied…."

"Why?" Our eyes locked, and I felt a hot flush rush to my face. He may have noticed it even though the light was dim. "Let's go to the clinic." He held my arm. "Can you stand on your other foot?'

"I'll try." I stood. I did feel a little pain when I put my weight on my left foot. If I had been alone, I could have stretched my legs. But he was here with me, and I wanted him to help me. So I held his arm tightly, but when I hopped on my right foot down to the next step, I lost my footing and fell into him.

"Don't move. I'll carry you downstairs."

I clung to his back. His hands carefully tugged the hem of

the dress down around my calves that I had wrapped around his waist. He bent himself slightly and began to pick his way down the flight of stairs.

My head touched the nape of his neck, and my chest was against his back. Suddenly, his body shook. I tightened my arms around him, and a giddy feeling spread through my body. I wished the moment could last forever.

Eventually he reached the main floor and put me down gently. His hand still held my right arm. "Can you move now?"

I looked at him; his face was sweaty. "Let me try," I said. He held my arm, and I pretended to be amazed. "I seem to be fine," I said. "I don't need to go to the clinic."

"Are you sure?" Viktor asked. He didn't seem as worried anymore. "Do I need to see your father?" he asked, with just a touch of sarcasm. He had finally seen through me, I thought. I cringed a little, but then shook it off.

"No." I shook my head. "Would you like to go back to the auditorium?"

He checked his watch. "Too late. The movie started half an hour ago, but I can walk you home." He still held my arm.

"Okay." I moved slowly. I was gleeful about his hand on my arm, even though we weren't quite hand in hand. "Is anyone waiting for you?"

"Who would be waiting?" His tone showed his surprise.

"Were you going to watch the movie alone?"

"You, little girl, are funny," he said. "A few of my classmates planned to go together, but you interrupted that."

"I'm not little. I'll be eighteen in two months."

"I know you're going to university next month."

"How did you know?" I was surprised.

"Hmm. You're my professor's daughter."

"So?"

"Congratulations on your acceptance into the university."

"Thanks," I said, taking my chance. "May I ask you a question?"

"Go on."

"Don't you feel cold when you wear those black cloth shoes in the winter?"

"Do you mean the cotton padded shoes?" He paused.

I nodded. "That Saturday morning when you came to hand in your laboratory report to my father, I noticed your shoes. It was a very cold day."

"I had been napping in the laboratory, and I forgot to put on my boots before I rushed out. When they got wet, I was definitely cold."

"Do Chinese people wear those thick cloth shoes for winter?"

"Some do. My mother made them for me."

"Can't you buy them from stores?"

"Yes, but the ones my mother makes are better."

"I don't think my mother can make shoes." I knew that in a few minutes we would reach my home. "Do you mind if we take a walk along the Moskva River?"

Viktor hesitated, but then he agreed to stroll for fifteen minutes.

While we meandered along Lebedeva Street, where my family lived, we chatted about his experiments in the lab and my preparation for my future studies. I learned that he had studied English in high school and Russian at a university in China.

"Where did you learn to play the *bayan*?"

"I played the accordion in high school. When I saw my Russian language instructor at the university play the *bayan*, I asked him to teach me to play it. The key board was only slightly different from the accordion, so I picked it up easily."

"Did you learn Russian songs from your teacher?"

"Yes, and I picked up some of them from films. I watched Russian films and listened to the music on the gramophone," said Viktor. "By the way, why do you want to study English?"

"Partly because I want to see the world outside the Soviet Union."

"These days, many schools and universities in China have

Russian courses instead of English courses. In my mind, Russian represents Bolsheviks and revolution, and English represents capitalism and imperialism."

I was astonished to hear his opinion about the languages. "Are you a revolutionary?"

"Yes and no." Viktor sighed. "My parents always expected me to become a doctor. Chairman Mao teaches us to be red professionals. It means I must follow revolutionary principles first and then become a good doctor."

I grinned. "I know the meaning of red. We had the Red Army, red flags, and Red Square."

"It seems China and the Soviet Union have many things in common." Viktor's voice was gentle.

A few lights glowed dimly along the river, and the breeze was cool. Suddenly some song lyrics came to mind: *My love is inside me/ He has no idea, not a single clue…"*

Viktor checked his watch again. "Oh no. We've wandered for about half an hour. I should get back to my lab." He insisted on walking me back home. I was thrilled when he said he was fond of my native Russian. My heart felt light as a feather floating on the running brook.

He said goodbye in front of my home and hastened away.

***

CHAPTER 17: A NOT SO YOUNG SPINSTER

KANG CORRECTED THE TYPOS and punctuation marks in the manuscript following *The Canadian Style: A Guide to Writing and Editing,* which she had borrowed from the library.

Kang wondered if there was such a thing as a Chinese style guide to writing and editing. She couldn't recall any except for the composition guidelines for students. She wondered if she could even write in Chinese on the computer in Canada. If so, she would be able to send an email to her parents.

She telephoned Fei to find out whether she wrote in Chinese on her computer.

"Sure. You just need to install the right software," Fei told her. "Haven't you ever written in Chinese on a computer?"

"I did in China, of course, on the school computer, but I can't do it on the computers at York."

"I have an idea! You should ask Shang to help you out. It would be a piece of cake for him. Don't forget he's a programmer. Ask him for help if you're not too shy," Fei teased.

"I'll think about it," said Kang.

She was hesitant about contacting Shang. When he drove her back home after Fei's party, he had suggested they meet again. She was afraid that calling him to ask for help might make him think she was interested in him, and she didn't want him to get that idea. She thought she could simply check with the computer technicians who ran York's labs about writing in Chinese on the computer.

As she sat down to continue with Tania's manuscript. The phone rang. It must be Fei, Kang thought, and picked up the receiver.

"Hi, Kang." It was Shang's voice. "Fei said you'd asked her about writing in Chinese on the computer. I think I can help you out."

Kang was surprised, but she was pleased by his offer. "What should I do?"

"Do you have your own computer?" he asked.

"No, but do you think I could use the computers at York?"

"I think the computers at York would reject any attempt to install software. Do you have access to any other computer? A friend's, maybe?"

She thought for a moment before it came to her: Tania. "Maybe my landlady would let me use her computer. I'll ask."

"Good. If she's okay with it, let me know and I'll give you an archive file with instructions. If you have any trouble using it, I can always help you."

She realized, suddenly, that she felt quite relaxed and at ease talking to him. She thought he had been helpful, but not forceful, and she felt like she was warming up to him. She realized that her attitude toward men was gradually changing. At the very least, she was becoming less wary and aloof.

She finished the proofreading and handed her four completed chapters to Tania that evening.

Tania took the pile and sat on the couch, leafing through the chapters. "Huh, a lot of marks," she said, checking the edited words. "Gosh! How did I make so many errors! Thanks for all your work on these. I'll give you more chapters shortly. How do you like my memoir so far?"

"I'm really enjoying it." Kang stifled the desire to ask about Tania's relationship with Viktor since she knew she'd learn more about it in the next part of the manuscript. Instead, she asked, "Would it be possible for me to use your computer occasionally for email?"

"Can't you use York's computers?"

"Yes, but I can't write in Chinese on those computers." Kang explained that she only wanted to borrow Tania's computer to email her parents and that her friend, Shang, was going to give her some software that would allow her to do that..

"Are you sure it won't give my computer a virus?"

"The friend who has the software is a programmer—he knows what he's doing." She added, "I would only use it once or twice a month, and only when it's available."

Tania thought a second and agreed. "Okay—as long as the Chinese characters won't kill my computer." She grinned. "I'm kidding."

Kang resumed her studies after the Christmas break. She had to take five more courses to complete her B.Ed., one of which was a science course. She knew she had to try hard in that one, because it was likely that, as a non-native English speaker, her chances of finding a job as a math or science teacher would be greater than finding a position as an English teacher.

When she entered the classroom for her second practicum, Luke greeted her and thanked her for covering his class before the holidays.

"How is your girlfriend?" asked Kang.

"Good. We had a baby girl. She was a bit premature but she's doing fine. I guess she wanted to join us in time for Christmas." Luke smiled.

"Congratulations!" said Kang, though she was puzzled about him becoming a father before he got married. She'd had no idea his girlfriend had been pregnant. In China, such a child would be called a bastard, and the mother would be referred to as "broken down shoes." She sighed. Even her sister had been called this shameful name, simply because she'd been raped. Kang sighed audibly and then thought that life really was much better for women in Canada.

Luke asked, "Is everything okay with you?"

"Very good. I'm wondering why you're taking this course."

"There are always more teaching positions available in science and especially in math," he replied.

The course required each of the student teachers to design a model demonstrating a scientific principle. After doing some research in the library, Kang decided to make a model of a gear in order to help students understand how wheels function, and especially how they create energy. She thought she could ask Brian for some help and wondered why she had not heard from him since he had missed Christmas dinner. She telephoned him that evening.

"Did you get my message?" he asked.

"What message?"

"I called you on New Year's Eve, but you were out. I spoke to Tania. Didn't she tell you?"

"No, not yet. What was it about?"

"I just wanted to say hi to you. Anyway, how was your party?"

"Very nice. It was good to speak Chinese and sing Chinese songs again."

"That's great," he said. "So what else is going on with you these days?"

She told him about her new project. He asked her about how she would use the model in class, and then he gave her some suggestions about where to get the necessary parts.

In a store named Science City, Kang found a tiny motor and two gears in different sizes as well as three axles and other items. Then she got a tube of school glue and two boxes of green-and-yellow popsicle sticks from a dollar store. When she placed all the items on the table, she felt relieved. She was thankful for Brian's help; he'd saved her a lot of time.

The software package from Shang had arrived, but Kang waited until Saturday to install it. In the morning, Tania told Kang that she was going for a walk with Hachiko, and that her computer was available. Following Shang's instructions, Kang inserted the CD into Tania's computer. When she typed

a couple of Hanyu Pinyin phonetics and saw Chinese characters appearing on the screen, she was delighted. Her parents
had finally gotten a computer, and she would no longer have
to worry about mailing her mother letters and waiting three
or four weeks to receive her response. Shang had been really
helpful and she was grateful that Fei had suggested it.

Later when Shang telephoned her and invited her to join Fei
and their other friends at his place for another Chinese New
Year party, she accepted without hesitation.

The following Saturday, as Kang was mopping the floor, she
thought about the party and wondered what she could bring.
She felt certain that there would already be a lot of Chinese
dishes, so she considered bringing something different.

As she opened the refrigerator to clean it, she found Tania's
leftover quiche and the spaghetti sauce she had made a few days
earlier. Maybe she could bring spaghetti or a quiche? Suddenly
she remembered that Fei liked an Italian cake called tiramisu,
made with ladyfingers and cream cheese. That would be good
and easy to carry, but where could she get it?

Tania suggested she search the phone book for bakeries that
might have it. After several phone calls, Kang found a place.
In the late afternoon, she picked up the cake from an Italian
bakery and could finally relax. To save bus fare, she decided
to walk the ten minutes to Shang's place. The whipping wind
nipped at her face; she grasped her coat tightly with one hand,
while her other hand held the cake. When she imagined how
sweet the cake would taste when they had it later in the evening,
the wind suddenly seemed less strong. Shang is a nice person,
she thought. She thought that Shang was a nice person, and
she wondered if she would grow to really like him when they
got to know each other better.

But when she thought about Shang, it was Brian's face that
she saw. She realized that with Brian she had never felt nervous. He was a *bai ma wang zi*—a prince on a white horse.

She sighed and thought it was really too bad that he was gay.

When she entered Shang's apartment, she was greeted by the cheerful melody of a Chinese New Year song called "Full of Joy." After Shang helped her take her coat off, he didn't immediately let go of her hand. "You're cold. I should've picked you up at the bus stop," he said.

"I'm fine now," Kang said, feeling warmed by his words. Fei, Bing, and Minla and her boyfriend, Yang, were all there.

"You are the VIP we've been waiting for." Fei handed her a glass of wine. "Let me make a toast. I wish every couple *hua hao yue yuan!*"

These Chinese words, literally meaning "beautiful flowers with a full moon," symbolized a happy marriage. Blushing at the toast, Kang knew that Fei's intentions were good. But Kang also knew that she a long way to go before she could even begin to think about marriage. She touched her glass to everyone else's. When Shang clinked his glass against hers, he looked steadily into her eyes. "I wish you all the best," he said. His tone was full of affection, and it made her heart pound.

Then he directed the guests to partake of the food laid out on a table. "Try my fish," he urged them, pointing at the largest plate in the centre of the table. He sliced the fish, picked up a pair of shared chopsticks, and began to serve each guest a piece.

Minla said, "It tastes so good,"

"You're a good cook, Shang!" Fei complimented him.

Kang took a bite and nodded. "I haven't eaten such delicious fish since I left China."

"I assume everybody knows why we eat fish on Chinese New Year."

"Sure," Minla answered. "The word for fish sounds the same as the word for surplus. So when we eat fish it symbolizes abundance, right? And if we want to eat more fish, then it means that we expect to be rich!" Minla laughed.

"I didn't know that," Bing chuckled. "It seems we Chinese are either greedy or starving."

Shang said, "My Jewish friend has a similar saying."

"You've never told me about him," Bing said. "What does he do?"

"He's my boss, actually. He told me that if you have one penny less, you're poor. But when you have one penny more, you're rich. His idea of having one more penny is similar to our notion of abundance," Shang explained.

"Wow, that's interesting," Fei said as she sipped a cup of tea. "So our culture also has something in common with the Jewish culture."

Kang thought that in this city, where so many cultures came together, it was true that people were more similar than they were different.

"Let's enjoy our food," said Bing. "It's not often that we're able to get together. Let's toast to our friendship—a friendship that would never have existed if we hadn't come to Toronto! We didn't even know each other before."

"Well, as Fei said at her party, Toronto is a meeting place." Minla gazed at Kang. "Am I right? Fate brought us together here in a place so far away from our hometowns."

Fei placed the tiramisu on the table. "Time to try Kang's dessert." She cut the cake and placed the slices on individual plates. "Come eat. Bing and I can't stay much longer. We have to call his parents in Taipei and my grandma in Shanghai."

"Me too," said Minla, pulling at Yang's arm.

All done, the guests bundled up for the chill that awaited them outside, laughing and wishing one another the best for the coming year.

Soon they were gone, leaving Kang and Shang alone in the living room.

"Don't worry. I'll drive you home," said Shang. His warm hand guided Kang away from the door and back to the couch. "I'll bring you something to drink—cranberry juice?"

"Yes, please." Kang was touched that he remembered what kind of juice she liked.

While she sipped the juice, Shang suggested a movie. He put on a DVD and sat down next to her. "I think you'll enjoy it," he said and picked up his own glass of juice.

The theme music sounded pleasant, and the sweet and sour cranberry juice made Kang relax. Her head was close to Shang's shoulder, and she could hear his breath. She wondered if this was a shoulder she could lean on. Her eyes pricked with tears at the thought that she might finally be able to get out from under the shadow of her sister's misery.

Shang's arm stretched around her waist. She shivered slightly but did not withdraw. On the screen, a young couple was strolling, hand in hand, along a street lined with flowering shrubs. The girl's hair floated in the breeze, and the man's smiling face shone in the sunshine.. The couple entered a house and sat together in a love seat. On the coffee table in front of them stood a vase full of pink peonies. As the slender woman began to unbutton her blouse, Kang was embarrassed and looked away. Shang's hand caressed her arm lightly, and she felt her breasts tingle in response to his touch. When she glanced back at the screen, the woman was naked. Kang suddenly realized that they were watching a pornographic film, but Shang had already pulled her onto his lap, thrusting his hands into her pants and his mouth onto her breast.

Without even thinking, she smashed her fist into his face and leapt to her feet, struggling to zip up her pants. Shang tried to hold onto her. "I ... I love you," he said. His breath smelled of the wine they'd used to toast to their friendship.

"Leave me alone!" she screamed, shoving him away with all her strength. On the screen, the naked woman and man were lying on a bed, entwined in each other's arms.

"I thought you were westernized, but you..." Shang stammered. "We should talk about this...."

Kang grabbed her coat from the closet, rushed out of the apartment, and ran down the stairs to the street. Outside, the bitter wind whipped her face. Clutching her coat tightly around her, she trudged to the bus shelter. After she finally climbed onto a streetcar and sat down by the window, she couldn't hold back anymore, and tears began to stream down her cheeks. She pulled a tissue from her pocket and wiped her tears, turning her face to the window so other passengers wouldn't notice her weeping. Then she saw a figure running toward the streetcar stop—it was Shang. He paused when the streetcar passed him. As she watched him disappear into the distance, she imagined him shouting, "I've lost her, a not-so-young spinster!"

CHAPTER 18: "I DON'T NEED A HUSBAND"

K ANG GOT HOME around eleven o'clock. She noticed that the light in Tania's study was still on, and tiptoed downstairs to her room; she didn't want to tell Tania what had happened. There was a letter taped to her door. Her eyes were still blurry from weeping, but as soon as she made out her mother's handwriting on the envelope, her face brightened.

Before opening the envelope, she went to the washroom and splashed cold water on her face. After drinking a glass of water, she felt better. She thought about what had happened. Shang had frightened her, and she realized he needed to find a woman who was ready for him. She was not that women.

For a moment, she banished him from her mind; she wanted to enjoy her mother's letter.

She set the pillows up against the headboard and lay back. Breathing a sigh of relief, she started to read.

My dear daughter,

Have you checked your email? I tried a couple of times to email you on our new computer, but my first few messages bounced back. Your father said maybe your email address was wrong. So we tried sending emails to each other. I got his, but he didn't get mine. In the end, your father noticed I had missed a dot in the email address. So careless of me!

I hope you will get my letter before Chinese New Year,

even though I know it's not a holiday in Canada. By the way, your father said eating raw vegetables is a better way to get vitamins, so I've started eating raw carrots instead of sunflower seeds when I watch television. But I won't try raw bok choy! I don't need to worry about your food anymore, but I'm still hoping you can find a suitable man. To live alone is something worrisome.

I have good news for you. Jian moved in with us on New Year's Eve—we thought her new life should start right before the new year began. She let Yaozu keep their apartment. He has applied for an apartment at his factory, but it might take six months to get one.

Jian was so miserable when she first came here. She was sad and exhausted, with salt-and-pepper hair. I couldn't help but cry when I saw her. Your father asked jokingly, "Do you want to scare our granddaughter off on New Year's Eve?" So, I stopped weeping. Then we went to do some last-minute shopping together.

Your father took Linling to look for her favourite toys, while Jian and I went to a hair salon. I suggested she colour her hair dark. I got mine cut. When we met your father and Linling afterwards, Linling said, "My mom looks younger," and your father said, "I almost can't recognize my wife."

Linling is a lovely girl, but too obedient and too quiet. I think it's because she has been growing up in an unhappy home with a father who is stupid and unkind. It stole her innocence. Now she is starting to be a little bit naughty. I like her better this way. She needs to be a child. In March, she will go to kindergarten. Your father will take her there in the morning, and I will pick her up in the afternoon. We are so thrilled to have them with us. Jian is much better now—smiling and relaxed.

Your brother Ming, his wife, and his son joined us for dinner that night. We had the most wonderful time together after so many years apart. The laughter of the two kids filled our home, and it reminded me of years ago when you were little ones.

For the coming Chinese New Year, we're going to gather in Ming's home. My only regret is that you are unable to join us.

Please say hello to your landlady. We're thankful that she provides you with a good place to live.

I look forward to your reply.

We all miss you. Your mother

Kang burst into tears again after she read the letter. As she thought about her family, her sadness faded, and she envisioned all of them together at that festive time. With that image in her mind, she fell asleep.

The following morning, she asked Tania's permission to use the computer before she went out to walk Hachiko.

"Go ahead," Tania said. "You can have it all morning if you want. I won't need it until the afternoon."

Kang checked her email, but she couldn't find her mother's message. She searched everywhere and finally located it in the spam folder. It'd come in about ten days before. Maybe the computer didn't know what to make of the Chinese characters, she thought. Then she wrote a reply.

Dear Mother,

I was happy to read your letter about your New Year's Eve dinner. I can imagine how joyfully all of you gathered around the table, especially now that Jian has left her abusive husband. But I'm worried about Linling. During my practicum, I noticed that a couple of students with single parents weren't very good at their studies—maybe because they get less help from their families or because they're financially and psychologically disadvantaged. I hope your

affection and support as grandparents will prevent Linling
from becoming disadvantaged.

I celebrated the Chinese New Year's Eve at a dinner
with friends. I even had black sesame dumplings, my fa-
vourite. In Toronto, you can find many kinds of Chinese
foods in grocery stores, but I'm too busy to cook.

Maybe I'm too old to find a man, but I'm old enough
to take care of myself. Don't worry about me.

Can you tell me Father's email address? I have some
medical questions to ask him. It's not for me, but for my
schoolwork.

Writing Chinese on the computer takes more time
than using a pen and paper! I've got to go. Please send my
best regards to everyone!

Love, Kang

Before sending the email, she translated the subject line into
English so it wouldn't go into her mother's spam folder. Then
she chuckled, realizing that her mother's computer would
obviously have no trouble with Chinese.

She glanced at her watch. It had taken her almost two hours
to write the letter. She needed more practice with the Chinese
keyboard. She sighed and clicked "send."

That afternoon, she tackled her science project. She had
already made a square box out of the green-and-yellow popsicle sticks. She put the two gears on the different axles and
connected the worm drive to the motor on the other axle, but
she wasn't sure where in the box the gears and motor should
go. Almost finished, she gazed at the model with a wide smile
on her face. She decided she would ask Brian about the model
later that evening. She felt lighthearted just thinking about
going to see him.

The doorbell rang at six thirty that evening. Knowing it was
Brian, Kang slid her project into a bag and quickly opened the

door. He was leaning on his car, waiting. As soon as she came out, he opened the passenger door for her.

They arrived at Tim Hortons and sat down at what had become their usual corner table. "My turn to pay," Kang said. "Would you like your usual large black coffee with a chocolate chip cookie?" She handed him her coat and gestured for him to tuck it into the corner while she got their drinks.

When she had returned and sat down beside him, she felt comfortable and happy.

"I see you still drink iced tea," he said.

"Why would I change?" She smiled and then took her project out. "Here's what I've done, but I need more help. How should I put all these pieces together?"

"Not bad," he said, smiling and examining the model carefully.

He explained what she should do next while she listened and took notes. "Your help has saved me a lot of time and trouble. Let me take you out for dim sum as a thank you."

"I would like that," he said. "Now tell me, how was your second Chinese New Year party?"

Her eyes widened. "How did you know I got together with friends?" She chuckled. "Did you follow me?"

"I went to Tania's house to fix the washing machine that evening. She mentioned it."

"Well, it was nice. We had a very good dinner and listened to traditional Chinese music." Thinking about what had happened with Shang, she paused.

"Then what?" he asked.

She blushed. "We... Shang and I..." she said, hesitantly.

"Who's Shang?"

"A computer technician Fei tried to set me up with at the first New Year's Eve party at her house."

She hesitated again, and then asked, "Do you think it's normal for a man to try to make love to a woman the second time they meet?"

"Hard to say. Some people have sex the first time they meet.

It really depends on whether both of them want to or not."

"Is it easier if both parties are the same gender?" asked Kang.

"What do you mean?" he asked, his eyes wide open with surprise.

"Sorry. What I meant is that women think about love, not just sex. They're more interested in feelings than men are."

A moment of silence set in. Brian seemed somewhat startled. He cleared his throat. "You don't think men have many feelings?" He smiled wryly. "We may not show our feelings as much as women do, but it doesn't mean we don't have them."

"Do you mean men don't use words to show their affection?"

"You're losing me. Can you be more specific?"

"Do men use sex to show their love?" she asked, feeling her face grow hot.

"Well, yes and no. Sexual desire is a biological thing. Some men can have sex with any woman, and vice versa. Funny—I am speaking as if I were a sex ed teacher." He sipped his coffee and eyed her curiously.

"I think I understand now. When sex workers have sex it isn't based on love—perhaps they're forced to accept it because they need money."

"That's another topic completely," Brian replied. "Anyhow, it seems that Chinese people have enjoyed cuddling up for a long time."

"What do you mean?"

"I mean that China has the largest population in the world. In other words, babies don't come out of nowhere." He gave her a lopsided grin.

"Very funny." Kang said, slapping his hand lightly. "Anyway, a man can have sex with a woman even if he doesn't love her—am I right?"

Brian nodded.

"But, as a woman, I wouldn't think of having sex without love."

"Have you ever been in love?" he asked softly.

"Hmm," she answered, "I haven't. I'm just curious about the link between love and sex. It confuses me a lot."

"I suppose that's because of your sister's experience. By the way, how is she now?"

She told him the good news about Jian. "I think I'm finally getting out of the shadow of her past."

"In what way?"

"I'm much less afraid of men than I used to be. I actually felt quite comfortable with Shang."

"Good," he responded without much enthusiasm.

"No matter what," Kang said earnestly, "I regard you as my best friend."

"Really?" He stretched his hand over the table to hers and held it.

His hand felt warm and firm to the touch, and her heart skipped a beat. She felt a pang of regret. She couldn't understand why she was so much more attracted to Brian than to Shang. Maybe she was just weird, she thought. She recalled what had happened with Nancy in that dark restaurant where they couldn't even see their food. She shook her head, remembering how she had wondered at the time if it was possible she was a lesbian. No, she knew better know. She chuckled.

"What's so funny?" asked Brian as he finished the last bite of his cookie.

"I was just remembering the time I went to that restaurant, O. Noir. Have I told you about that?"

"Is that the one where you have to eat in total darkness?"

"Yeah. I was thinking about how I ended up sitting on the floor."

"You fell because it was too dark?"

"No, no. I'm too embarrassed to tell you what happened. I think I'll keep this one to myself."

"By the way," he said hesitantly, "are you going to see Shang again?"

"Why?"

"I'm just curious."

"I don't think so. He's a good person, but ... what is it that people say? There's no chemistry between us ... or his chemistry is different from mine."

"Interesting. That makes sense," he said. He suddenly seemed more cheerful.

"It's funny—I had more friends and acquaintances in China"—she sipped the last drop of her iced tea—"but many of them really didn't understand me. In Toronto, I don't know many people, but they seem to understand me." She stood. "We should be getting home now."

"Yeah, we'd better. Tomorrow is a work day."

"Thanks so much for your help. I really enjoy being with you."

"I'm flattered," he said with a smile.

As they drove, Kang asked, "How's Eric?"

"He's busy with school."

"Does he enjoy your pecan pie? I liked it very much."

"I'll make one for you some day."

"You shouldn't go to so much trouble," she told him. "I think it's really amazing that you can bake pies."

"It's not a big deal. I like cooking if I have the time."

"Does Eric cook, too?"

"Sometimes." He chuckled. "Nowadays, I wouldn't be surprised if more men than women can cook."

The car stopped in Tania's driveway. Kang thanked him and went into the house; her heart was full.

Tania was still in her study. Kang said good night and went downstairs to her room.

As she got ready for bed, she hummed an old song: *When young friends get together, they feel more joyful than anything else.* In 1988, when she had first heard Kris Phillips singing it, she was seventeen. Now she was thirty-three, almost thirty-four. She still remembered the lyrics, though she was now twice as old as she had been when she'd first heard it. She wondered if the song would come to mind in another seventeen years. She also wondered if Brian had seen *Miss Saigon* when he lived in New York. Kris Phillips had played a solider in the show. She would ask him about that when she saw him next.

CHAPTER 19: EIGHTEEN-YEAR-OLD TANIA

K ANG WAS HAPPY with her grade on the science project; she got an A-minus, the same as Luke. She checked the calendar; the next practicum was eight weeks away.

Two weeks passed, but she had not yet received a reply from her parents. She worried that she might have made a mistake when she typed the email address. Or that her message somehow gotten lost. She thought about Viktor Liu and was happy in early February to get back to reading Tania's memoir.

***

I moved into a student residence on campus in September and usually came home once a week. One Saturday evening, after supper at home, I was in my bedroom rummaging through my closet to find something to wear for the next day—17 November 1957, my eighteenth birthday. Viktor had booked tickets for *Swan Lake* two weeks in advance. I had been anticipating this day, my eighteenth birthday. I was about to become an adult—an adult with the right to have a lover. My heart seemed to melt as I imagined standing face to face with Viktor, my hands in his and his lips on mine. But so far Viktor had only ever kissed me on the cheeks. Were Chinese men shy? I wondered. He said he was waiting for me to be an adult.! I felt like I would do anything for him, even become the mother of his child—though I certainly wasn't interested in the domestic work that wives were expected to take on.

While I was indulging the fantasy, my mother knocked on the door. "A phone call for you."

I picked up the receiver and was surprised to hear Viktor's voice, since we had already decided to meet at a bus stop tomorrow. I worried that he might have called to cancel our date, or that something bad had happened.

But his voice sounded cheerful. "I have good news. Something important is happening tomorrow."

"What is it? Tell me!" I asked eagerly.

"We ... I mean all the Chinese students from the different universities in Moscow are coming to our auditorium for an important assembly." He paused. "I'm hoping you'll come, too."

"Why?" I felt disappointed. Why would I be interested in a meeting of Chinese students?

"You must have heard that Chairman Mao's delegation arrived in Moscow two weeks ago for the fortieth anniversary of the October Revolution. Well, they're still here, and they'll be coming to address the gathering."

I didn't understand how that could be more important than our date.

He seemed to be able to read my mind. "Your birthday is very important to me, dear Tanechka."

That was the first time he had called me by my nickname, and my heart softened. "Maybe I'll come," I said, although I didn't feel very enthusiastic about something that sounded so boring. "I'm looking forward to seeing you at the bus stop, as we had planned."

It was Mother's routine to go grocery shopping on Sunday mornings, so Nadya and I took turns helping her carry her purchases, even though I only had meals at home on weekends. Most of the time, we got our food from the staff canteen, but my mother thought we should have something better on Sunday. That morning it was my turn to go with Mother to the nearby market. As we walked, she asked me why Viktor had telephoned me the night before. I told her it was about the Chinese leaders' visit. I asked her how she knew it was Viktor. She said she had recognized his voice, and besides, he had told her who he was. I understood her curiosity, but I didn't feel like telling her more. I wasn't even sure how he felt about me since he had only kissed me on the cheek—it wasn't very different from the way my father kissed me.

When we got back home, an idea occurred to me and I told my mother that I would go to the Chinese students' assembly. Then Nadya said she wanted to go with me. Mother wanted us to stay for lunch, which would be ready soon, but I was afraid the meeting might be over. So we grabbed some biscuits and candy and hurried away along the snow-covered road toward the auditorium.

Besides Chinese students, we also spotted students from Hungary, Poland, and other Eastern European countries that had gathered around the auditorium. Some of my fellow Soviet students were there too. My classmate, Oleksiy, told us excitedly, "Chairman Mao might come."

"That's wonderful! I watched him and Stalin shaking hands in a film once," responded Nadya. Her voice was filled with excitement. "I want to see Chairman Mao in person!"

"Hasn't he arrived already?" I had seen the clock on the tower as I entered the building, and assumed that the meeting was almost finished, and that I had missed seeing those important Chinese leaders. "It's already eleven thirty. Who told you he's coming?" I asked Oleksiy.

"My Chinese friend told me half an hour ago."

"Why are you interested in this?"

"I have a pen pal in China," he replied. "I'm thinking about going to work there someday. How about you? Why are you here?"

"I have a Chinese friend here in the hall. Someday I may go there, too." I felt overjoyed when I imagined going to China with Viktor.

"Let's go inside." Nadya pulled my arm.

I looked around, wondering where Viktor was. The hall was lit with bright lights, and all the seats were filled with students singing Chinese songs, one after the other. We stood in the lobby, waiting for Chairman Mao. I was worried that the meeting wouldn't finish in time for Viktor and me to catch the bus and go to the ballet as we had planned.

"Where is your Chinese friend?" Oleksiy yelled over the roar of the singing crowd.

"Inside, but I don't know where."

"Let's go in," said Oleksiy, beckoning to us.

I held Nadya's arm as she followed the tall and slim Oleksiy, who squeezed himself into a middle aisle packed with people. He made his way forward slowly and waited for us to follow. After passing five rows, he couldn't go any farther; Nadya and I were stuck several steps behind him. It was lunchtime, but nobody was leaving. It was clear that if you did, you wouldn't be able to get back to the same spot.

A Chinese officer approached the podium and began to speak. Nadya asked the people around us who he was, and we were told he was Lu Dingyi, the minister of the Central Propaganda Department of China. After his speech, the Chinese students around us chatted and sang again. Even though I couldn't understand what they were saying, I could feel their fervour and frenzy. I folded my coat into a makeshift cushion and sat on the floor in the aisle, trying to practise my English by writing down what I was seeing.

Other people in the aisles started to sit on the floor. Nadya joined me, and we ate our biscuits and candy; we were very hungry since we had skipped lunch. Gradually I fell into a dreamy state; I felt as though I were floating on a babbling brook. Just as I began to imagine Viktor's smiling face, his mouth close to mine, a sudden roar of applause woke me up. A Chinese girl helped me as I tried to struggle up from the floor. I asked her what the people were shouting about. She said Mao had arrived and they were greeting him with, "Long live Chairman!" Now everyone around me including Nadya was standing up on their seats. I could hardly see who was on the stage through the forest of heads in front of me.

I joined in the cheers—the Russian word "hooray" began to rise in the clamour and echo in the hall. The entire audience was shouting.

As Mao began to speak, one of his sentences sounded like a slogan, and the crowd clapped and cheered. Then I heard him say the word "world" in English. But I couldn't understand the rest of the sentence or why it had such an effect on the audience. Did he promise them something? I remembered a similar scene—when Stalin and his wife appeared in the Red Square and fanatical voices rose above the sea of people.

Nadya tugged my arm. "I've seen him now. Let's go home. I'm starving."

"You go. I'm meeting a friend after."

She left. I waited, hoping that I would find Viktor. It felt like this was longest meeting in the world. I finally asked another student what time it was, and he told me it was 6:37 p.m. I had to go, so I picked up my coat and squeezed myself out of the hall. When I stepped out of the auditorium, I looked up at the clock on the tower outside of the building. It was a quarter to seven in the evening, the time we were supposed to meet. Panicked, I started to run, even though I felt weak from hunger.

Then I heard someone running behind me. As I quickened my pace, a voice called out, "Tania, it's me, Viktor." Before I could stop, he caught me in his arms from behind. Suddenly, he slipped and we both fell onto the snow. I turned to face him, and suddenly his mouth covered mine. Then he kissed my eyes, my cheeks, and my neck. I shivered with hunger, cold, and delight.

"Are you cold, my dear?" he asked, his Beijing accent melting my heart. He untied his scarf and draped it around my neck even though I already had my own. I held him tightly, my face pressed against his, and we both shook. I felt the warmth of his body but also the coldness from the snow. "Let's go to the theatre," he said, standing and pulling me up.

Arm in arm, we walked to the bus shelter. My stomach was empty, but my heart was full. By the time we arrived at the theatre, the performance had begun, so we got some popcorn and crept to our seats. It was the best popcorn I had ever eaten in my life!

As I listened to the music, my eyes began to grow heavy. With Viktor's arm wrapped around my waist, I fell into a sweet dream. Suddenly a burst of rousing applause woke me up. *Swan Lake* had ended and most of the audience was leaving.

Viktor teased me, "What did you enjoy more, the ballet or the nap?"

"Why didn't you wake me up?" I asked as I followed him out of the theatre.

"You were tired and needed the rest."

"Aren't you tired?"

"Not really. I'm still excited about seeing Chairman Mao and the other leaders."

"Who were they?" I asked him as we strolled along the street.

Viktor told me those leaders' names, but the only one I can still remember is Deng Xiaoping.

"What did Mao say about the 'world'?" I remembered how the crowd had responded with wild applause and cheers.

"He said, 'The world is finally yours.'"

"Oh," I replied, but I didn't feel excited about it.

We entered a restaurant where we filled our empty stomachs with *pierogies*. Suddenly he tapped his forehead. "I almost forgot!"

He walked over to where his coat was hanging, pulled something out of his coat pocket, and handed me a gift wrapped in a light blue handkerchief. "Happy Birthday!"

I took the package, which felt soft to the touch. "Should I open it now or at home?"

"It's up to you. I hope you like it."

I opened it and found a palm-sized, stuffed white bunny with red eyes and perky ears. I pressed it to my cheek in delight. "Thank you so much! It's a charming gift!"

"Do you know why I gave you a rabbit?"

I shook my head.

"Because you were born in the Chinese zodiac year of the Rabbit. Rabbit people are gentle, elegant, and independent."

"And under what sign where you born?"

"The Rooster."

"What are Rooster people like? Tell me more."

I found the Chinese zodiac fascinating, and we talked about the animals and meanings of the signs on the way back to campus.

It was quiet. Viktor walked me to my dorm, and then he pulled me out of sight behind some shrubbery where we stood, hugging and kissing each other for a long while. When a few snowflakes dropped on my face, he licked them off. I enjoyed his warm tongue and I thought to myself that he was more like a dog than a rooster.

Finally, he took my hand and led me to the entrance. "Good night. See you in three weeks."

We had decided on the way back not to see each other too often because he said he needed to focus on his studies. I wasn't very happy about this, but as long as I knew he loved me, I respected that he needed to try to balance his time. I also knew his studies were important to him. My eighteenth birthday was the most marvellous, because he, a determined Chinese man, began to treat me as a lover.

* * *

Kang thought about what she had read. Viktor's perspective on education was familiar to her—he sounded just like her father. Her father had also attended a university in the Soviet Union, but he had never told her which one. She wondered if he had been in Russia around the same time as Viktor had. She even toyed briefly with the thought that Viktor might actually be her father. But her father was born under the sign of the dog; Victor was a rooster; and Viktor's family name was Liu, and not Wang. She doodled on her notebook on the table as she thought and decided she would have to ask her father which university he went to next time they spoke.

Kang continued the manuscript, eager to find out what would become of Tania and Viktor.

**

I was still hesitant about introducing Viktor to my family as my boyfriend. That would have been a big step. In those days, being introduced to your partner's family was like an announcement of an engagement. My parents liked Viktor, but that didn't mean they would accept him as my boyfriend or fiancé. I had to wait for the right time, but I didn't know when that would be.

I felt so joyful every day when I thought about his kisses, which seemed to have cast a spell on me. I felt like I finally understood the kind of love that I'd read about in novels.

I was tortured by the long wait before I could see him again. Three weeks seemed like three months, or even three years. I had never read any stories in which a man chose to meet his lover only every three weeks. Even Don Quixote was sleepless when he imagined his lady love, Dulcinea. I decided I would suggest to Viktor that we watch the new movie, *Don Quixote*, which was made in the Soviet Union, and I circled the date of our next meeting on the calendar: December 8.

I thought about my roommate, Nelly. She was from Leningrad—which had recently been changed back to its original name, St. Petersburg—and a year older than me. She majored in geography, and her boyfriend, from the same city, was in his third year of the engineering program. They saw each other a couple of times a week and spent most weekends together. I was envious and wished that Viktor and I could see each other as often.

One Sunday when I came back from my parents' house, I put the key in the lock, but couldn't open the door. I realized it was locked from the inside. "Nelly, open the door. It's me, Tania." I waited a few minutes before the door opened. When I asked her if she had been sleeping, her face reddened in embarrassment. And then I saw her boyfriend sitting in the chair behind the open door. It was awkward for all of us. "I'm joking," I said, trying to diffuse the situation.

In those days, sex before marriage was taboo. After her boyfriend left, Nelly went to great lengths to explain to me that they hadn't slept together. It was the 1950s, and remaining a virgin until marriage was the most important moral standard that a "good" girl had to adhere to. Nelly told me her boyfriend had simply touched her to explore her body. She wanted me to understand that she and her boyfriend had not crossed the line. Suddenly I understood why I enjoyed Viktor's kisses. He touched me, too, but not everywhere.

Young people were very naïve in those days. Although we had natural sexual desire, we did not have much knowledge about it, either physically or psychologically. We were constrained by traditional moral values and discouraged from enjoying physical pleasure. As a matter of fact, Nelly and her boyfriend, and Viktor and I, were all in the same boat; we were more or less following the principle of self-sacrifice in order to serve the communist cause. Viktor seemed to be the most self-disciplined. Premarital sex was considered a kind of moral corruption that was harmful to the communist revolution.

Since Nelly was so open with me, I told her about my first kisses. She asked, "Hasn't he seen your body and touched it?"

I shook my head. "Should he?"

She nodded. "Maybe soon."

I began to imagine how it would feel if Viktor were to see my body and touch it. Just thinking about it, made me light-headed.

* * *

CHAPTER 20: "KATYUSHA"

THE LAST WEEK IN FEBRUARY was reading week; students had no classes, but were expected to complete readings—both articles and books—for their courses. Kang started with Tania's manuscript first rather than her reading list. As she leafed through the pages, she felt closer and closer to Tania, as though she had lived through those years with her.

***

The winter was over, but I still could not find the right time to introduce Viktor to my family. Meanwhile, we continued to meet every three weeks. On our dates, I helped him with his Russian pronunciation, and then we would talk about the articles and books I had read. One article in particular brought up a few questions for me; it was about Hitler's fondness for German shepherds and his attempt to train them to speak. It reminded me of the true story of a feral child in India, Dina Sanichar, who, at the age of six, had returned to human society after being raised by wolves, but had never learned to speak. I told Viktor that I doubted that a dog could learn to speak a human language. He agreed with me; he had read in Frederick Engels's work that the transition from ape to man had taken hundreds of thousands of years of labour, and that the evolution of human languages had happened over a long period of time. We agreed that Hitler was insane for believing that he could train his dogs to talk.

The first of May was the Celebration of Spring and Labour. I asked Viktor if he could spend the day with me. He said he needed to do some work in the lab that morning, so we decided we would go to the Red Square to watch the annual parade after lunch.

Nelly went home to Leningrad the day before the celebration. Alone in our dorm, I did my schoolwork; I had to read one of the "Fragments" in *The Canterbury Tales* by Geoffrey Chaucer. I was up until midnight reading "Fragment III: Wife of Bath, Friar, Summoner," and then continued the next morning. Then I left for the canteen to get some food before noon.

Back in my dorm, I waited for Viktor. It was noon, but he did not appear. It usually only took five minutes by bicycle from his laboratory to my dorm. I tried to focus on the book, but couldn't read much. Instead, I listened intently for any sound in the hallway. Half an hour passed, and the food in the enamel container turned cold. I heard steps pass my door a few times, but every time I was disappointed. My stomach began to growl, and still Viktor had not shown up. I wondered if he had forgotten. Or if his bicycle had broken down. Then I wondered if I should go to his laboratory and see if something had happened.

Suddenly there was a knock, and I threw the door open as quickly as I could. Viktor stepped in, pulled me into his arms, and kissed me. "Sorry for being late." He took a breath. "But I got a good result from my experiment." He lifted me, and then set me down on my bed. "I'm really tired. I only slept a few hours last night." He tried to stifle a yawn.

"Aren't you hungry?" I asked.

He nodded.

"The food is cold. I'll go to the kitchen to reheat it."

He said he didn't mind eating it cold, so we ate the *pierogies*.

I noticed his exhaustion and asked him if he would like to take a nap on my bed. He lay down with his clothes on. In two minutes, he was fast asleep, so I took his shoes off and covered

him with a blanket. I knew we would miss the parade, which
usually finished at three o'clock, but I didn't care very much.
I sat in my chair and resumed Chaucer's "Fragment III: Wife
of Bath, Friar, Summoner."

Soon I felt sleepy and decided to lie down on Nelly's bed.
Half asleep, I felt a warm hand on my forehead, so I opened
my eyes. Viktor was bending over me. "Are you okay?"

"I just took a nap like you."

"It's half past three. Shall we go to the Red Square?"

"It's too late." I smiled at him. "Do you have enough energy
to carry me to my bed? I'm too lazy to walk."

He lifted me and placed me on my bed, but I kept my hands
around his neck, seeking his mouth with mine. He kissed me,
but kept his body from touching mine. I thought of Chaucer's
"The Wife of Bath's Tale"—the knight didn't want to kiss the
ugly old hag. I was young and surely better looking than that
hag, but Viktor didn't want to touch me. Tears welled up in
my eyes. "You don't love me."

"What do you mean?"

I told him what Nelly and her boyfriend did together. He
said he admired Nelly's boyfriend.

"Why?" I asked.

He grinned. "I wouldn't be able to resist if I did that."

"You can imagine that I'm just your patient." I unbuttoned
the upper part of my dress.

"You're so beautiful." His voice trembled while his hands
gently touched my body. "You have a strong heart, good muscles,
a healthy bone structure, and you're gorgeous...." He paused.

"What?" I stared at his face.

"Your breasts are perfect," he murmured as he buttoned my
dress. "Am I a good doctor?"

I nodded with satisfaction. I was glad that he had seen and
touched my body, even if it was only parts of it. From his voice,
I could feel his affection. I sat up and pulled him down to sit
with me, my head on his chest. I heard his heart pounding.

"Tell me about your laboratory results." I wanted to understand what he was working so hard on.

He talked about his research, but then astonished me by changing the subject. "Would you be willing to go to China with me?"

"I ... I don't know. Yes, I would. But why don't you stay here?"

"Because my government paid for me to study here. In return, I'm expected to go back to serve China. If you'd like to go with me, you could teach Russian or English there. There's a city called Haerbin, northeast of Beijing, which has a large Russian population. If you like it better than Beijing, I'll try to get a job there and wait for you, or you can transfer to a Chinese university and study there."

I was ecstatic about these plans because they meant that he took our relationship seriously.

Time seemed to move very fast, and suddenly it was June. I had my last exam on a Friday morning, and, afterwards, I lay on my bed thinking about my relationship with Viktor. Since I would be back at home for an eight-week summer break, it was going to be hard to see him without my parents knowing. I thought that maybe I should introduce Viktor to my family after my parents' vacation.

I was interrupted by a knock on the door. When I opened it, I was surprised to see Viktor, since we usually only saw each other on Saturdays.

"I must talk to you now, Tania." He looked wearied. Noticing Nelly at her desk, he asked if I could go outside with him for a few minutes.

I followed him outside and into a small shrub-enclosed garden, where we sat on a bench.

"Tania," he said, "I have to say goodbye."

"I don't understand," I said, clutching at his arm.

"The Party Secretary told me I have to go back to Beijing immediately."

I reached for his trembling hand. "When will you come back?"

"I may not be able to come back."

"What?" I exclaimed. Then I realized we were in public, so I lowered my voice. "Why?"

He shook his head. "I don't know for sure. The Party Secretary told me I may have made a certain mistake. In China the Anti-Rightist Campaign has been going on for a year, and apparently the Communist Party is now checking up on the Chinese students in Russia."

The blooming chamomile flowers in the garden were spreading over the ground like a white blanket, but to me they looked like a sudden snowfall, one that froze my heart and blinded my eyes.

I asked him if he could refuse to return. He smiled wryly. "I am a Chinese Communist Party member, like all the other Chinese students. I'm obligated to obey the Party." Like a trapped fish, my heart struggled in the net; I didn't understand why the Chinese Communist Party had such control over his life.

"Will you tell my father? He might be able to help."

"I'm supposed to leave next Saturday. Your father is going on vacation next Monday. Besides, he's not Chinese, so the Party probably won't listen to anything he says."

I told him my father was one of the most respected professors at the university and insisted he talk to him.

Finally promising that he would, he said he had to go back to his experiment in the laboratory. It was hard for me to understand how he could just calmly follow his routine under such dire circumstances.

When I got back to my dorm room, I lay in my bed and eventually fell asleep. Then someone shook me, and I opened my eyes. It was Nelly asking me if I was sick. I shook my head, tears in my eyes.

We went to the canteen together to get something to eat, and I told her what had happened. She, too, was shocked. She suggested that Viktor and I get married so he could stay. She herself was planning to have an engagement party in July and to get married before the end of the year.

"You should at least get engaged right away, so he has a reason to stay. Or maybe you could go with him."

Nelly's words opened my eyes; I felt a glimmer of hope. But I would have to tell my parents first.

That night, my mind was full of stray thoughts, and I couldn't stop picturing what might happen with Viktor: he was holding my hand in front of my parents; the two of us were strolling through Tiananmen Square like we had once meandered through Red Square; we were kissing each other in his apartment in Beijing; I was studying Chinese at Beijing University.

The following morning, Nelly's boyfriend came to help her pack to go home. Seeing them together and happy, I began to get very worried that I would lose Viktor forever. I felt my heart ache. Saying goodbye, Nelly hugged me and wished me the best of luck.

As soon as Viktor got to my dorm that afternoon, I asked him what my father had said. He told me that my father had promised him to talk to someone at the university. "He's going to postpone his trip till he gets a response. Let's wait and see."

We went on an outing as planned. He lifted me onto the front bar of his bicycle, and we rode down toward the Moskva River. The road sloped downwards, and we flew along it, even though Viktor wasn't pedalling at all. The wind blew, and my hair floated around my ears. In his arms and leaning against his chest, I felt a rush of excitement.

As we approached Luzhniki Metro Bridge, which was still under construction, I asked Viktor to stop, and we strolled quietly along the river. There were wildflowers here and there. I picked a few bright orange ones named scarlet globemallow. Viktor put one in my hair, and we sat on the bank, resting against a large boulder, his arm around my waist.

"You look so beautiful."

I caressed his hand in response and prayed silently for God

to help us. I was reminded of M. Isakovsky's "Katyusha," and its heroic lyrics and romantic melody began to echo in my ears. I started to hum:

> *Pear blossoms are blooming*
> *The river is in the mist of morning*
> *On the steep banks Katyusha is standing*
> *Spring sunshine is with her, singing.*

Viktor joined me, singing:

> *Her song is about a grey eagle*
> *Her true love at a remote post*
> *Her greetings are like moonlight*
> *Accompanying her beloved soldier at night.*

I was not surprised that he knew the song since he loved Soviet movies and had probably learned to play all the songs on the *bayan*. Since the day I had heard him playing "Viburnum in Bloom," I had always felt as if he had grown up in the Soviet Union like me. The only difference was that he could speak Chinese.

The song touched our tender, young hearts. We had no clue what would become of us, but we cherished that brief moment of sunshine.

Later, at supper, Father told Mother he could not grasp why the Chinese authorities demanded that Viktor return to China to join the Anti-Rightist Campaign.

I asked Father to do everything in his power to help Viktor. He asked me why I cared so much. I gathered my courage and said, "Because I love him."

Everyone was shocked, including myself. It was Nadya who finally broke the silence. "He plays the *bayan* beautifully." I looked at Nadya thankfully.

Later, my father told us he had talked to a member of the

university committee and would get an answer next week. When Mother reminded him that they were leaving on Monday, he told her that he had cancelled the train tickets, and that they wouldn't leave until he received a response.

On Tuesday morning, my father brought back some good news. The Chinese Student Committee had agreed to grant Viktor two more months at the university since my father needed him to complete his experiment. However, the committee had warned my father that the final decision on whether he could stay till he graduated had to be made by the Chinese Embassy.

My parents invited Viktor for dinner on that same day. At the dining table, Viktor acted a bit nervous; I was tongue-tied. Nadya stepped in again and chatted with Viktor, putting him at ease. Father told him not to worry too much and said he would discuss the issue with his committee friend, and maybe the university would contact the Chinese Embassy directly to work out some kind of solution.

I assumed we would have some peace and quiet for the time being. The following day, Viktor returned to his work, and my parents went on their vacation.

On Thursday morning, I woke from a decent sleep and went to get a pile of books from the library. Before I had a chance to start my summer reading, I got a call from Viktor. As I listened to him, my hand started to tremble.

He had been told to leave on Saturday as planned. I didn't understand how the Chinese Student Committee could break its promise. Many years later, I came across the answer in *The Art of War* and *The Thirty-Six Stratagems* by Sun Tzu. The Chinese Student Committee had adopted the scheme known as the "delaying tactic." They had postponed their plans while my father was present, but they had moved quickly as soon as he was out of the way.

As a loyal Party member, Viktor did what he was told to do. He promised that, even though an ocean could dry out and a stone could crumble, his love for me would never change. Touched by this Chinese saying, I told him in tears that I would wait for him. I was lucky to have Nadya, my dear sister, who did all she could to comfort me in my misery. Finally, we saw Viktor off at the airport.

When Father returned home and learned what had happened, he was outraged. "Someone lied to me!" He met with his contact at the university, even though I told him there was no point. He was told that the Chinese Student Committee regretted the situation but they'd had no choice but to obey the Embassy.

A year later, Father himself would be accused of interfering with Chinese internal affairs because of his effort to keep Viktor in Russa. This would lead to Father's decision to leave for Israel to avoid further persecution.

I waited for a letter from Viktor, but nothing came. Then, in early August, the phone rang. After a few seconds, my mother passed the receiver to me.

I heard Viktor's voice! He asked if I'd gotten his two letters. I said no and asked how he was. He then explained to me that he had been forced to return home because he had broken the rules—no Chinese students were allowed to have love affairs with Russians. Now labelled as a rightist because he had requested a foreign professor to interfere with Chinese policies, he was to be banished to Southwest China for thought reform. He asked me to forgive him for bringing so much trouble and unhappiness into my life. I could detect dismay in his voice.

"You take care! I love you," I said, over and over again. I could not call him since he didn't have a telephone. He never called again.

I fell ill for a long while, and I resumed my studies in September. Nelly wept with me when she listened to my story. I started to have nightmares and woke up screaming a few times, disturbing Nelly. After that, she avoided talking about her engagement party. Years later, whenever I recalled my student life at Lomonosov Moscow State University, I felt appreciative of Nelly, my dear roommate.

* * *

Kang put down the manuscript and wiped her eyes with a tissue.

CHAPTER 21: DIM SUM AND JIAOZI

KANG HAD A PRODUCTIVE WEEK. She proofread another four chapters of Tania's memoir, completed a paper for her course, and prepared some lessons for her future practicum.

On Saturday at noon, she and Brian took the subway down to Chinatown for the dim sum she had promised him. They made their way along Spadina Avenue to the Dragon City mall, and Kang led Brian into the restaurant on the top floor.

The huge room was packed. They waited for ten minutes before they got a table. "Oh, they have a smart way of cleaning tables," said Brian.

"What is it?"

He pinched the layers of thin plastic tablecloths between his fingers. "They only need to take off the top sheet after a meal is finished."

"You're observant," she said with a smile and picked up the teapot the waiter had brought to the table. After she filled Brian's cup, he tapped his fingers lightly on the table.

"What are you doing?"

"You don't know?" he asked in surprise.

"I haven't learned your secret codes." She blinked her eyes and smiled.

"It's Chinese tea etiquette to say thank you."

"I never heard of such a thing. Where did you learn this?"

"From my ex, who picked it up from some Chinese Americans. We ate dim sum in New York's Chinatown all the time."

"I guess Chinese Americans may have kept more Chinese traditions," said Kang. "Or maybe this is a Cantonese tradition. I didn't learn this tea etiquette back home."

"Interesting."

"Chinatown in New York must be more exciting than here."

"Not really. It's smaller. Toronto's Chinatown is one of the largest in North America." He paused. "I learned that from my ex, too."

It turned out that he knew better than her what to order. Kang tried a slice of turnip cake that tasted totally foreign to her. "I've never eaten this before." She chuckled. "You seem more knowledgeable about Chinese cuisine than I am."

Just then a familiar male voice called out, "Hi! Kang!"

She turned her head, and there was Shang, smiling. "Can you take a photo of me and my fiancée?"

He already had a fiancée? It had only been a month since Kang had last seen him. She raised her eyebrows. Before Kang could answer, he pointed to a young woman at his table. "Here she is." Behind her was a red wall decorated with a large Chinese character which stood for double happiness. It was flanked by a golden dragon and a phoenix. "You're with someone," he said.

"A friend," Kang said and introduced him to Brian.

"I'll be back in a second," she told Brian, following Shang to his table.

He handed her a camera and asked his fiancée to stand beside him. "Would you mind taking a few photos?"

"Say cheese!" Kang said as she pressed the button. After taking a second picture from a different angle, she handed the camera back.

"We're going to get married on the Victoria Day weekend. I'll send you an invitation," he said loudly. Then he followed her a few steps toward her table and asked, "Is Brian your boyfriend? Can he...?" He paused.

She waited.

"Can he *wait*?" he asked, a hint of sarcasm in his voice. "I hope he's a better man than me."

"He's not my boyfriend. Just a friend, like I told you before. I don't need to lie," she replied hastily. Then she strode away.

When she sat down in her chair, Brian asked, "Are they going to get married?"

"It seems so," she replied.

"Well, now you don't have to feel guilty about rejecting him," Brian said smiling widely.

"That's for sure." She shook her head and smiled back at Brian. She didn't want to think about Shang at all.

As a server wheeled a cart of dim sum past their table again, Brian asked for his favourite wonton soup, and Kang asked for a plate of rice noodle rolls. "You said you'd tell me why you decided to move to Toronto."

"Well, it's a long story. Like most teenagers in North America, I was eager to get out from under my parents' roof to explore my own life. They had always been easy going, so after high school, my folks were willing to pay for college in New York City. I spent thirteen years there, studying and then working— pursuing the American dream, just like my mom expected me to. She'd never even taught me Russian, her mother tongue. I was very happy until Ingrid and I broke up— I took it pretty hard. Then in the following year my parents died in a plane crash. It was the darkest time I've ever gone through." He paused, his hand clenching. "If death had been something I could touch, I would've crushed it into bits."

"When was that?"

"In 1999. For a long time, I drowned in my sorrow and regret that I hadn't spent enough time with my parents. Once I left home, I'd only visited them once or twice a year. I was young and self-centred at the time. I guess I'd always assumed they'd be there—or at any rate that they'd live well into their eighties or nineties.

"After they died, I went through their house to put it up for sale and I found my dad's diaries. Reading them gave me a chance to learn so much more about him. I found out that he had a secret: he'd fallen in love with Aunt Tania at the State University of New York in Buffalo. After graduation, he got a job, but Tania left for the University of Toronto to pursue an M.A. My old man waited for two years for her to return, but then she decided to stay in Toronto and earn a Ph.D."

"I know the rest of the story," Kang interrupted him with a grin. "Later your dad met your mom, Tania's sister Nadya, in the hospital where she worked as a nurse. They fell in love and got married in 1967."

Surprised, Brian accidentally dipped his soup spoon into his tea cup. "How did you know that?"

"I'm proofreading Tania's memoir."

"Well, you probably know more about Tania than I do."

"It's so sad that Tania missed her chance to fall in love again," Kang said, her voice sorrowful.

"It may have been bad for Tania, but it was good for me."

"How?"

"Well, if my dad had married Tania, their child would've been another person. So I wouldn't have existed."

"Life is mysterious." She nodded, then sighed and asked him to continue with his story.

"After reading Dad's diaries, I decided to move to Toronto to be close to Aunt Tania—she's my only close relative. The sudden loss of my folks at the age of thirty forced me to grow up fast. I think I've become less self-centred."

"Very interesting. According to Chinese tradition, people normally establish themselves and settle down by the age of thirty," she remarked as she sipped tea. "And how did you like Toronto?"

"It wasn't a totally new place to me. When I was a child, I used to visit Aunt Tania almost every summer. Have you noticed the Boston ivy on the front wall of her house? I planted those vines about twenty years ago. So moving here was just like returning home. They even have Broadway shows here, just like New York."

"But if your parents were still alive, you probably wouldn't have moved here."

"I guess not."

The link between Tania and a Chinese man had intrigued her, and now the broken romance between Tania and Brian's father added another element of fascination. Kang thought again about the fact that Brian was the first man she'd met that she hadn't been afraid of. She wondered if that was because Tania had told her he was gay, and so she had never felt he would demand anything of her. But she found him so attractive and she wondered fleetingly if maybe there was a chance that Tania might be wrong. She was curious about Brian's relationship with Eric, but didn't know how to broach the subject.

When he asked if she would have a meal at his place the next Saturday, she smiled. "Will Eric be okay with that?"

"I don't think I need his permission," Brian responded in amusement. "He can invite a friend, too, if he wants."

"Okay, I'd like that. Can I bring some *jiaozi*?"

"You don't have to, but it'd be great if you wanted to," he said, delighted.

One day after class, Kang went to the computer lab to do an assignment. When she was done, she went home and checked her email. She was pleased to find messages from both of her parents. She opened her mother's first.

Dear Kang,

I was excited to receive your email and intended to write back soon, but Linling got pneumonia after Chinese New Year. She stayed in the hospital for a few days, and it took several weeks for her to recover. We were so scared, especially since last year's SARS outbreak is still fresh in our minds. Your father is a senior now and getting more vulnerable to such diseases, but he insisted on monitoring Linling every day at home. I cooked special food for her and cleaned her items separately from ours. It was so exhausting. I don't understand how we managed when the three of you were kids and developed liver problems after eating dates from Iraq. I think we must be getting old.

Jian really appreciated our help because she did not have to miss many days at work. I told her that's what family is for.

During the winter holiday, we also helped Linling catch up with the schoolwork she had missed. There are so many assignments. Kids nowadays seem to work harder than adults! Now Linling is well again and back at school, and we can relax a little bit. So I'm able to reply to your email. It takes me more time to write on a computer than with a pen and paper. I'm not so familiar with Hanyu Pinyin. Anyway, we're back to our normal life.

Love, Mother

Her father's message was terse.

Dear Kang,

I hope your mother's letter finds you well. Here are my answers to your questions.

I earned a B.M. from Beijing Medical University in 1956 and went to study at Lomonosov Moscow State University in September of the same year.

I was labelled a rightist in 1958. The news about me becoming the enemy of the revolution let my parents down and destroyed their souls—at the time, a rightist was regarded as a counter-revolutionary. They died that same year. My father was sixty-three years old, and my mother was sixty-two.

I hope this answers some of your questions.

Your father

Kang held her breath as she read her father's message. She was stunned to discover that he attended the same university as Viktor Liu, but she reminded herself that there were so many Chinese students studying at that university at the time. There was no way he and Viktor could be the same person—they were born under different signs, and they had different family names—but maybe they had crossed paths at some point.

On Saturday afternoon, Brian insisted on picking her up. "It'll save you some time," he said on the phone.

It only took ten minutes to reach his house, a bungalow on a crescent-shaped street. The evergreen hedge surrounding the front lawn reminded her of a holly hedge in a campus garden where she had played as a child.

He gave her a quick tour of the two-bedroom house and told her to take a seat at the kitchen table. There was no sign of Eric. The aroma of cheese and tomato drifted in the air. He took a white oval-shaped casserole dish out of the oven and placed it on the table next to a large bowl of salad.

"Compared with a Chinese meal, this is pretty simple. I hope you like it."

She pointed to the container of *jiaozi* she had brought with her and asked, "Can I reheat the dumplings in the microwave?"

"Sure," he answered as he set out the plates.

When they sat down, she asked, "Where is Eric?"

"He went out with his girlfriend."

"Girlfriend?" She tried to make sense of the situation. She wondered if Eric was bisexual. She had read about people like that. Hesitantly, she asked, "Are you okay with that?"

"Why not?" he asked. "Wait a second. What do you mean?"

"Are all gay men open-minded like you?"

"What?" Startled, he accidentally dropped his fork into the salad bowl. "What on earth makes you think I'm gay?"

"You mean you're not?" she asked, her eyes wide.

"What the heck? I can't understand why you would think so."

"Tania said you were."

He burst out laughing. "Now I understand why you always ask about Eric. This is too funny!" He took her hand and kissed it.

She blushed. "Well, I'm ... I'm really glad you're not," she murmured.

Then he gently tilted her chin up and pressed his lips to hers; her heart melted in his embrace.

When they started to eat, he said, "My aunt is so cute. Now I finally understand why she keeps asking me to bring Eric over to her house."

"She thought that the breakup with Ingrid had changed your sexual orientation."

"Do you believe her?"

"I did," she said. "Why wouldn't I? I had no reason not to believe her, and she seemed so certain."

"Maybe now that we've cleared this up we can see each other more often, like every weekend?"

She smiled up at him and nodded. She thought of Tania and Viktor on the Moskva River bank, and the lyrics, "*Pear blossoms are blooming/ The river is in the mist of morning*," resounded in her ears.

It was different for her and Brian, she thought. They weren't saying goodbye to one another; their story was just beginning. Giddy with happiness, she returned his kisses.

CHAPTER 22: TO LIFE!

K ANG'S FIRST DAY of her practicum at Lawrence Public School started with a staff meeting before classes began. The principal introduced the student teachers to the staff and then went on to deal with regular school business. That day, Kang was to observe the three classes she would teach: the second grade in Health and Physical Education, and the second and third grade in Science and Technology.

At lunch hour in the teachers' lounge, she said hello to the people around her and sat down to eat a ham sandwich she had brought with her. Kang thought she recognized the woman sitting across from her from the staff meeting. She was an educational assistant, but Kang couldn't remember her name, so she said, "Hi, I'm Kang. Nice to meet you."

There was no response. Kang thought she might have been mistaken. No one seemed to notice her embarrassment; they were all busy talking about a new movie called *Chasing Liberty*.

Then she heard a familiar voice. "Is that you, Kang?"

"Oh, Nancy!" she exclaimed, astonished but happy to see her former roommate. "Do you teach here?"

"Yeah. I think you're a student teacher, right? I missed the meeting this morning."

Kang happily chatted with Nancy until the bell rang, and then she headed to Ms. McKinnon's second-grade class for Health and Physical Education. When she got there, she saw that the woman she had greeted at lunch was also in the classroom.

She had finally remembered her name—she was someone she had met through Nancy—and, wanting to be friendly, she said, "Good afternoon, Rita." Again, the woman did not acknowledge her. Kang was annoyed, but she wasn't sure how to handle the situation.

Ms. McKinnon began the lesson with a story about a girl who recovered very quickly from surgery because she followed her doctor's advice about exercising every day. She then explained how muscles grew stronger through regular exercises and answered the children's questions.

After that, the students were taken outside. They ran one lap around the playground before choosing to play on the slide or the swings, or in the sand.

Kang supervised the children on swings and made sure that nobody ran in front of or behind them. Ms. McKinnon warned her, "The children know the rules, but still forget them when they're excited and playing." Kang nodded and kept a close eye on the area.

When the exercise period ended, she held the door open to let everybody back inside. Rita passed her, carrying a tote bag on her shoulder. Kang had noticed earlier that the straps kept slipping off of Rita's shoulders when she bent down to talk to the children. "Why don't you hang your bag in the closet?" Kang suggested with a smile.

"I prefer not to," responded Rita, brushing past her.

Stung by this rejection, Kang wasn't sure if she could work with her. She didn't know what to say. After class, she decided to consult Nancy about the problem. She found her in the middle of training a group of students to sing in chorus. She waited until she was available.

Nancy told her not to take Rita's rejection personally. "She had a run-in with a Chinese supply teacher last year—maybe that's the problem." She added, "Let me talk to her. What time is your class tomorrow?"

"The second period in the morning."

"Okay, I'll speak to her before your class starts. Try to be patient. In a multicultural situation, it's easy to misunderstand one another. Sometimes adults are worse than kids when it comes to getting along."

Kang had an anxious night. She tossed and turned for hours, even though she kept reminding herself that her conflict with Rita was nothing personal.

The next day, when she entered the classroom, Nancy was already there, chatting with Rita. "Oh, hi, Kang," she called out. Turning to Rita, she introduced them. "Do you remember that Kang and I used to be roommates? Now that you two are working with the same class, I'm sure your experience will be a great help to her."

"Good morning," said Kang. "I'm glad I have someone to call on if I have any problems."

"Good morning." Rita forced a smile.

Before leaving, Nancy said to Rita, "I'll phone you when I get the tickets for *Mamma Mia!*" After that, Rita started to talk to Kang, and things began to go more smoothly between them. To thank Nancy, Kang offered to help her with her after-school music group.

When Kang was nearing the end of her practicum, the principal offered her a supply teaching position that started right away. Kang almost jumped up and down with joy, but she managed to contain herself and she thanked the principal as calmly as she could.

On the last day of her practicum, Rita congratulated her on her new position, and the students clamoured to know when they would see her again. "In a week," she told them. "I have to return to the university for my final exams, but then I'll be back."

Tania's health issues finally caught up to her. Her doctors had discovered that one of her arteries was blocked, and Tania was scheduled to have surgery at St. Michael's Hospital on the first Monday in May. She had to be at the hospital by eight the next morning, so Brian planned to come to get her early.

When Kang heard her moving about, she climbed out of bed and went upstairs to check if she needed any help.

"Go back to sleep. I'm done," said Tania, pointing to a small suitcase on a chair in the living room. "The rest is the doctor's job."

"Well, I can at least see you off," Kang said. "And don't worry about Hachiko. I'll walk him twice a day."

Tania took a sip of apple juice, but, following the hospital's instructions, ate nothing else. When Brian came, Kang picked up the suitcase, and the two of them went to the door. Hachiko trailed behind, whimpering as if to say goodbye. Kang put Tania's luggage on the floor of the back seat and then waved goodbye as Brian drove away.

Kang ate her breakfast and took Hachiko out for a quick walk. On the bus to school, her mind darted back and forth between her excitement about the first day of class and her worry over Tania's surgery.

At noon, she went to the teachers' lounge to call Brian. "How was the operation?"

"I'm still waiting to hear." His voice sounded tense.

"I'll come to the hospital as soon as school is over."

"If you're not too tired."

Kang reached the hospital before five o'clock and bought a flower basket in the gift shop. When she got to the intensive care unit, Tania, who was hooked up to several machines, gestured for her to sit on a chair by her bed. Kang placed the flowers on the table. "How are you feeling? And where's Brian?"

"I'm okay. I asked him to go walk Hachiko." Tania spoke slowly. "The poor dog will be upset. It's the first time he's been without me for an entire day."

Hearing Tania speak so tenderly, Kang recognized her motherly affection for Hachiko and marvelled that she seemed more worried about her pet than herself.

A nurse came to give Tania some medicine and take her blood pressure. "Ms. Shapirovski, how do you feel?"

"A little more pain than an hour ago."

"I've just given you a painkiller," she said as she replaced the intravenous bag. "It should take effect within half an hour. I'll be back soon to check on you again."

Tania looked pale, but she seemed relaxed. "I'll get up and walk around as soon as they remove the tube."

"Tell me what you need," Kang said, holding her hand.

"Nothing else. I only wish I could move around." She looked over Kang's shoulder and her face lit up. "You're back so fast! How was Hachiko?"

Kang turned her head and saw Brian.

"I called him up," he said. "He told me he didn't need me; he said I should stay with Tania."

"Ha!" Both women laughed.

"You need some rest, Brian." Kang noticed his drawn face.

"I'll have a good sleep tonight. How was your first day of class?"

"I was a little bit preoccupied by Tania's surgery, but I think it went well. Can you get tomorrow off?"

Instead of answering, he put his hand over his mouth to cover a yawn. Tania began to drift off to sleep. Not wanting to disturb her, Kang and Brian went out into the hall.

"Well, you can go home now," Brian said to her. "I'll wait till Tania wakes up in case she needs something."

"But you're tired. I can stay."

"It's okay. I just want to make sure she's all right before I leave. And yes, I've gotten tomorrow off." He held her hand. "Don't worry. You seem more terrified than the patient."

"Heart surgery is scary. Do you think she'll be okay?"

"Yeah, she's a tough cookie. The nurse says they'll be getting her up to walk tomorrow. I switched to the night shift so I can come to the hospital at noon. So I can help with that."

"And I can come by after school."

The two of them continued to make plans for Tania's care until Brian saw Kang off at the bus stop.

It was a hectic week for Kang. In addition to teaching, she walked Hachiko twice a day and visited the hospital daily.

When she was with Brian, she felt lighthearted, like her tiredness had gone away. Once he said, "We'd enjoy life more if we could take the blue pill sometimes."

"What's the blue pill?"

"The pill of blissful ignorance. It's from *The Matrix*."

"So, if I'd taken the blue pill when I was younger, I wouldn't have been aware of my sister's suffering," Kang said and grinned.

Tania was scheduled to be discharged from the hospital on Friday afternoon, and Kang was eager to get home quickly. When she caught sight of Brian's car in the driveway, she knew Tania was back. As soon as she entered the house, Hachiko ran toward her with his tail wagging and led her to Tania, who was sitting on the couch.

"Welcome home," said Kang. "It's so good to have you back."

"No kidding. The hospital is my enemy." Tania smiled and took the glass of juice Brian had poured for her. "Thank you both so much for taking care of Hachiko and me."

"I'm just sorry I couldn't spend more time with you," said Kang.

"Brian, stay here," Tania called out when she saw him go to the closet for his jacket. "I'll order a pizza." She noticed his surprised face. "Not for me, but for you and Kang. I'll just have some soup."

"Sorry. I've got to go. I have to work very early tomorrow." He bent to kiss his aunt and got ready to leave.

Kang walked him to the door with Hachiko close behind her. "You're coming Sunday afternoon, right?" she whispered.

"Don't worry, my dear. I won't forget. But don't tell her

about it." He pulled the door open and left.

She returned to Tania. "Now let me make that soup for you."

"No, I can do it myself. I picked up some canned tomato soup; it's easy to make. What kind of pizza do you like?"

"No, no. I don't need it. I have leftovers from yesterday." Tania stood. "It seems like you and Brian like each other." She sighed. "I just wish he were straight." She went into the kitchen and took a can from the cupboard and a bag of peas and diced carrots from the freezer.

With a grin, Kang picked up her backpack from the floor.

"What's so funny?" asked Tania as she turned and caught Kang's smile.

"Nothing. I was just thinking about my leftovers. Whenever you need my help, please let me know," she said as she went downstairs.

On Sunday morning, Kang walked Hachiko to the Real Canadian Superstore on Gerry Fitzgerald Drive and bought a chicken, and some vegetables and fruits. On the way home, Hachiko raced ahead of her and strained so hard on his leash that she could hardly keep up. As they crossed Steeles Avenue West, she suddenly remembered how she had felt when she had walked home in the dark on the day of the blackout. Now, a new chapter in her life had begun, and the spring sunshine was driving away the shadow that had been hovering over her for years. She hummed a song, thinking about its lyrics: *My love is the sunshine shining. My joy is the flower flowering.* Hachiko galloped like a pony beside her.

When they reached home, Tania was pacing back and forth in the living room. "This afternoon, I'd like to stretch my legs for fifteen minutes. Can you come with me?" she asked.

"Sure. We can take Hachiko with us, too."

Their stroll along David Lewis Drive was very pleasant. Purple-and-white crocuses, buttery daffodils, and brilliant red tulips dotted the front gardens of the houses they passed.

Kang exclaimed, "I didn't even notice these flowers yesterday."

"You probably have a lot on your mind. I often don't notice things around me when I'm preoccupied," said Tania. "Once I drove right past my house because I was so focused on the final exams I was about to mark."

After a brief walk, they returned home and were greeted by the aroma of Kang's chicken soup simmering on the stove. While Tania went to have a quick nap, Kang started to make a couple salads—a vegetable one and a fruit one.

Brian arrived as planned, bringing with him a big bouquet of pink and red carnations and a nicely decorated box of chocolates. He put the flowers in a vase, asked Kang to sign a Mother's Day card, and taped it to the box.

When Tania walked into the living room and saw the flowers, her eyes lit up. "Lovely!"

"Happy Mother's Day!" Their greeting startled her. Brian handed her the box of chocolates. "This is sugar free and low fat, but you're still only allowed to eat one piece a day. It's from my girlfriend Kang and me."

Speechless, Tania gaped at Brian and then Kang and then exclaimed, "Your girlfriend? But…"

"Yes, I know." Brian laughed. "You thought I was gay."

"You're not?"

"Definitely not!"

"I can vouch for that," Kang chimed in.

"But you never seem to date women. And you live with a man. I just assumed…."

"Well, you assumed wrong. Eric is just a housemate."

"Oh … Oh, I am an idiot!" she exclaimed.

She wrapped her arms around them both. "Brian, you're not gay!" She patted Kang's head. "Kang, you're not afraid of men anymore!" She laughed until her eyes blurred with tears. "I'm so thrilled for both of you, and for me. Thanks so much for this wonderful news. Let's celebrate this moment." She got a bottle of wine out of the cupboard and put it on the table

Kang ladled the soup into three bowls while Brian poured wine for Kang and himself, and juice for Tania.

Brian raised his glass. "Cheers!"

Tania said, "*L'chaim!* To life!"

"Bottoms up!" Kang smiled while their glasses clinked together. As Kang sipped her wine, she imagined how surprised and delighted her parents would be when she told them she finally had a boyfriend.

CHAPTER 23: A PARADE

K ANG GAZED AT HER FIRST PAYCHEQUE. It was triple what she used to earn at the Tim Hortons. Without thinking twice, she sent four hundred dollars to her sister along with a note: "*This is my contribution to Linling's education. I'm too busy to write more right now, but you and Linling are always in my heart. I'm thrilled to hear about your new life.*"

A few days later, as she leafed through the *Toronto Star* on her lunch break, a travel ad caught her eye: *Hot Flight Deal: $1,119.99 from Toronto to Moscow.* She stared at the word Moscow. She could afford that now!

Victoria Day fell on May 24 that year. It was a beautiful day, so Kang and Brian went on a long walk along the Don River. He led the way across Dufferin Street and then along a path leading south.

"Where does this go?" she asked.

"I think it will take us to G. Ross Lord Park." They crossed a small wooden footbridge, and he stopped and gazed over the brook.

"What's that?" Leaning on the railing, she peered at the sun-dappled stream.

He put his arm around her waist. "Once, probably about twenty years ago, I watched two fish swimming in the water, and I wished I were one of them. Now the fish are gone, but we're here. We're those two fish."

"Do we look like fish?" She snickered.

"You're my little fish." He laughed.

They continued along, passing into the shade of the trees. "This was my paradise," he said. "I used to come here to cool off after cycling."

After crossing Steeles Avenue West, they continued along the path. Kang pointed to a heap of large heart-shaped leaves still clinging to roots. "Who did this?" She looked around, but didn't see anyone.

"Maybe an animal. A beaver can cut down a whole tree. Animals are capable of many things."

"But they can't be as capable as human beings."

"We human beings have learned many things from them. Animals can be so amazing. Like chameleons, for example: they change colours to camouflage themselves. We imitate them when we camouflage ourselves by changing clothing."

"Human beings have different colour skin, and we don't need to change colours. I'm yellow. You're white. Other people can be black or brown."

"That's different," Briand said.

"All humans originated from the same race, didn't we? And then we changed according to our environments, right?" she asked, reaching out to pluck a blossom from a crab apple tree.

Brian stopped her hand. "You're destroying nature. Don't pick something you don't need."

"Don't change the subject," she teased.

"I'm not sure about human skin colour, but I'm serious about the natural environment. Every animal or plant is a part of nature, a link in the food chain."

"I heard about the food chain in high school, but I don't know much about it." Kang noticed a woman squatting to pick something up, and she walked toward her.

"Good morning," Kang said, watching the woman pluck what looked like weeds from the ground. "What do you do with this plant?"

The woman continued pulling up the roots of plant, not looking up. "I use them to make soup."

"Are those your plants back there?" Kang pointed back to the clump of small plants that they had passed.

"Yes, I'll gather them on the way back."

Brian bent down to smell the plant.

"Do you like it?" asked the woman. "It's burdock. It is very good in soup." She turned to Kang. "Do you have children?"

"No." Kang picked several leaves and handed them to the woman. "How do you cook them?"

"I add the peeled roots to some broth with mushrooms, ginger, and a bit of meat. It's good for children. You can also eat the leaves in a salad if the leaves are young. Burdock is also medicinal."

Kang thanked her and followed Brian back to the path. "I'm inspired. Maybe we can find some herbs for Tania's high blood pressure."

By the time they reached the park, it seemed as though everyone had out come to enjoy the sunny holiday. People either picnicked under the trees or strolled across the meadow; Kang and Brian heard the sound of cheering in the distance.

"They're playing cricket," Brian told her.

"What's that?"

"It's a bat-and-ball game with two teams. It's a traditional game from Britain. That's why it's popular in British colonies—like in India and the West Indies. It's the immigrants from those countries who continue to play this English game in Canada."

"Interesting," she said, as she spotted a man rooting around in the meadow. "Let's go to find out what he's doing."

As Kang got closer, she saw him collecting snails and dropping them into a bucket. It was already half full.

She stooped to gather a few. "Hello," she addressed him. "Here are a few more." She dropped them into the pail.

In China, she had eaten snails that grew in rice paddies, but she hadn't realized that people could eat snails that lived on grass. "How do you cook them?" she asked.

"I not speak many English," the man said with a Russian accent.

Brian glanced into the bucket, wrinkling his nose. "They look like garden snails. Do they taste good?"

"Taste good." The man put his hand into the snails and swirled them through his fingers. "Wash them. In water for one day. Cook them."

They thanked the man, and Kang said, "*Do svidaniya.*" The man waved his hand. "Goodbye."

"Where did you pick up Russian?"

"Back in the elementary school. I heard one of my classmates say that, and when I asked my father what it meant, he told me it was goodbye in Russian. Later I learned some more words from the same girl. Her mother taught Russian in the 1950s when the Soviet Union and China were still on good terms."

"I picked up a bit from my grandmother as a kid. Whenever I visited her, she would tell me stories in Russian. I understood quite a bit at the time, but now I've forgotten most of it."

"I'm thinking about visiting Moscow this summer."

"Really? Why?"

"Well, Tania's memoir makes me feel drawn to the place."

"Are you serious?"

"Why not? Your mother came from the Soviet Union. Wouldn't you like to see where she grew up? Why don't you come with me?"

"My parents went there once, but it ended up costing them their lives. So the word 'Moscow' stirs up a lot of very unpleasant memories for me."

"I understand. But maybe if we go together, we can make a new and pleasant memory. Please think about it!" She felt excited, imagining herself and Brian visiting the places where Viktor and Tania had met, fallen in love, and parted. "I'll be starting my new job in September, so I can afford to take a summer vacation." Several scenes from Tania's autobiography crossed her mind: the theatre where they'd gone to watch *Swan Lake*, the garden where Viktor had told Tania his dreadful news, and the path along the Moskva River where they'd cycled.

"I'll think about it," said Brian, but he didn't show much enthusiasm.

On the way home, he recollected one of his grandmother's stories. "It's about a poor fisherman who catches a talking goldfish. The fish begs to be set free and promises to make any of the man's wishes come true if he lets it go. So the fish gets freedom and then changes the man's hut into a mansion, just like it promised."

"Yes!" she exclaimed. "I know the story. The greedy wife wanted to become a queen, and to live in a palace with the goldfish as her servant. So the goldfish turned the mansion back into a hut. The moral of the story is not to be too greedy."

"Did you read it in Russian?"

"In Chinese. It was a poem by Pushkin. Maybe he just retold the fairy tale."

"Fascinating. We learned the same story in childhood, but in different countries. I only read Pushkin when I was in high school—I thought he was so cool, and I especially liked the dueling parts of *Eugene Onegin*. So when do you plan to go on this trip?"

"At the beginning of July, I think."

Kang stayed in the office after school and googled wild plants that could help with blood pressure problems. She found a few, and then also looked up burdock. According to the article, burdock was used to cleanse toxins in the blood. She printed the page and then googled tours to Moscow, but didn't find much. She jotted down a few phone numbers of travel agencies, thinking that she would call them to find an affordable flight as soon as possible.

When she gotd home and opened the door, a delectable aroma drifted out of the kitchen. She went into the kitchen and found Tania standing at the stove, stirring a large pot. "Your chicken soup smells delicious," Kang said, her stomach suddenly growly and hungry

"Did you miss the bus?" asked Tania as she chopped up carrots.

"No, I stayed at the school to use the computer. Have you ever heard about a plant called burdock?" She got the printed page out of her backpack and showed it to Tania. "Maybe you should try it."

"Maybe, but I have to check with my doctor first. Maybe I will be able to find it at the Shoppers Drug Mart."

"Shoppers Drug Mart?" Kang hadn't seen any fresh produce in the drugstore.

"Yes, in pill form. It might be in the vitamin and supplement aisle."

"But you can get free burdock roots and leaves in the park." She told Tania about seeing the woman they had met in the park.

"We don't know how it tastes."

"She said it made good soup. Maybe I should try some first to find out if it tastes okay." Kang smiled. "I can sense that you don't want to eat something that might taste awful."

"My main concern is that the city sprays pesticides on those weeds, so it could be dangerous to eat them." She carried a bowl of soup and a toasted slice of twelve-grain bread to the table. "For now, I'm enjoying my soup."

Kang took some leftover spaghetti and sauce out of the fridge and reheated them. "I'm planning a trip to Moscow," she said as she sat down at the table beside Tania.

"Wow!"

"Have you ever gone back?"

"Not yet. I thought about going a long time ago, but I changed my mind when my sister and her husband died in the plane crash. Is Brian going with you?"

"He feels the same way you do. I've been trying to persuade him."

"I don't blame him. But why do you want to go there?"

"Your memoir has stirred my interest." She hesitated, but decided not to mention her father's training in Moscow. "I've noticed many similarities between Red China and the Soviet Union and now I'm very interested in Russia's history and culture."

"Sounds good. Maybe I should go on a tour someday. Let me know after you book the trip."

Kang telephoned Brian again to ask if he had made up his mind. He said, "I'm sorry, Kang. I'd love to go with you, but I don't have the heart for it."

After the phone call, Kang debated with herself, trying to decide if she should still go. Then she lost herself in thought. She wondered if she would do something that she wasn't interested in, if Brian had asked her to. Then she wondered if he really cared about her. Eventually she convinced herself that she should go whether Brian accompanied her or not. The trip wasn't only for sightseeing and learning about Russian history and culture; it was also a chance for her to search for the footprints her father might have left there.

The next day she contacted a travel agency and booked a five-day tour. Back home, she began to browse the brochure she had gotten from the agency.

Brian called to ask about the trip and offered to take her to the airport when the time came. She felt reassured that he really cared about her, but she still wished that he was going with her.

It was mid-June when Nancy invited Kang to get together with her and her partner on the last Saturday of June. "School will be finished and we can have a leisurely lunch. And then, if you'd like, you can join us for a parade."

"A parade? What for?" asked Kang.

"A lesbian parade."

Kang was surprised. "Is that ... is that the same as the Gay Pride Parade?"

"It's a short one. It'll be on the day before the Gay Pride Parade. It will be a lot of fun."

She was hesitant, but curiosity took over. "Okay, I'm in."

"We'll expect you at about eleven thirty in the morning."

Final exams were keeping Kang busy, but there were still many details of her trip to be worked out. At last, school was over, and she had a lunch date with Nancy and her girlfriend. As she approached the building, she remembered the flower beds she had seen that day in March when she had first met Nancy. Now nothing remained of the tulip blossoms but brown stems, but yellow-and- purple pansies were still in bloom. She took a deep breath. So much had changed over the last year. She was a different person now, not a scared spinster anymore. She had a good job and a boyfriend! Nancy opened the door and ushered her in to meet her partner. "This is Sue, a song writer. Sometimes we play music together."

"Nice to meet you." Sue turned to Kang and smiled, but did not extend her hand as she was spinning the salad for their lunch. "I'll be done in a minute."

Kang joined them in the kitchen and helped Nancy peel tangerines for a fruit salad. "I know you enjoy escargots. Have you ever eaten the snails you can find on grass?" she asked Tania. Then she told them about the Russian man picking snails in the park.

"Can't say that I have," replied Nancy with surprise. "I suppose wild snails might taste better. Maybe later in the summer we could gather some. By the way, is Brian okay with you joining us for the parade?"

"Of course he is. Why would he have a problem with it?" Then hesitantly she asked, "Do you think it's okay that he doesn't want to come with me to Moscow?" Nancy turned to look at her quizzically, so Kang added, "His parents died in a plane crash when they went there."

"I understand why he might not want to go," Nancy replied. "He's probably trying to avoid a trip that would stir up painful feelings. It's a kind of self-protective behaviour," Nancy stated then added chunks of honeydew melon into the fruit salad bowl.

"You're right." Kang sighed.

"Cheer up! It's holiday time." Nancy laid three plates on the table. "Let's eat."

They had quiche for lunch and fruit salad for dessert, and then Nancy pulled three wigs from the closet and showed them to Kang. "Which one do you prefer?"

"Are we going to wear these?"

"Believe me, this is the simplest thing we can do," Nancy said. "Wait till you see the costumes people wear to the parade."

Kang took the green one, Nancy, the red, and Sue, the blue. The three of them set out for the event, which was just a few minutes' walk away on Church Street.

Nancy was right—there were many colourful costumes. Two teenage girls were dressed in pink satin ball gowns with yellow sashes and flower wreathes on their heads. Several women wore black or red bikinis, and others wore sequined tuxedos. Kang was not surprised when she noticed a few topless women in the crowd.

They joined the marching throng, walking in step with the accompanying drumbeat. Kang walked next to Nancy, who held hands with Sue. Some of the onlookers burst out laughing at a man who was walking beside her. She glanced at him and saw that he was wearing artificial breasts over a red T-shirt. Suddenly his breasts shot liquid toward the onlookers, who started to scream and laugh. When she noticed the big bag of water on his back and the tube running down to a pump on his shorts pocket, she chuckled. Kang wondered if Brian would be that naughty. Would she want him to be?

CHAPTER 24: KUPALA NIGHT IN MOSCOW

O N THE DAY OF KANG'S FLIGHT, Brian arrived with plenty of time to take her to the airport. He wheeled Kang's suitcase along the driveway and placed it in the trunk, and Tania saw them off at the door. "Enjoy your trip!"

They headed to the parking garage of Lester B. Pearson International Airport, and Brian found a spot and unloaded Kang's luggage. She was surprised to see him reaching in and pulling out a second suitcase.

"Whose is that?"

"Mine."

"Yours?"

"Yes. I'm going with you!" Grinning from ear to ear, he looked for the way into the terminal. Kang could not help but throw her arms around him. "I'm so surprised! And so happy!"

Brian held her and smiled. "Let's go. We don't want to miss the plane." He picked up the suitcases. As they made their way to the terminal, Kang pinched herself. It wasn't a dream! He was really going with her.

Their seats were a few rows apart on the plane, but the girl next to Kang offered to switch with Brian, so they could sit together.

"How do you feel?" Kang asked, knowing that he didn't like being on planes. "Are you nervous?"

"I'm trying to imagine I'm on a train. It'd be easier to do if I had a blue pill to take."

"Still thinking of *The Matrix*? You're fond of that movie, I guess."

Brian rocked slightly in his seat. "Don't worry. I feel fine now. And I'm thrilled that you're with me, not with someone else." He gently caressed her hand. Then he closed his eyes and smiled. "Now I'm imagining we're watching *The Time Machine*."

It's probably another one of his favourite movies, Kang thought. Peeping through the small window and seeing white clouds flying past, she felt joyful and peaceful.

Finally, their plane arrived safely at Sheremetyevo International Airport. Following the signs, they found their Moskva Tour group and followed their guide, Igor, onto the bus that would take them to the Blues Hotel.

Kang followed a hotel attendant to her room on the second floor. Almost everything in the room was red: a light red curtain on the window, a dark red sofa against the wall, and two beds also covered in red velvet. Maybe this was the revolutionary style, she thought as she wheeled her luggage in.

She plopped herself down on one of the beds, enjoying the luxury of being able to stretch out. The sleepless journey had made her tired. Within minutes, she fell asleep, dreaming that she was on a boat exploring an endless turquoise sea. Suddenly the sound of a mosquito buzzed in her ears. She shook her head, but the whizzing noise continued. As she forced her heavy eyes open and spotted the red sofa near her bed, she remembered where she was and realized that the buzzing sound was coming from the phone. She picked up the receiver. "Hello."

"Supper time," said Brian. "I'm in the cafeteria. It's on the main floor."

"Okay, thanks. I fell asleep, but I'll be there in a few minutes."

As she entered the cafeteria, the cashier checked her room card against his binder and directed her to a round table where Brian sat by himself. He stood up to greet her and pointed to a plate full of food beside his half-finished plate. "The staff was getting ready to leave, so I filled a plate for you."

She gave him an appreciative smile and sat down to eat, starting with a stuffed bun. "They seem a little bit like Chinese *jaozi*—steamed round dumplings."

"Oh, yeah. They're called *pelmeni*," explained Brian. "You eat them with sour cream. Here you go." He spooned some cream onto her plate from a small bowl.

"Ha! How did you learn about Russian food so quickly?"

"My grandma used to make these when I was a kid."

She took a bite. "Tastes good."

He picked up the last piece of bread from his plate and opened a small pack of butter. "You might like the black bread with jam."

"You mean rye bread? Why do you give it a different name?"

"Russians call it black bread because of the colour."

"Russian food seems similar to Canadian food," she said, glancing at her watch. "We should hurry up if we don't want to miss the bus to the theatre."

"I'm going to have a cup of tea. Would you like some?" he asked as he walked over to a *samovar* on the serving counter.

"No, thanks," she said. "I'm still trying to finish the potato and fish." She noticed that Brian brought a cup of tea back but then placed a second empty cup on the table. Then he absent-mindedly poured the tea from the cup in his hand into the other one on the table. Kang wondered if he was bored just waiting there

"Is the tea too hot?" she asked.

"Not at all," Brian answered and then poured the tea back into the first cup.

Kang though his behaviour seemed odd. Assuming he might simply be restless, when she finished her meal, she got up and motioned for him to get up as well. "Let's go," she said, linking her arm in his.

They joined their tour group on the bus and got to the Moscow Stanislavsky Theatre for the performance of *Swan*

Lake. Listening to the graceful dance music, Kang pictured a fairy tale world, and her heart softened. When the black swan spun onto the stage toward the prince, she felt her heart leap, and she remembered a scene from Tania's manuscript. Tania and Viktor had sat in the same theatre, and Tania had slept through the show. Now, almost a half century later, she and Brian were watching the same ballet. Did history repeat itself? Could the black swan be a bad omen? She tightened her grip on Brian's arm. "Take it easy," he whispered, patting her arm. "It's just a show."

"Thanks." She nodded.

Her eyes blurred with tears as the white swan and the prince danced together and then leapt into the lake. "It was very sad, but beautiful," she commented to Brian, still sniffling.

On the way back to the hotel, people on the bus were still talking about the ballet performance. Brian chatted to the person across the aisle. As they walked into the hotel, he whistled one of the melodies from *Swan Lake*. He seemed different, Kang thought. He was more energetic and talkative than she'd ever seen him.

"I think you've gotten drunk from the vodka-filled chocolate we had at the intermission," she teased him, remembering the sweet and bitter taste of the chocolates they had been given.

"Can I stay with you?" Brian asked when they reached her room.

She hesitated for a second and then opened the door, gesturing for him to sit in the armchair. After turning on the light, she went to the window and pulled the curtain closed. As she turned around, she almost tripped over Brian, who was kneeling down on the floor in front of her.

"What are you doing?" she asked and then caught sight of what he held in his extended hand. It was a small velvet jewellery box.

"Will you marry me?" he asked.

She was speechless. It was as if she were watching herself

from another place and another time.

"Will you?" he had to ask again.

She was tongue-tied, but she nodded.

Brian held her hand and slid the ring onto her finger. It was a bezel-set diamond flanked by two blue gems on each side. Then he stood up and wrapped her in his arms. They kissed, and she lay her head against his chest and closed her eyes.

"We've had enough excitement for today," he murmured, carrying her to her bed. He kissed her gently. "We'll have an engagement party in Toronto. Good night, my darling," he whispered as he tiptoed quietly away.

Half asleep, she opened her eyes and asked, "What should we do for the party?"

There was no answer. The image of the black swan flashed across her mind. She wasn't sure if the whole thing had been a dream. Where had Brian gone? She got up and walked to the other bed. He was lying flat on his back with his eyes closed, snoring lightly.

He must have been exhausted, she thought. They both were. Gently pulling the blanket over him, she tiptoed to the washroom.

When she lay in her bed and turned off the lamp, she was startled by his voice. "*Rodnoy gorod moey mamy*," he said. "My mom's birthplace."

Kang turned in bed. She wondered if he was speaking Russian in his sleep. First, he surprised her with the engagement ring, and now he was talking in his sleep.

The following day, Igor took the group to the Red Square and the Kremlin. The names of the places excited Kang, who had seen these iconic sights in *Lenin in October*, a Soviet movie she had watched many times as a child. In her memory, there had been a huge red star on the Kremlin's highest cupola, but today there was a shiny cross atop each dome. It was different from how she'd imagined it.

The evening's entertainment was a festival in Gorky Park.

Kang had read Gorky's autobiography and enjoyed *Part I, My Childhood*, the most; she was eager to visit the park that was named after him.

At the front of the bus, a microphone in hand, Igor asked the group, "Does anybody know what tonight is called?"

"Kupala Night!" Several people answered since it had been scheduled in their brochure.

"That's right! July seventh is the famous Kupala Night," Igor said, his grey eyes glowing. "It's a performance of Russian folklore. It's said that if a young couple leaps through the fire holding hands tonight, they will stay together forever!"

Kang gazed at the ring on her fourth finger, which sparkled in the dim light of the bus. Brian held her hand up and kissed it. Forever, she thought happily.

"There's more." Igor continued. "Girls will throw flower diadems into the water. If a young man can retrieve it, the girl will spend a night with him. However, I have to warn you all not to jump over the fire or jump into the water."

"Why not?" several passengers called out.

"Because our insurance policies don't cover any injuries," Igor answered.

The audience laughed. Kang wasn't sure if Igor was kidding.

Once the bus stopped in the lot at the entrance to the park, Igor pointed at a line of huge birch trees. "Remember—our bus is near the first birch. You should look for this line of trees and the streetlamp over there to find it. If you get tired, you can get on the bus early. Please be back by nine thirty. Be careful and watch out for each other."

Kang followed Brian and the others off the bus. The crowd meandered along a path toward an open area near the woods. A ferris wheel appeared in the sky and the screams of roller coaster riders echoed through the park. The dancing and singing crowd glowed orange in the sunset. Her heartbeat following the rhythm of the *bayan* music, Kang quickened her pace.

"Slow down. Are you going to the fire?" Brian called out.

She laughed. "Yes! Just like Igor said."

A man strolling ahead of them began to hum, his voice full of joy. Drawn to his cheerful voice, Kang asked, "What are you singing?"

"'Dark Eyes'—my favourite song." The man sang a line in English: *Dark and burning eyes, dark as midnight skies.* He was perhaps seventy, pudgy and had a comb over hairstyle. "I won my wife's heart with this song. Right, my darling?" he said and slipped his arm around the waist of his female companion.

They approached the bonfires; the crowd watched and cheered as young couples stood hand in hand in front of them.

The flickering flames reminded Kang of when she and her classmates used to collect trash and fallen leaves to be burned in the schoolyard. She would race to throw more trash on the fire, imagining herself to be Sui Ren, who was sent by the fire god Zhu Rong to keep the flames going. She had learned about them from studying Chinese mythology.

The young people's passionate shouts brought her back to the present. A burning smell mixed with a light floral scent hung in the air.

Brian handed Kang a flower diadem he had bought from one of the vendors. She buried her nose in the blossoms and then placed it on her head. Several other women in the tour group also had flower wreaths on their heads.

She tilted her head toward him, asking, "Are we going to jump through the fire?"

"Shall we? Looks kind of dangerous, and the guide advised us not to."

"Yes," she agreed, not able to contain her sigh of disappointment.

They locked eyes. "Let's do it anyway," said Brian with a lopsided grin.

Holding hands, they waited their turn, watching other

couples successfully leaping over the flames. Suddenly it was their turn, and the fire pit in front seemed to blink at Kang. She took a deep breath.

"On three," he said. "One, two, three!"

She started to run. As they jumped over the fire, she caught the scent of rose and honeysuckle from the wreath. Their hands were clasped, she thought with delight. But as they landed on the ground, her flower wreath fell off and she dropped Brian's hand to grab it. He reached out for it too, and they found themselves on the other side of the fire, both of their hands clutching the wreath.

"We..."—said Kang, drawing a breath—"we didn't hold our hands together."

"But they were joined by the wreath." Brian tried to comfort her. "The wreath is round like a wedding ring. That symbolizes our togetherness."

"Why didn't I think of that? You're very wise."

"But I burned my foot." He sighed and placed the wreath back on her head.

"You need some cold water." She noticed a whisp of smoke drifting up from his loosened shoelace. "There's a pond over there. Let's go."

They reached the nearby Pioneer's Pond, where girls with flower diadems were wading in the waist-high water, hand in hand, humming to the melody emanating from the bank.

Kang pointed to a patch of grass near the water. "Sit here. I'll check your foot."

They sat down, and she took off his shoe and noticed a red patch on his ankle. She touched it. "Does it hurt?"

"A little," he said, sucking in some air.

"Your skin isn't broken. Soak your foot in the cold water."

Following her instructions, he stretched his foot out into the pond. "I feel better now. Thanks."

She shook the ashes off his shoe. "I'll put a gauze bandage on your foot when we're back at the hotel."

He pulled her to him and began to kiss her. "You look so beautiful in that wreath," he murmured.

The Russian music mixed with cheers flowed past Kang's ears. She felt as light as a feather.

Then they heard a familiar voice on the breeze. "Moskva Tour members, it's time to go back to the bus."

Kang sat up and got a tissue out of her pocket to dry Brian's foot.

"Thanks," he said, "but I can do it myself."

A couple walked past them, and the man called out, "Let's go back to the bus, young couple." It was the same man who had sung "Dark Eyes."

"Yes, thank you," Kang answered. "Do you know what song the people are singing now?"

"Sure. It's called 'I'm Fire and You're Water.' A nice one, huh?"

"Very nice," she replied.

Brian stood up. "I've gone through fire and water today."

"You haven't jumped into the water yet," said the man's wife with a chuckle.

"Well, his foot went in." Kang laughed.

On the bus, she thought about their hands coming unclasped after they jumped over the fire. Was Brian right? As she stared at her ring, she wondered if it was enough that they held onto the wreath together.

CHAPTER 25: THE TIME CAPSULE

THAT NIGHT KANG DREAMED she was wading in the Moskva River and searching for her wreath. She couldn't see anything in the darkness, so she pried her eyes open until she finally woke herself up. Still groggy and confused, she noticed a figure seated at the desk in her room. Startled, she blinked and realized it was Brian, with his elbows on the desk and his head in his hands. She watched him rocking back and forth, the dim light caressing his wavy hair.

"Are you okay?" she asked.

He raised his head and then turned to her. "Sorry. I woke up and couldn't get back to sleep," he said as he fumbled toward her bed. "But I'm sleepy now."

She slid over to make room for him, and he draped his arm around her shoulder.

"Is your foot hurting?" she mumbled.

"Not anymore."

Then sleep overtook them.

The following day, the bus drove them up to Sparrow Hills. As Kang watched the scenery unrolling outside the window, she forgot about Brian's odd behaviour. Instead, she was thinking about Tania's manuscript. The road seemed broader than she had described, and there were more buildings.

The bus stopped at a place called Vorobyovy Gory, which was adjacent to the main building of Moscow State University. "This is Sparrow Hills," Igor informed the group. "If you have read Tolstoy's *War and Peace*, you may have heard of this place. Sparrow Hills is mentioned four times in that novel."

He had a good memory, Kang thought. She could barely remember the plot of that novel.

"This is one of the highest points in Moscow," Igor continued, "so it gives you a bird's eye view of the city."

As soon as they got off the bus, most of the group, including Brian, began snapping photos. Kang walked along the railing and gazed over at the gently flowing Moskva River. She called out, "Brian, that must be Luzhniki Metro Bridge." She was excited and pointed at the double-decker structure spanning the water.

"Yes, I see. We'll be going there this afternoon," he reminded her and took another picture.

She wondered whether Tania had ever stood there. Had she and Viktor ever been there? Kang decided that when she returned home, she should write to her father about Sparrow Hills and see if he had anything to say about it.

"Let's follow the crowd." Brian's voice dragged her back to the present. The group was heading toward the university's main building. Looking up, Kang recognized the clock tower above the auditorium where Tania had listened to Mao speaking. She followed the group, but her mind wandered back to forty-five years earlier, and she pictured young Tania walking across the campus. She felt like she had been there, watching Tania. If she hadn't read Tania's memoir, and if she hadn't known that her father had studied here, all these things wouldn't be so fascinating to her, Kang thought, realizing that Tania's story had brought all of this to life for her.

"Sweetheart," Brian said gently, nudging her arm. "What are you thinking about?"

"I've realized the power of writing."

"Do you mean Tolstoy's writing?"

"No, I mean Tania's. I can feel her life here."

He smiled. "I'm sure we'll feel more of it this afternoon."

Later, they had lunch in a restaurant where, according to the guide, Tolstoy had often dined. Then the group headed to Arbat Street, a pedestrian street in the historical centre of the city. But Kang and Brian had made other plans. She talked to Igor. "Brian and I will leave the group for a while, but we won't get lost."

"No problem, but you'll have to get back to the hotel on your own. Do you have a map?" He handed them his business card. "If you have any difficulty, call me."

A taxi took the couple to the Luzhniki Metro Bridge. As they walked down to the ground level of the overpass, Kang imagined the scene that had taken place several decades before: Tania perched on the crossbar of Viktor's bicycle, passing the very same spot. Kang pulled out her camera and took a few photos of the bridge across the Moskva River, the boats on the water, and the buildings in the distance. She thought Tania would be thrilled when she saw the photos.

Enjoying the pleasant scenery, she looked at Brian and said, "This is the riverbank Tania used to walk along. Everything seems familiar to me. Let's walk west. " Pulling his arm close, she asked, "Do you feel it, too?"

"No, can't say that I do. But it does seem exotic." He looked around. "Things are real, but I'm not sure if I'm travelling back in time."

She chuckled. "Are you in a science fiction mood or what?"

"It's odd that I don't feel as much of a connection to this place," he said, "given that my mom was born and raised here."

"Maybe because I've read more Russian novels than you. Besides, I've read Tania's memoir."

"Probably. What are you searching for?" he asked.

"I assume Tania and Viktor had their last outing somewhere around here, but I can't find the boulder she mentions in the manuscript."

"Take a picture. Then you can ask her if she recognizes the place."

"Good idea." She looked around and spotted a bush with yellow-and-white blossoms. She ran to it and stuck her nose into the branches. "This is honeysuckle. It smells so good. Oh, look at the flowers over there. They could be the scarlet globemallow that Tania wrote about." Kang took a photo of the wildflowers with the river in the background.

"Come on," said Brian. "I think Park Vorobyovy Gory isn't too far. We might find something interesting there."

"What do you want to find? Exotic plants or aliens?" She took a few more snapshots.

"Something more interesting than aliens."

"What's that?" She followed him.

"We'll see." He sped up, holding a compass in his hand. "There's an exit to Kosygin Street off the park. It's only a few minutes by a cab to reach my grandparents' house."

"Wow," she exclaimed. "You sound like you're coming home. Did you get the information from Tania?"

"Yup, plus, I did my homework. Want some water?" he asked, patting his small black backpack. She noticed that his pack was full. He pulled out two water bottles and handed one to her.

"Thanks. I'm thirsty."

They walked quickly, and soon they found the entrance to the park. He put his compass back into his pocket. "This way," he said, turning right.

They meandered along a path, and soon they came to a meadow where some teenagers were playing football. She followed him past the meadow and into a pine forest. Then he started to look around.

"What are you searching for?" she asked.

"A stone monument."

"I only see brushes and trees. There's no sign of a stone monument."

"It's small, only knee-high."

"A monument to whom?" she asked. "Does it have something to do with your grandparents?"

"No, no. It's something Tania asked me to find."

He continued to root around under the bushes while Kang, her feet sore, sat down to rest on a patch of grass and began to look through the bushes. Then she spotted something moving in the distance. Is that an animal? she wondered. Watching carefully, she realized there were people rambling around in the bushes. She stood up to find Brian and walked over to him quietly. "I saw two people in the woods," she whispered, patting his shoulder.

"Maybe they're searching for treasure, too." He pushed some branches out of the way. "I found it!"

A stone tablet covered with yellow-and-green moss stood there. She went around to the front and recognized the inscription in Russian.

"What does it say?"

"Sparrow Hills Park," he told her as he pulled out a trowel and mini mattock.

"Do you want to dig it out?" Kang's mouth dropped open. "You'll get us in trouble!"

"Definitely not. I'm going to dig for a time capsule that Tania buried," he said, going behind the tablet. He stepped back about one metre and started to cut through the soil.

She couldn't remember reading anything about a time capsule in the memoir, or anything about Tanya burying something in the woods.

He made a hole in the ground and then used the trowel to turn up the soil around it. Then they heard the sound of metal on metal—Brian's mattock had struck something. "Huh, I've got it!" He continued to scrape away the earth until he was able to pull out a small metal cylinder. From his pack, he took out a paper towel. "Can you clean it? I need to fill this hole."

She wiped the loose soil off the rusty metal tube. She couldn't find a way to open it, so she shook it to find out what was inside. She heard a little rustling sound. "Can you tell what it is?"

"Something written on paper, I think," he answered as he stood. "I'm done. Tania will be thrilled to see it." He took a paper towel from her to clean his hands.

"Why didn't you tell me about this?"

"I thought it would make our adventure more fun. Don't you think so?"

"Oh yes." She put the cylinder into his pack, and they walked back through the woods. When they reached a garbage bin near the meadow, he placed his digging tools on the ground beside the bin. He told Kang he didn't need to carry them back to Canada, and that perhaps someone who needed them would find them and take them home. She nodded, then raised her head and spotted the two figures she had seen earlier at the edge of the woods.

"It's almost four thirty now. We'd better get to my grandparents' place," said Brian. They bent their heads over the map in Brian's hand. "Let's head north to Kosygin Street."

She turned her head and saw the same two men walking out of the woods. "We're being followed," she said apprehensively.

Brian turned around, but saw nobody. He laughed. "Don't be nervous. My digging was far more suspicious than us walking."

"Have you forgotten what Igor told us? He said that there have been robberies recently, so we have to be careful."

They reached Kosygin Street, which was lined with birch trees. Standing in the shade, they hoped to find a taxi, but only saw cars driving rapidly past them. She looked again. "The two men aren't far behind us."

He noticed them too. "Maybe they think we've found buried treasure. Let's cross the street."

When a gap in the traffic opened, they hurried across the road. Looking back, Kang noticed the two stalkers starting to run, too.

"I know a short cut." Brian checked his map and compass. "Let's run. The traffic will stop them for a while."

Her legs pumping, Kang started to run, and anxiety made her forget her sore feet. After they crossed the meadow, she turned her head back, panting, but now the two men were nowhere to be seen. "Hurray! We're faster."

They crossed two streets and turned left. "Here's the beginning of Lebedeva Street," He looked back. "They're still behind us, but we can get on a bus to get rid of them if necessary."

Before they reached the bus stop, he found the street number 16. "My grandparents' house is number eighty-nine. We need to get to the other side. There's a crosswalk ahead."

When they reached it, the traffic light turned green.

Running on the sidewalk, Kang felt her heart pound faster when she saw their followers waiting at the red light on the other side of the street. They were in their late twenties, wearing blue T-shirts and jeans.

"Here we go!" said Brian when they reached a two-storey building. He stared at it. "Why is it a duplex?"

They went up the steps, and he knocked on the door to 89A. There was no response, so he knocked again.

Kang noticed a peephole in the door. Was someone eyeing them before they opened the door? She wondered if they should try the door to 89B.

"Mr. Anosov!" Brian called.

The door opened, and a man in his sixties appeared. "Come on in."

Feeling relieved, Kang followed Brian into the sitting room.

"Are ... are you Mr. Vsevolod Anosov?" Brian asked with astonishment—the man appeared to be much younger than the person he was looking for. Brian opened a notebook and pointed at a name and address to show him. The man shook his head and tapped his chest. "Ivan Anosov." Gazing at Brian's puzzled face, he pointed grimly to the floor. "Vsevolod Anosov."

Kang interpreted his body language. "I think he means un-derground—that Vsevolod Anosov is dead."

"I guess so." Brian nodded.

Suddenly a woman about the same age as Ivan shuffled into the room. "Vsevolod Anosov is dead. He was Ivan's father." She pointed at the man. "Ivan is my husband." She gestured for Brian and Kang to sit down.

Kang realized that Vsevolod Anosov was the brother of Tania's mother, and therefore Tania's uncle.

"You are Brian," said the woman in heavily accented En-glish. Before Brian could respond, she walked over to a desk and picked up a small, framed photograph. "This is you," she said and pointed at the picture. Brian looked at the photo of himself with his parents and passed it to Kang.

"I'm Vera. Ivan is a cousin of your mother. Your parents visited us in 1999." Vera turned to her husband, speaking Russian.

Vera told Brian, "Ivan does not speak English, so I will inter-pret." Then the couple told them that Brian's parents, Nadya and Charles, had given them the photo when they had visited the Anosov family five years earlier.

"Did you meet my mother before her family left Moscow?" Brian asked.

Vera interpreted what Ivan said: "One day in July 1959, Aunt Dina, your grandmother, came to my father and told him that she was going to Minsk, in Poland, for a ballet performance with her daughter Nadya. Aunt Dina asked him to take care of some documents related to the family's property including a *prospiska*—a residency permit in English. At that time, Aunt Dina's husband and Tania had already gone to Israel to look after your grandfather's ailing brother, and she didn't want to leave the papers at home since nobody lived there. I wasn't aware they were leaving for good, but I remember Nadya told me they were planning to join her father and sister later. Aunt Dina probably told my father that they wouldn't come back, but it had to be kept a secret."

Kang glanced out the window. To her relief, the two men had disappeared from the gate.

"After the family left," Ivan continued, "the house was taken over by the government. Later it was demolished and replaced by this building. But my father did not dare to make a claim until Gorbachev came to power in 1985. Then he used the documents left by Aunt Dina to prove that he had the right to the property. An apartment was given to him as compensation. Years later, when your mother came back with your father, she did not see her family house. My father had died, and she met us in this apartment that my father had left to us. We had lost contact with your grandparents. In those days, in the Soviet Union, anyone who had a connection with non-communist countries were considered enemies. It was easy for people to lose contact with family members. We hadn't heard anything about them at all until your parents' recent visit. We were so happy to be reconnected. But then my letter to your parents was returned. We had no idea that they had passed away, until now. We feel terrible about their deaths, but we're very happy to finally meet you."

"It's supper time," Vera said. "You must stay and eat with us."

Back in the hotel, Kang recalled the eventful day. Life, she mused, is sometimes stranger than fiction. Brian should write about the reunion with his second cousin. Tania would be very interested to hear about it, too. Then she remembered the time capsule. What was inside it?

CHAPTER 26: YELLOW AND PURPLE FLOWERS

AS SOON AS THEY RETURNED to Toronto, Kang and Brian went to Tania's house first, eager to find out what was in the time capsule.

Tania's hand trembled as they handed her the copper cylinder. As she gazed at it, her grey-green eyes beamed and brimmed with tears. "I thought I'd never see this again." Then she asked Brian to open it.

"I need a hacksaw," he said.

"There's one in the garage," said Tania, passing him the capsule. Several minutes later, Brian returned and handed the opened capsule back to Tania.

Gently she reached into the tube and drew a small paper scroll out with her fingertips. After unrolling it carefully on the table, she separated the two pages, putting one next to the other. The faded writing looked mysterious on the yellowish paper. A wry smile on her face, Tania said, "I need to get my magnifying glass. You can take a look."

Kang and Brian bent their heads over the first page. "It's in Russian. Here's Tania's name." Brian pointed to the lower right corner of the paper.

Tania came back with the magnifying glass and put it over the name. "You're right. It's my signature." She moved the glass to another page. "Here is Viktor's."

Kang and Brian examined the words. Underneath his Russian name were the Chinese characters: Wang Peihan. Kang's eyes widened. That was her father's name! Even the signature looked the same. But he was born in the year of the dog, Kang thought. What did this mean? Finally, in a weak voice she asked, "What does the rest say?"

Tania's words seemed to float over Kang's head. "Viktor copied two lines of Qin Guan, his favourite poet in the Song Dynasty. As *long as two hearts join each other/ Their eternal love is blessed night and day.* Then here are his own words: *Sparrow Hills witnesses our love forever. The sparrows might fly away, but the hills will remain. We have to say goodbye, but our love will be the same.*

"I copied two lines of my favourite poet, Alexander Pushkin: *I still remember that amazing moment/ When you appeared in my sight.* Then I wrote: *I'll wait for you to cross mountains and rivers, so we can read those words together. Our hair may turn grey, but our hearts will be young forever. Although we have to say farewell, we will always belong to each other.*"

Tania's voice faded away. Kang opened her tear-filled eyes and saw Tania staring into the distance. Her still image was like an open book to Kang. It told a wordless story of joy and sadness, lifelong expectations and moments of desperation, and love across mountains and oceans. Her heart deeply touched, Kang embraced Tania. Brian put his arms around both of the women, stroking each of their backs gently.

"I hope my story doesn't depress you two. I'm old, but you'll have a long time together," said Tania. "When are you planning on having your engagement party?"

Kang gazed at Brian. "Well, we talked about having it after my convocation."

"Yeah." Brian went to check the calendar. "How about October 16? It's a Saturday, a week after your graduation."

Reaching into his backpack, he took out a Red Army hat called a *budennovka* that he had bought from Lzmailovsky Market and put it on. It was dark brown with a red star and a pointy top, and it made him look ridiculous. Tania and Kang burst out laughing. "You look like a revolutionary," Kang said, "so I dare not disobey you. Let's have it on October 16."

Tania picked a pen and circled the date on her calendar. "Okay, I've marked it down. And I'll help with the arrangements."

The following day, Kang googled the Chinese zodiac years. She looked up her father's birth year and was shocked to learn that the year of the dog ranged from February 14, 1934 to February 3, 1935. Her father's birthday, February 10, 1934, was not included. How come? She was puzzled for a few moments, but soon remembered that the Chinese zodiac was based on the Chinese lunar calendar, not the Western one. Of course! Her father's birthday was still in the Chinese lunar year of 1933, the year of the rooster. Suddenly she understood: Viktor and her father were one and the same.

Later, Kang wrote a letter to her parents.

Dear Parents,

I'm writing to tell you good news. I've been dating a man named Brian Cole for several months. He's my landlady's nephew, and he is an engineer. We're engaged and plan to have an engagement party on October 16 and I really hope you can come. I'm enclosing an invitation along with an application form for a Canadian visa. It usually takes at least one month to process, so you should get your paperwork ready and apply for the visa as soon as possible.

Mother, now, you can tell people proudly that I'm no longer a spinster. And Father, I'm sending some photos we took in Moscow where Brian proposed to me. I hope you'll enjoy them and recognize some of them.

I'll be busy teaching summer school for the next four weeks. How is Jian? Did she get her apartment back?

Can't wait to hear from you.

Love, Kang

She decided not to mention that she had found out about her father's secret love affair. She didn't think it was the right time to say anything, and she decided not to tell Tania either.

Kang was busy at work and feeling cheerful, and the days began to pass by very quickly; she didn't notice until Friday that the week had already slipped away. After school, she arrived at Boston Pizza on Yonge Street ten minutes early. As planned, she would have supper with Brian and then go to Cineplex Odeon, a movie theatre next door. Instead of going in, she waited outside in front of Boston Pizza and watched people coming and going through the subway entrance. He was a little late, but she wasn't worried. Any minute now, she would spot him in the crowd, she thought.

A rotund, middle-aged man walked past her and then returned. Leaning over, he took Kang's hand. Her reflex response was to clench her hand into a fist; she was prepared to punch him in the face if he touched her again. "Oh, married," he mumbled in accented English after seeing the ring on her finger. His wrinkled face looked disappointed.

What a stupid man! she thought. Did he think this was an acceptable way of meeting women? She recognized the tight feeling in her chest that she had not experienced for a long while.

She entered the restaurant, found a table for two, and sat down. She started to feel anxious. Brian was always on time. What had happened to him? Ten minutes passed, and the waitress came by twice, but still Brian was nowhere to be seen. Kang stepped into the phone booth at the entrance.

To her surprise, he answered, sounding sleepy. "Sweetie, where are you?"

"Boston Pizza."

"Hoops, I forgot! I'm so sorry. Why don't you go ahead and eat without me? I'll catch you at the theatre."

Kang ate pizza alone, puzzled about how Brian could have forgotten their date. She wondered if he thought he didn't need to make an effort now that he was certain about their relationship. In the theatre, they watched American Wedding, a romantic comedy. Kang was shocked by the explicit sexual scenes, but she laughed during the part about the bachelor party. She realized that North American weddings were completely different from Chinese ones, and she wondered about having a bridal shower and the role her parents should play on that day. Preoccupied with all these questions, she did not ask Brian why he had forgotten their date.

The next morning, a Saturday, after cleaning the house as usual, she started to read a wedding magazine to see if she could get some tips for their upcoming engagement party. She was dismayed to learn that the bride's father was expected to make the first toast. Someone would have to show her father how that was done, and he would also need to practise giving the toast in English, or they would need an interpreter.

"Can I speak to you?" Tania's voice broke into her thoughts. Tania stood on the stairway.

Kang came upstairs to the living room where Tania gestured for her to join her on the couch. "Have you seen Brian recently?"

"Yes, we went to see a movie last night."

"And was he okay?"

"We were supposed to have dinner before the movie, but he forgot until I called him." Her voice quivered slightly when she noticed Tania's worried look. "Why?"

"Last night," said Tania, "Eric phoned me to say that Brian was acting a little strangely. Once he asked Eric whether he'd run away or fight back if an alien on the street attacked him. Twice in the wee hours of the morning, Eric heard footsteps in the living room. He got up to check and saw Brian pacing back and forth with a tiny flashlight in his hand."

"Have all these things happened recently?"

"In the past week. Did anything unusual happen during your trip?"

"Not really. There was one night when we thought we were

being followed by two men." Kang told Tania what had happened. "And one night I woke up and found him sitting in a chair rocking back and forth." She held Tania's arm. "Do you think it might be insomnia?"

"I'm not sure. But you should keep an eye on him," said Tania, patting Kang's hand. "Maybe he's tired from going right back to work after the long flight. I'll try to get him to come for lunch tomorrow. Can you join us?"

"I'd love to, but I've promised to get together with Nancy—she wants to hear all about the trip."

The following day, over a lunch of a pasta salad and grilled cheese sandwiches, Kang gazed closely at Brian. "You didn't get enough sleep, did you?"

Tania watched them both closely. Kang had decided to forgo the lunch with Nancy to be with Brian when he came over to visit Tania.

"What gave it away?" Brian asked, his eyes flitting from Kang to his aunt.

"Your bloodshot eyes," Kang said.

"Don't worry. I'm okay." He hesitated. "I have a question for my aunt."

"Go ahead," Tania said, and locked her eyes on his.

"Did you ever think about going to China to locate Viktor?"

Kang was surprised that Brian was so forthright with his aunt.

"What a question!" She sucked in air. "Yes, sometimes I did, but the circumstances were never right."

"How about now? China is open, and you have the time," said Brian before biting into a sandwich.

Kang squirmed in her seat. She wasn't ready to tell them what she had discovered, and she was perplexed by Brian's insistence on this line of questioning.

"Well, I'm too old. Why do you ask such questions?" Tania smiled wearily.

"I guess the trip to Moscow sparked my imagination." He

chuckled. "If I could find a time machine, I'd travel back in time and find out where Viktor went."

"I don't think you need to be thinking about this," Tania said firmly.

Kang let out a small sigh of relief.

"What did I say?" Brian asked, staring into space. "Sometimes my mind feels very hazy."

"Your mind?" Tania paused. "Can you pick me some flowers from the garden after the meal?"

"Of course! Which ones would you like?" he asked, taking a sip of Pepsi.

"Pick some black-eyed Susans and the purple coneflowers."

He finished his Pepsi, got a pair of scissors, and dutifully went out the side door. Tania watched him from the kitchen window. Kang stood beside her. Neither of them knew quite what to think.

They watched Brian make his way along the path between the flower beds. Several startled sparrows rose from the shrubs as he passed, one of them almost hitting his head. He jumped and his arm swept in the air as though he were trying to catch it. He stepped past the black-eyed Susans and then coneflowers. Finally, when he reached the end of path, they saw him jump again, one hand clenching into a fist, the other holding the scissors. "My gosh! What's wrong with him?" Kang cried out.

Tania shook her head and started to clear the table. "He needs to see a doctor," she said. "Something is wrong."

When they finished cleaning the kitchen, they made their way to the living room. Kang had prepared some tea and she was sipping from her cup, wrapped up in her thoughts and worried about Brian. Tania had almost dozed off when they were both startled by Brian, who had slipped into the room quietly. "Aren't they beautiful?" he said. He was holding a vase filled with white flowers of different colours. "What do you call this white one?" he asked.

Suddenly wide awake, Tania looked the flowers. "That's a dahlia! In fact, they're all dahlias!" She tried to speak without panicking. "My dear, didn't you find the black-eyed Susans or the purple coneflowers?"

"You said yellow and purple. Plus I got some white ones." Brian sounded innocent. "Don't you like them?"

"They're very nice. Thank you." Tania asked, "Where are my scissors?"

"I washed them and put them back in the drawer."

Kang was sitting very still on the couch. Brian hardly paid attention to her. She could feel the hair rise up on the back of her neck as she watched this man who suddenly seemed like a stranger.

Kang watched Brian attentively as he placed the vase on the table. It was as though she wasn't even in the room.

"Have you had a checkup lately?" Tania asked.

"No. Do you think I should see the doctor because I'm flower illiterate?" Brian laughed.

"When was your last checkup?"

"Probably four years ago."

"You should have a physical every two years, Brian. You know you're going to get married soon. It's important to do this."

"Are you my mother?" he teased her. Then he suddenly turned toward Kang and said, "And you are going to be my bride! Do you think I need to see a doctor too?" He laughed uproariously.

Kang's eyes widened, but she didn't respond.

She saw that Tania's eyes were full of tears. "If you don't take care of yourself, I will," Tania said to Brian, placing her hand on his arm.

"Okay, okay, I'll make an appointment," Brian said. Tania and Kang exchanged glances and then Kang got up to make a cup of tea for everyone.

One day after school, Kang was pleased to get an email from

Jian. She had finally written her a long letter and she was eager to read it. Jian told that her bosom friend Yezi had come
back to China for a visit after having lived in the U.S. for
twenty-three years. After chatting with her, Jian was feeling
encouraged, inspired, and stronger than before. The sense of
inferiority she had experienced after being raped, abandoned,
and divorced had more or less gone away. She had learned
about women having more equality and freedom in North
America. She told Kang that someday she would visit her and
Yezi and see these countries in person. "I can imagine your
spinster's hat being blown away into the Pacific Ocean," she
wrote, making Kang laugh.

Her sense of humour has come back, Kang thought. She was
also glad to hear that Jian had gotten her apartment back from
her ex-husband, and that Linling had won a prize in a math
contest. Things were looking up for all of them. She breathed
a sigh of relief.

Before long, Kang also received a letter from her parents.
She shook her head, wondering why they kept using the mail
service instead of email. She shook her head as she opened it.

They said they'd sent their visa applications to the Embassy
of Canada. And her father had enrolled in an English class.
Kang thought this was wonderful news. She was happy to
think that her father would be able to make the toast. There
wouldn't be many guests at the wedding, so her father shouldn't
be nervous. But, she wondered, what would her father think
when he saw Tania? What would Tania think? And what about
Brian? She was worried about all of it, especially as Tania had
finally told her that her grandmother had schizophrenia, and
the gene may have passed on to him.

The following day, she came straight home from school. Tania
was in the kitchen making a salad. "Are you going to meet
Brian this weekend?"

"Yes, we're going for a walk tomorrow evening."

"Can you find out whether he's going to see a psychiatrist?"

"A psychiatrist?"

"I've sent a note explaining my concerns to my family doctor—she's his doctor too. I asked her to refer Brian to a psychiatrist."

"Did the doctor think that was a good suggestion?"

"I'm Brian's only family, and as I told you earlier, I think he might have inherited the illness from his great-grandma," she said as she sat down for her supper. "This problem only occurs in one percent of the population. But there's a higher risk for people whose family has a history of schizophrenia." Noticing Kang's tense facial expression, she tried to smile. "Maybe I'm the one who is paranoid."

"I'll talk to him. Thanks." Kang put away her backpack and picked listlessly at the leftovers in her plate. She had lost her appetite for supper.

When Kang thought about schizophrenia, her heart jumped. She had learned that people with the disease were violent, but she had never even seen Brian lose his temper, let alone hit anyone. Devouring multiple articles and books on the subject, she learned that its symptoms included hallucination and paranoia—fears not based on reality. Recalling Brian's nervousness in the airplane, she concluded that his fear had been related to a real accident, and that therefore he was not paranoid. Was he having hallucinations, though? She wondered about why he kept talking about alien attacks. He also seemed suddenly disorganized. He had forgotten their date, and then a few days ago he had told her he couldn't see her on the weekend, but then yesterday asked to meet her on Friday evening. Kang sighed deeply. She was worried that their unclasped hands on Kupala Night might have been a bad omen. But she reminded herself that they had both held onto the wreath, which was a good sign. But she could not quell the butterflies in her stomach, and she even forgot to brush her teeth before she went to bed.

After supper on Friday, Kang was going to meet Brian.
On her way across Dufferin Street to the park, she wondered
what Brian would say to her.

CHAPTER 27: THE SPINSTER'S HAT

K ANG REACHED THE PATH, but couldn't find Brian. Walking over to the wooden bridge, she leaned against the railing, expecting him to show up any second. She hoped he hadn't forgotten again that they were supposed to meet. She didn't know if there was a phone booth nearby if she had to contact him.

The dappled sunlight cast orange patches of light on the bridge; the tree branches shook slightly in the breeze. Canada warblers chirped in the trees as though they were singing in a choir. The sound of splashing water came from under the arch. She wondered if there was a big fish down there, but she didn't think that was possible. Then she detected a voice. Was it a mermaid? She was amused by her own thought, but the splashing grew louder, and a few drops of water landed on her head. She turned around to look over the railing, and to her surprise, she saw Brian standing in the middle of the stream, grinning at her. Then he bent down and splashed her again.

"Were you daydreaming?" he asked. "Didn't you hear me at all?"

"I thought I heard the voice of a mermaid," she joked, even though his strange behaviour was worrying her more and more. "Why are you in the water? You're getting soaked."

"I'm just cooling off. Too bad I haven't seen any fish." He scrambled up the bank and put his shoes on. When he joined her on the footbridge, water was still dripping from the cuffs of his cargo shorts. "I can't wait for the day to come."

"What day?"

"The day of the engagement party. Did you forget?" He patted her on the arm, and his cold hand felt good on her skin.

"No, no." She hesitated. "What was the important question you had for me?" she asked as they meandered along the path.

"I need a break from my project. Walking with you will relax me, sweetheart."

"How's the project going?" she asked. "Is your supervisor satisfied?"

"So far so good." He chuckled. "What does 'Red October' suggest to you?"

She wondered why he had changed the subject. Maybe he was disoriented, she thought. She remembered that was one of the symptoms of schizophrenia. "It sounds like it might be referring to the Russian Revolution."

"Your graduation and our engagement will be in October. Maybe 'Green October' is better." He gazed into the distance. "Well, here's my question: if I could travel back in time, would you want me to stop Viktor from returning to China?"

Startled by his question, she answered, "But you know time only flows forward."

"Maybe. Maybe not."

"Why would you want to do that? Would you have liked Viktor to have stayed with Tania?"

"Yes, so she would've been happier."

A thought instantly crossed her mind: If Viktor had stayed in Russia, she wouldn't exist. And she and Brian wouldn't have met.

"Maybe you should let things stay as they are," she said.

"But don't you feel for Tania?" He stopped walking and locked his eyes on hers. "Why not?"

"It's a secret," she responded, thinking if she used this as bait she might be able to get him to stop fixating on Viktor and Tania.

"Hmm, let me guess," he said, clapping his hands. "If Viktor had stayed, there wouldn't have been a time capsule for us to find."

"Try harder," she urged.

"If Viktor hadn't left, Tania's family probably wouldn't have left the Soviet Union."

"Why?" Kang went a little further, trying to determine if his mind was clear.

"If he'd stayed, Tania's dad wouldn't have taken her away from the Soviet Union. The family's departure wasn't only because of the persecution of her dad; it was also because of Tania's nervous breakdown. And if the family had stayed in Moscow, my mother never would've met my dad, and I would've never been born." He laughed.

"I agree with you, but that isn't my secret."

"I wasn't thinking about your secret; I was just imagining."

"What were you imagining?"

"If you could travel back in time, what would you do?"

"I'd catch an alien and teach him how to speak Chinese," Kang said with a wry smile.

"Wow! I think you have a very good imagination. You could write science fiction."

Kang frowned. She had hoped to bring Brian back from his fantasy world. "Your aunt is worried about your health. She wants to know if you've seen your doctor."

"Then she should ask me herself."

"She phoned you and left a message, but you didn't call her back."

"A message? I didn't get a message. Anyway, can you tell me your secret?"

She hesitated. She thought that if she told Brain that Viktor was her father, it might confuse him more. "I will, but on the condition that you go see the doctor."

"I don't have a medical problem. And I don't have time to see a doctor, either."

"Think about Tania. You don't want her to have a nervous breakdown again, do you?"

"What makes you think she's going to have a breakdown? She's tough."

Before Kang could respond, an elderly woman approached them on the path. "Excuse me, did you happen to see a puppy?"

"What does he look like?" Kang asked. The desperation in the woman's voice made her forget what she and Brian had just been talking about.

"Piebald. She's about this size." The woman gestured with her hands. "Her name is Beans."

"Don't worry," Brian told her. "She can't have gone far." He turned to Kang, pointing to the left side of the path. "I'll check the other side."

They scoured the bushes along the path. "Here, Beans!" the woman called out as she too searched along the path.

A cluster of mosquitoes buzzed around Kang's head, so she picked up a branch to drive them away. Several minutes later, she heard a dog barking. She pushed the branches aside and emerged into a little clearing where she was surprised to see Hachiko. Then she heard Tania's voice calling out, "Is this your puppy? She's so cute with her little red bow." Kang saw that Tania was at the edge of the clearing, holding the little puppy in her arms.

"Thank you so much!" The woman took the leash from Tania and hurriedly pulled the puppy from her arms. "I thought I'd lost her. Thank goodness."

Then Brian arrived at the clearing and greeted Tania.

"You all know one another?" asked the puppy's owner. "Well, thank you all for helping me. He's very cute, too," she said as she patted Hachiko's head, who had run over to her, and was wagging his tail energetically at the puppy. The woman said goodbye to the three of them and then left with the puppy still clutched in her arms.

"How nice to meet you here," Tania said, gazing up at Brian.

"Did you get a referral from the doctor?"

"Ha! You're acting like my mother." He grinned and ignored the question. "Good bye, Aunt Tania!" He waved and walked away.

Kang looked at Tania and shrugged her shoulders. She ran to catch up with Brian. "You shouldn't be disrespectful," she admonished him.

"I wasn't, darling," he said. "I just don't want to be nagged. Besides, I need to go home to work on my project."

Kang couldn't sleep. She tossed and turned all night, worrying about the possibility that Brian might be ill. Engrossed in her thoughts, she compared the symptoms of schizophrenia that she had read about to his recent behaviour. She'd noticed his restlessness, the strange things that came out of his mouth lately, and occasionally he forgot things. He'd been busy with a project, but he was very secretive about it. She wondered if rocking back and forth was a symptom. He never mentioned hearing voices and that reassured her somewhat. But why didn't he want to see a doctor?

Thinking about what to do, she jotted down some notes to remind herself to spend more time with him after she finished summer school, and to continue to encourage him to get a psychiatric assessment. She tried to imagine the worst-case scenario. In China, when the Cultural Revolution was over, she had witnessed people who had been traumatized traipse up and down the street, ranting or raving and shouting out quotations from Mao's works. Her father had told her these people were ill, and possibly even schizophrenic. If he was diagnosed with schizophrenia, should she put off the engagement party? Or cancel it?

She decided to ask Nancy's opinion. On a Saturday afternoon, Kang met with her in a coffee shop and shared her concerns.

"First thing's first: You need to find out if he actually has the disorder," Nancy suggested.

"But how? He didn't even respond very well when his aunt tried to find out if he'd seen a psychiatrist."

"Another question you need to ask yourself is: are you willing to live with him if it turns out he does have schizophrenia?"

"Rationally, I should say no. But the truth is I don't feel threatened by his odd behaviour."

"How do you feel when it seems like he's avoiding you?"

"I feel sad."

"Maybe he's avoiding you in order to force you to leave him?"

"I don't think so. One day he showed me his design for the engagement party invitation. He also told me not to worry about the cost, that he would take care of it. That doesn't sound like someone who doesn't want to get married."

The two women sat quietly for a minute, and then Nancy said, "Tell you what. I have an acquaintance, married with two kids. She was diagnosed with schizophrenia five years ago, but she seems to function well as long as she takes her medication. And she even teaches a painting class. Luckily she has a very supportive husband."

"What kind of symptoms does she have?"

"None that I can see. I don't feel like she's very different from anybody else, actually. I think I can arrange for you to meet with her. She would be able to answer your questions better than I can."

"That would be great. The sooner the better, because I have to decide what to do before it's too late."

"Before what's too late?"

"My parents are coming to the engagement party. I have to decide whether I should cancel it before they book their plane tickets."

"Here's an idea. Why don't you tell him how you feel. Tell him he has to be assessed and that you might have to put off the party if he doesn't follow through. Anyway, did you have to consult your parents before you agreed to marry him? Do they know your concerns?"

"Not really. I haven't told them anything, and I didn't need their permission to make my decision. I decided on my own to come to Canada and I think I can choose my own husband."

"Well, you're strong, but think about yourself. I mean, think about whether you can live with Brian if it turns out that he is schizophrenic. It will impact your life as well."

"It would help me make up my mind if I could meet your friend."

"Okay, I'll phone her and let you know when she's available." Nancy took the last sip of her latte and then got up to leave.

The iced tea had cleared Kang's mind. She thanked Nancy and they left the café together.

On the way home, she thought about how to convince Brian to see a doctor. When she got home, she was surprised to see his car in the driveway. Brian was sitting on the front step. When she approached, he stood and greeted her with a kiss and a hug. "Why are you sitting outside?" she asked.

"Nobody's home," he smiled. "But I figured you'd be here eventually, so I waited."

"I'll get a cell phone soon," she said and unlocked the door. "That way you can always reach me."

They stepped into the living room and sat down on the couch. "So what's new?" she asked.

He handed her an envelope.

"What's this?" she asked, wondering if she should talk to him openly about her fears and his need for a psychiatric assessment.

"Read it. I did it for you."

She took a single sheet of paper from the envelope and scanned it quickly. To make sure she understood, she reread it.

MENTAL STATUS EXAMINATION: Brian Cole is a 37-year-old male, alert and oriented, and cooperative with concentration. Thoughts are clear and language is appropriate. No symptoms of depression, but experiences anxiety related to writing a science fiction novella. No auditory or visual hallucinations or delusions noted, but he is in a highly imaginative and creative mood. He has clear insight into his situation. His judgment is good.

After reading the document, Kang was silent for a moment before she understood that the psychiatrist's report confirmed that Brian did not have schizophrenia. His odd behaviour was merely a product of his creative mind. As relief flooded over her, she began to sob. Brian immediately jumped up and took her in his arms.

"*Green October* is a science fiction novella?" asked Kang.

"You got it, sweetheart," he said, smiling. "I wanted to surprise you."

"But if you knew you were fine, why did you decide to see the specialist?"

"You and Tania made me. What choice did I have? I didn't want to lose you and I didn't want you to worry." He grinned. "Besides, I also have a persuasive aunt who thinks she's my mother."

"Will we be able to see each other more often now?"

"Well, I'm still working on my manuscript, but I'm hoping to finish it by October." He paused. "Now can you tell me what your secret is?"

"I hope you won't be shocked."

"Don't worry." He laughed. "My heart is in good condition, according to my family doctor."

"Viktor is my father."

"I know."

"You know? How?"

"Well, Tania told me."

"I don't understand."

"She told me that she'd made an educated guess. First of all, you have the same family name as Viktor's, right?"

"But Viktor's family name was Liu."

"Turns out that was a pseudonym."

"A pseudonym? Shouldn't everything be true in a memoir?"

"I have no idea. You and Tania can discuss it." He continued, "You were born in Kunming, which is in Southwest China, where Viktor had been sent. Like Viktor, your father was a medical doctor. And finally, when you stared at Viktor's signature in Chinese, the look on your face affirmed Tania's suspicion. She put two and two together."

Kang was speechless.

"Since then, she's claimed to see a lot of your dad in you. It was as much for your sake as for mine that she insisted I see a psychiatrist. I guess realizing you were Viktor's child must have awakened her protective maternal instincts."

"But what am I going to tell my parents about this? I'm relieved that Tania knows now, but what am I going to say to my mother?"

"Don't worry. We'll find a way."

"We?"

"Yes. Tania, you, and me."

The cool evening breeze whispered outside the open windows. The sunset glow filtered in, covering them in golden light.

In her mind's eye, Kang saw a vivid scene: a wide-brimmed spinster's hat had been thrown up in the sky. It was gradually falling into the deep ocean, just as Jian had described in her letter. She smiled. It was the sweetest smile.

ACKNOWLEDGEMENTS

I am deeply grateful to my publisher and editor at Inanna Publications, Luciana Ricciutelli, for her dedicated editing and suggestions that have helped bring this novel to the world.

I would like to thank the Ontario Arts Council for its grant assistance to this writing project.

My thanks also go to my critique pals: Magdalena Ball, Phyllis B. DePoe, Anita C. Dermer, Amanda K. Hale, and Noreen C. Olive. They read through the manuscript in its earlier versions and provided me with honest and helpful feedback. I owe personal notes of thanks to Marie E. Laing, Carol Mortensen, Dorothy Rawek, and Penelope Stuart, who are always there for me.

Last, but certainly not least, I am thankful to my husband and son, Jean-Marc and Shu, for their patience and unwavering support of my writing.

Photo: Jean-Marc Roy

Born in China, Zoë S. Roy, an avid reader even during the Cultural Revolution, writes literary fiction with a focus on women's cross-cultural experiences. Her publications include *Butterfly Tears* (2009), a collection of short fiction, and two novels, *The Long March Home* (2011), and *Calls Across the Pacific* (2015), published by Inanna Publications. She lives in Toronto, and taught with the Toronto District School Board for years.